TOTAL POSSESSION

THE DUFORT DYNASTY
BOOK THREE

JULIETTE N. BANKS

COPYRIGHT

Author: Juliette N. Banks

Editor: Jen Katemi

Cover design by: Elizabeth Cartwright, EC Editorial

ABOUT THE AUTHOR

Juliette is a bestselling indie steamy romance author who has taken the paranormal romance genre by storm with her bestselling vampire series, The Moretti Blood Brothers. Not all of her sexy and powerful heroes are supernatural—Juliette now has a series of hot, page-turning contemporary romances readers can't get enough of.

Juliette also has a vast background in consumer marketing and previously published with Random House. She lives in New Zealand with Tilly, her Maine Coon kitty.

Juliette N. Banks website:

DEDICATION

To Jeannine, without whose guidance and healing I would never have reached this place in my life. You are wise, kind, and very magical. I am forever grateful you showed up in my life.

Juliette x

ALSO BY JULIETTE N. BANKS

The Dufort Dynasty
Steamy billionaire romance
Sinful Duty (**FREE**)
Forbidden Touch
Total Possession
Desire Unbound

The Moretti Blood Brothers
Steamy paranormal romance
The Vampire Prince (**FREE**)
The Vampire Protector
The Vampire Spy
The Vampire's Christmas
The Vampire Assassin
The Vampire Awoken
The Vampire Lover
The Vampire Wolf
The Vampire Warrior

The Moretti Blood Wolves
Steamy paranormal shifter romance
The Alpha Wolf
The Unbound Wolf

The Protective Wolf

Realm of the Immortals
Steamy paranormal fantasy romance
The Archangel's Heart
The Archangel's Star

TOTAL POSSESSION

CHAPTER ONE

Hunter stepped into the elevator and tugged on the sleeves of his black Prada blazer.

He was late.

On purpose.

Which was an asshole thing to do, given it was his brother Fletcher's engagement party.

He wished they'd all stop getting engaged. By *they*, he meant his two brothers. Both had. Which left him as the sole Dufort bachelor.

And didn't the New York media know it, and regularly mention it.

He hated the spotlight being on him and had been relying on Fletcher to remain single and uphold his title as the Playboy of Manhattan. Then he'd gotten all hot and heavy with his PR manager and was now engaged, a stepfather to Olivia's daughter, Sammy, and expecting a child.

Their older brother, Daniel, was getting married to his Kiwi girlfriend, Harper.

How in the holy fuck did that all happen?

The brothers had all sworn off marriage in their late teenage years after watching their philandering father destroy their mother.

Well, he wasn't going to lose his mind like those two airheads.

The likelihood of that happening was very low given his tastes.

And he wasn't talking about whiskey.

Which he very much liked.

His bedroom tastes, if one could call them that given he rarely made it to a bed when fucking women, were darker than that of most people.

He wasn't a sadist.

He just needed to be in control.

Complete control.

His style wasn't for everyone. Nor were the women who enjoyed being submissive to a dominant lover the type, generally, to be looking for marriage.

Although those who learned his surname quickly changed their mind.

Dufort.

He was a billionaire.

So were his two brothers.

As equal majority shareholders of the Dufort Dynasty, a legacy that included the global Dufort Hotel group, the three brothers were all the penultimate bachelors.

Or had been.

With good looks and charm on their side, along with their bank balances, thanks to their father Johnathan Dufort, who had created the company, women wanted to marry them, and men wanted to be them.

Or fuck them over.

It was the cold hard truth they had all learned very quickly.

So, no, Hunter wasn't concerned about falling into matrimonial bliss. And that wasn't why he had purposely delayed attending Fletcher and Olivia's engagement party this evening.

The elevator doors opened.

He was immediately greeted with the smells and scents of a cocktail party, along with Fletcher's multi-million-dollar view.

"Good evening, sir." A roaming waiter with a tray of champagne greeted him.

"Evening. I'll have a whiskey please. On the rocks," Hunter replied.

"Yes, sir."

He didn't bother smiling as he made his way through the crowd. Everyone knew he was the brooding type, so why prove them wrong? He hated large groups, much preferring one-on-one time with people, or smaller social events.

This was just the tip of the iceberg. There were two big weddings to follow these damn engagement parties. Daniel's would be in the middle of summer which was only a month away.

"Nice of you to finally arrive, dickhead," Fletcher said as he joined his brothers in the living room.

The waiter arrived with his whiskey.

"Cheers. Happy engagement and all that." He ignored his brother and gave Olivia a grin.

Broody he may be, but he had all the Dufort charm and knew his hazel eyes and dimples worked their magic.

"Thank you, Hunter," Olivia said and accepted his kiss on the cheek.

They weren't strangers. Olivia had worked for their company for over two years now and as the director of sales, he worked closely with Fletcher and his marketing team.

"Welcome to the family," he added.

"Right where she belongs," Fletcher said, wrapping his arm around Olivia's back, and kissing her forehead.

The two stared into each other's eyes like total idiots so Hunter turned away and surveyed the crowd for the woman he was avoiding.

Because he was avoiding her, very much.

It had been a month since he last saw her.

Since he met her one night at Olivia's when her daughter Sammy had been kidnapped by her ex-husband.

It was the most inappropriate time to meet a woman and want to fuck her into complete submission.

But that was what had happened.

Not that Hunter had fucked her. And likely never would.

He suspected Addison Hill was as vanilla as they came. Someone needed to tell his cock that.

Hunter had dropped her off home that night and it had been awkward. She was clearly overwhelmed by his wealth and being so close to him. He'd lost count of how many times she'd blushed and looked away from him.

Yet, he'd had an erection the entire drive home and if he hadn't had a t-shirt on covering his damn jeans, she would have seen it. Although he doubted she had the courage to look at his groin without dying of embarrassment.

He'd made small talk with her, casting looks down at her, as he worked his way through the New York traffic, and she'd chatted easily enough.

Addison was gorgeous, there was no doubting that. Her short wavy blond hair looked more suited to California than New York, but he could tell she was a stylish woman. She wore a pair of distressed jeans, a white crop top and a long dark cardigan, with boots.

That hint of skin above her jeans had been fucking with his head since he walked in the door of Olivia's house.

While he wasn't completely disengaged from the trauma of finding the missing child—because the situation had totally infuriated him—his eyes kept drifting to Addison.

Given the opportunity he'd unzip those jeans, rip up her top and suck on those breasts while fucking her with his fingers.

Then he'd make her wait.

And the games would begin.

She'd caught him looking and he'd snuck her a slow dirty smirk. Her blush had given him pause. She could be the perfect submissive, but something told him she wasn't.

He probably could have left it there, but when he pulled up at her building Addison had turned to him from the front seat of his Aston Martin and lowered her eyes.

Fuck, his cock had fought to get out of his jeans.

She'd tugged her bottom lip between her teeth and those eyes of hers had slowly lifted and locked on his, looking for instruction.

He'd taken her chin in his hand. "Be careful what you ask for, Addison."

Her lips had parted, and he couldn't look away from the glistening invitation inside.

"I will take everything you have to give if you want to play. If not, I recommend you hop out of the vehicle now."

As Hunter watched her mind swirl, trying to calculate the risk versus pleasure—if she even knew what he was offering—the clock ticked.

He began to think she was going to nod.

Her eyes had dropped to his crotch.

He'd smirked.

"You want to try before you buy?" he asked, raising an amused brow.

Then her gaze had shot to his, and he'd known. She had too much fire in her. She would be fun to break, but she was Olivia's friend. It was too close to home.

He dropped her chin and leaned back in his seat.

"Goodnight, Addison."

"Wha—"

"Goodnight, Addison," he repeated. "Trust me. This is for the best."

The dark look she had given him only confirmed he'd made the right decision.

Except those lips, that skin, and her sexy ass as she'd run into her building had haunted him.

Now, tonight, he would see her again.
And he wasn't sure he could say no a second time.

CHAPTER TWO

Addison took a half step back and leaned a quarter of an inch to the left. She wasn't hiding...

Okay, fine, she was hiding.

Hunter Dufort had finally arrived, and she wasn't sure if she was relieved or more anxious now that he was here.

Olivia was her best friend, so it wasn't like she couldn't be here for the engagement party. Nor would she dream of not showing up. She was so happy for Liv and Fletcher after years of believing they couldn't be together.

Who knew *her* bestie would be the one to snag the *Playboy of Manhattan*?

Now Addison had met Fletcher and gotten to know him a little, he wasn't at all what the media made him out to be. First, his love for Olivia was like something from a romance novel—which their friend and Fletcher's soon to be sister-in-law Harper would know all about because she was a bestselling author.

He was as much in love with Olivia's daughter Sammy as he was her mom. The two of them had a bond which rivaled some birth fathers. Unsurprising, after Sammy had been abducted by her own mentally unstable dad and Fletcher had been paramount in saving her.

No one had told Addison the full story, and she didn't care. She was just pleased Sammy had been found safe and unharmed. And that Olivia's ex was now serving time.

Sammy was the same age as her own daughter, Sienna. The two were close friends. Tonight, both girls were with her ex-husband, Rob, most likely watching *Frozen 2* over and over and driving him crazy, while she was hiding from a billionaire.

Hunter probably hadn't thought about her for a single second after she climbed out of his car a month ago.

She had.

She'd thought about him a lot.

Far too much. The way her body reacted to him should be illegal.

When he'd walked into Olivia's house that day, Addison had been shocked by the shiver that traversed her skin.

She knew who Hunter was. Most people in New York City did. The third Dufort brother.

Hunter was the youngest of the three, and the director of sales for the global Dufort hotel chain. Fletcher, she knew, oversaw the marketing and PR because Olivia worked in his department as the chain's PR manager, and Daniel, the eldest Dufort, was the CEO.

She wasn't sure how long Liv would continue to work for the Dufort's, but given the engagement, she suspected that situation might change over time.

Olivia had introduced her to Harper, and she'd instantly liked the New Zealander. She was learning how to deal with the media now she was in the spotlight as Daniel's fiancé and soon-to-be wife.

The media had always been obsessed with these brothers and their love lives. As a PR expert, Olivia was coaching Harper, and she'd invited Addison along to some of their lunches.

Being a newbie in Manhattan was tough for anyone. Being under the media spotlight was even harder.

Not that Harper didn't have all that money could buy as well as Daniel's complete commitment and protection. That man was one powerful individual and a bodyguard all on his own.

Addison eyed the men in dark suits standing in the shadows. They were a constant presence in the two women's lives now.

She didn't envy Olivia or Harper.

Although the penthouses they lived in were spectacular and award-winning, and probably worth more than she'd ever see in her lifetime.

Ten lifetimes.

Addison was happy in her brownstone, a few blocks down from Olivia's old home. She missed living so close to her friend. Now the girls weren't neighbors, they had to actively make time to get together.

And they did—for each other, and for their girls. Recently they'd had a girls' night at Daniel and Harper's penthouse with two bottles of wine—okay fine, it might have been four–and ended up dancing to old eighties music.

It had been a blast.

Until the moment she'd drunkenly asked, "What's the deal with Hunter?"

Both of the others had gone quiet, lifted their glasses to their lips, blinked and stared at her.

"What do you mean?" Olivia asked.

If there was ever a moment in life she wished for a time machine to go back and do it over, it had been then.

Stupid drunk mouth.

"Oh, I just mean, is he single or getting engaged next?" She had laughed. "You know, because Daniel and Fletcher have, so he must be next to put a ring on it."

Harper had choked on her wine before spitting it across the room. Olivia had patted her back, giggling.

"What?" Addison had asked, her cheeks heating because now she felt stupid.

As Harper tried to get her words out, still coughing, Olivia turned to Addison. "He's, um, into a different lifestyle."

"Ring…" Harper continued laughing. "Sorry. As a romance author I know things I shouldn't. I just imagined him putting a cock ring on a girl's hand while proposing."

The two of them had burst into laughter.

Addison knew what a cock ring was, too, but didn't think she should say that out loud. She kept those things to herself for a reason.

"But why would that stop him from finding Miss Forever?" Addison asked, when they stopped laughing.

Harper had shrugged. "Daniel said he won't. And he doesn't even date. He spends a lot of time at clubs."

"Clubs?"

"Not the kind of clubs we went to when we were younger," Olivia had said, nodding.

Addison had raised a brow, aiming for humor. "Who are you calling old? I'm only twenty-nine."

"You missed the point," Olivia had replied. "Let me spell it out. He goes to *sex* clubs. He's into a whole lot of kinky extreme things. So I doubt he'll be walking down the aisle anytime soon."

"Or if he does it could be in some bondage gear." Harper giggled.

"Oh my God," Olivia said. "I am never getting that image out of my head. Stop. He's our brother-in-law."

"To be." Harper grinned.

"To be," Olivia nodded, giggling again.

Addison had tuned them out and wondered if what they were saying was true or rumor. Goodness knows she had been subject to rumors once upon a time.

It explained some of the things he had said to her in the car and why her body had flared to life. Even if it had shocked her.

And by the way her friends were reacting, it was clear they both weren't into anything kinky. Another reason to zip her lips.

She wasn't going to share that she'd been fantasizing about being on her knees in front of Hunter Dufort as he forced his cock down her throat while her arms were tied behind her.

Nope.

No damn way.

She'd lost too many people already.

If they'd known the truth, perhaps they would have understood, but none of them stuck around long enough to allow her to explain.

Not even her father.

And for that, she would never forgive her ex-husband.

Sure they had a good relationship when it came to co-parenting their daughter but that didn't mean she wasn't resentful deep down inside.

He hadn't wanted to experiment in the bedroom at all. She'd felt their sex life was lacking and his silent performance during sex had bothered her. Aside from a few moans and his declaration of love when they'd first fallen for each other, it was very standard love making.

Which perhaps she should have been okay with.

But she hadn't been.

The day she sat down with him and had a serious conversation, sharing how she felt and asking if he would be interesting in trying something new, he'd looked at her like she was some kind of sex fiend.

It wasn't like she wanted to go to a sex club.

Although a part of her was curious.

Curious also about what people like Hunter did in those places. In his car he'd challenged her, and she'd felt his dominance.

And she liked it.

A lot.

Her body had craved… something. Him. More. For days.

Yet, after experiencing the judgment and rejection the last time she tried to own her desires, Addison refused to go there.

Not at all.

She needed to focus on being a mother and career woman. If it got out…

Nope.

Not happening.

While she had been sad to lose her friends—and thankfully, Olivia had been the one person Rob hadn't told—it was her father that had devastated her most.

For good reason.

Her father had confronted her about leaving Rob. She loved her dad, but he was a typical male, siding with the man in this instance. The truth was Rob was a good husband and father so she kind of understood her dad's concern and questions. He had been part of the 'older' generation; her parents had her later in life. So he very much thought women had their place in the home and a duty to their husbands.

But it was worse than that.

Rob told him why she'd left.

They had agreed to say they were no longer compatible. Which was true. It wasn't just the sex and their lack of passion. That had filtered through their entire relationship.

But Rob told her father she was into a kink lifestyle and needed therapy.

The last words her father said to her had been cruel and hurtful. "*How can you leave your husband and be involved with all that disgusting stuff? You are a mother. You need to grow up and go back to Rob. Sort this out.*"

A few weeks later he died.

Then friend after friend had disassociated with her. After one of them shared what Rob had told them, she had been furious.

Addison questioned whether she had done the right thing leaving her husband. After he'd told her she was mentally ill for having sexual desires different from him and finding herself in the position of no longer wanting her husband to touch her, it had to be a sign something was very wrong.

What she didn't know was whether it was just her.

So she'd gone to therapy.

It hadn't helped. The woman had tried to analyze the hell out of her interests and twisted her inside out. She believed there was some complicated reason because of her relationship with her father, on top of the fact that her mother had died early.

Ah... no. She just wanted someone to tie her up and fuck her brains out until she screamed.

Was it so wrong?

She had believed so until the moment Hunter Dufort had looked at her with pure unrestrained dominance and soaked her panties.

God, she wanted more.

And God, she was terrified to go near him.

Now, he was standing across the room. His hair was mussed in a sexy way, and his designer pants fit his tight ass perfectly.

Even the way he stood screamed confidence and control.

Shit.

She swallowed.

Addison needed to stay away from him. She might have all these needs and desires swimming inside her but if he looked her way, she would likely blush like a virgin.

And die from embarrassment.

After all, he had told her to get out of his car.

The last thing she wanted him to know was she'd been masturbating like crazy since that night.

And if he looked at her, she just knew he'd sense it.

Hopefully she could navigate the room and keep away from him. Just a few more hours and he would be gone.

Hunter Dufort was infamous for leaving parties the moment it was appropriate to do so.

Then she could breathe again.

CHAPTER THREE

Where the fuck is she?

Hunter knew Addison was here and now that he'd arrived, he wanted to see her. To see that her sexy neck, blushed skin and the rebellious spark in her eyes that craved to be tamed, had only been in his imagination.

He needed to see he was wrong.

To know he'd fantasized over something that didn't exist and that he could forget about her.

Addison was in his head and if he had to toss off in the shower imagining her mouth around his cock one more time, he was going to punch a hole through the bathroom wall.

This was the thing about being a dominant. He had to have control. When he got a hint of something he wanted, well, he'd go to great lengths to get it.

And he wanted Addison.

Nearly as much as he wanted to prove to himself that he didn't.

Because he couldn't play in his family circle. Her best friend was marrying Fletcher, and he'd heard Addison was becoming a good friend of Harper's, too.

Fuck, the last thing he needed was Daniel on his case.

His brothers knew he had a taste for things more erotic than most.

That was it. That was all they knew.

He'd been told to keep his lifestyle away from people they knew, and the media.

Fair enough.

They did run a multi-billion-dollar global organization. Like his brothers, it wasn't something he wanted the high quality Dufort brand aligned with.

But for the most part, they left it alone.

At least, they did these days. When they had been maturing, he'd been discovered, so to speak. God, he'd never forget the day Daniel found him. He had been seventeen and caught with two girls of the same age in his room. They hadn't been doing homework.

He'd tied them both up with his silk ties and was taking turns at licking their pussies.

Daniel had walked in, not knowing he was... entertaining.

While there had been a degree of shocked pride in his big brother's eyes, there had also been a ton of judgment. He knew why. Shelley, one of the girls, had been his steady girlfriend. For like a month.

Shelley had taken some convincing, but once Caroline had taken her top off, they were both into it. Being caught had freaked her out, as it had all of them, but rather than own what she'd been doing and admitting her part in it, she had burst out into tears and said he'd bullied her into it.

He hadn't. Not at all.

Daniel had pulled him aside and told him he was no better than their father. And that he needed to keep his antics private and not get into another relationship if this was who he was.

And to this day, he felt that conversation had been fated. A warning.

Hunter wasn't to marry. If he did, he'd no doubt end up a cheater like their father. So, as he watched his brothers break their own vows to never settle, Hunter knew he'd be the only brother to keep it.

Forever.

His needs, as a Dom, were specific. He was demanding and couldn't imagine a relationship where that need existed inside a loving relationship.

Daniel and Fletcher were both dominant men, anyone could see that, and he had no doubt they expressed that sexually.

But his interests were different.

He used whips, leather, and punishment. But it wasn't just physical. True domination existed in playing a psychological game, too. If you could master both physical and mental, it was a purely pleasurable experience for all involved—if they were consenting, that is. It was who he was.

He'd never been entirely sure what his brothers thought about his *lifestyle,* but a few years ago, he'd invited them to the sex club he owned. Daniel had raised a brow.

So that was a no.

Fletch had simply said *yeah, no thanks man. You go hard though.*

The pun had been intended.

Knowing they considered him just like his father caused him a lot of shame. Johnathan Dufort had hurt their mother terribly for many years, taking hundreds of women to his bed. She had turned to the bottle and now had a serious alcohol problem she still hadn't kicked.

And that was where the line was drawn for him.

For all of them.

Fletcher and Daniel might turn a blind eye to his kink life, as long as he kept it out of the media, but they'd never forgive him cheating on a woman.

And he would never forgive himself.

If that hadn't been bad enough, when his father had found out about the Caroline-Shelley moment, he'd slapped him on the back and said, "It's okay, Hunter, you and I are alike. We love women. We need more to satisfy us. It's the way we're built."

Well, he would prove his father wrong.

He'd never be a cheater like his dad.

It wasn't long after that he had begun to look for alternative lifestyles and discovered sex clubs. First, he had visited, then he had invested in them.

Now he owned the most exclusive sex club in New York City. *Pendulum.*

"Did you see the email I sent you?" Fletcher asked.

Hunter let out a laugh. "Fletch, it's your damn engagement party. Stop working."

The guy was a workaholic. He was better now Olivia was in his life, but he suspected the two, because they worked together, talked shop a lot at home.

"Whatever," Fletcher said. "This app guy is only in New York for a week. I want you to meet him with me."

He'd seen it.

Another app developer wanting their business.

"You really think we need it?" he asked.

"I do. With our corporate traveling clientele, being able to manage bookings and check in, without having to ring or speak to their assistants, it will be a great offer."

Fletcher headed up the marketing for Dufort Hotels so the final decision was his, but they had always worked collaboratively. As sales director, a big part of his portfolio was looking after their largest corporate clients. And suppliers.

Both would need to be engaged to buy into a new system if they were to go ahead with it.

"I'm not entirely sold. Our clients get their personal assistants to do it. These people don't have time," Hunter replied. "Just like you and me."

Fletcher looked thoughtful.

"I know but that doesn't mean it will be that way forever. People are doing self-check-ins at airports and the cost saving has been tremendous for both the airports and airlines. Let's ensure we're moving with the times. I want to hear him out."

Maybe Fletcher was right.

He wasn't sure the time was now, which meant it was a great time to start researching.

"Okay, set it up," Hunter replied, his eyes roaming the floor.

"Are you waiting for someone?"

His gaze shot back to his brother. "What?"

Fletcher's brows raised slowly. "I hope you're not planning to leave early. This is my engagement party, for fuck's sake. At least stay until ten."

Ten?

Fucking hell.

"I wasn't eyeing the exit." He lifted his whiskey to his lips. "Where is your fiancée, anyway?"

Fletcher indicated with his chin. "Over talking with Addison."

Hunter's hand froze, and then slowly lowered, as his eyes followed the direction Fletcher indicated. And there she was, in a stunning green cocktail dress which finished mid-fucking-thigh. Her blonde hair curled around her face and her rose-colored lips were glossy.

His eyes drifted to the nude stiletto heels that wrapped around her ankles, making her already long tanned legs look sexy as hell.

Jesus.

She was as hot as he remembered, but dressed up like this, Addison was smoking. He lifted his glass to his lips again and blinked as those feet began to move toward him.

"Hunter, you remember Addy, don't you?" Olivia asked as they stopped in front of him.

The dark rich liquid slid down his throat and he swallowed slowly. Cobalt blue eyes that belonged to the ocean met his.

"I do," he said, finding that same rebellious fire within her gaze.

"Hello, Hunter." Addison's cheeks warmed.

Had he heard a note of challenge or was she trying to cover up her nerves? Because he'd seen the little shake of her glass as she held it with both hands. But if she was serious about the challenge, then, my dear, challenge accepted.

ADDISON had been lying to herself that she could avoid Hunter all evening. He was Olivia's fiancé's brother. Part of the close circle she found herself now in.

Those eyes of his had completely undressed her, and she felt, with one gaze, she had bared her soul to him.

Again.

She had no idea how she'd greeted him with such confidence. On the inside she was jelly, while her mind swirled with all the things she wanted him to do to her.

Hunter smirked.

Damn him.

He damn well knew, didn't he?

"Oh yes, he drove you home," Olivia said. "That day was such a blur."

"Sammy was missing, so of course it was," Fletcher said, and out of the corner of her eye she saw him throw his arm around Olivia.

Hunter hadn't shifted his gaze. His eyes were still holding hers.

Curious.

Bold.

Daring her to show him more.

She refused.

"Make sure he doesn't leave," Fletcher said as a couple approached the happy couple, and they were swept away into a new conversation.

Olivia shot her an apologetic look.

Oh, God.

It was one thing to face him with the others as a buffer, but being left with Hunter Dufort on her own was quite the other.

Her confidence faded.

Hunter's lips curled up. "I remember that drive quite well."

"What?" she asked, feeling her cheeks heat.

She knew what he meant but questions could buy time to plan an escape, or at the very least give the impression you weren't quite as impacted by the sexual prowess of the powerful man in front of you.

Because Hunter Dufort was powerful.

He was a billionaire.

Rich, powerful and he held all her sexual desires in the palm of his hand.

Not that she would ever let him know.

Aside from it being written all over her face.

Or so it felt.

CHAPTER FOUR

Hunter's smile shifted to a smirk.

That blush of hers had his cock stiff as a plank and ready to play. He shouldn't, but his body wasn't interested in all the rules of his family.

He tried to work it out.

How often would he actually see Addison?

The weddings, sure. But Fletcher and Olivia were going to wait at least a year because she was pregnant. There might be a special birthday or two, but otherwise she would rarely be in his life.

She was unlikely to attend Harper and Daniel's wedding because she barely knew them.

Hunter could act now, and with a year's distance, their dalliance, as it were, would be water under the bridge. And what he was planning to do to her, she wouldn't be sharing with anyone.

He grin widened, and she lifted a brow.

If Addison Hill could accept what he was offering, she had desires he could fulfill. Because it took a certain type of woman to react to him.

And she was reacting.

Right in front of him.

Her chest lifted a little more than normal, showing an increased breathing rate. Her hard nipples pressed against the fabric of her dress.

She could pretend to be aloof, but he wasn't buying it.

And she had no idea, yet, just how committed he was to pleasure.

Very.

Very fucking committed.

"How many times have you thought about it?" he asked, moving his body closer to hers, forcing her to lift her eyes and expose her neck to him.

Submission.

"I—"

"I apologize," Hunter said slowly. "That was completely inappropriate."

The blush on her cheeks deepened, her hands gripping her glass tighter.

He wasn't really sorry at all. She could lie to herself all she liked, but he could see the need he evoked within her. Still taunting her was a fun game.

"There's no way a woman like you has imagined my hand running up your thigh, and... well, other things."

"Other things?" Addison swallowed.

Hunter wanted to throw his head back at her wide eyes full of curiosity. She was gorgeous.

Instead, he leaned in so his breath was hot on her neck.

"Delicious other things. Things I think you would like. Very much. But... I don't think you're ready for them."

The fire in her eyes returned.

"You have no idea what I like. Or what I'm ready for." She took a sip of her drink and looked away. "Anyway, this is not appropriate, as you said."

A slow smirk spread once again across his face, and she shook her head when she saw it.

"What?" he asked, thoroughly enjoying the way he was impacting her.

"Why do men like you always have dimples?" she scoffed.

"Sweetheart, it's not my dimples you should be afraid of. Trust me."

ADDISON'S body was an inferno.

She had to get away from this man. One second, she wanted to slap him, the next she wanted to lift her skirt and beg Hunter Dufort to touch her.

She'd never felt so insane.

And by the way he was watching her, studying her, he knew exactly how he was affecting her.

And was enjoying it.

"Hey, Addy," Harper said, joining them.

Thank God.

Hunter shot her a last devious smirk and then moved an inch away.

"We so need to ramp up this music. Get some dancing started," Harper said. "Do you know how to work Fletcher's spaceship?"

Hunter coughed out a laugh.

"Spaceship?" Addison asked.

"Yes. Look at all the buttons," Harper said, pointing at the Backes & Müller stereo system as Daniel stepped up behind her. The two were rarely separated when in the same room. Like two magnets.

Addison glanced between the two brothers and Hunter slightly narrowed his eyes.

Dominance.

It ran through both of them.

His eyes darkened, surprising her, with what she felt was a challenge. As if he were saying *keep those thoughts of yours to yourself.*

"Honey, before you turn this place into a club, why don't we make our announcement?" Daniel said.

"Oh?" Addison asked.

"Christ don't tell me you're pregnant. Am I living in a reality TV show?" Hunter groaned.

Three sets of eyes glared at him.

"Sorry, wrong audience. But come on already," he added. "Weddings, babies, what next?"

Addison tried not to smile, but she saw it from his point of view. His brothers were all shaking up and settling down.

"Hunter, you're fucking lucky that's not what we're announcing because if my fiancée *was* pregnant, I'd be smacking the shit out of you right now," Daniel growled.

Addison leaned away. When Daniel was protecting his girl, he was mean. And this was mild.

"Stop it," Harper said, noticing her reaction.

"Except we aren't thirteen anymore." Hunter laughed, draining the rest of his glass.

"Irrelevant," Daniel replied. "I can still take you."

"Okay, you two." Harper rolled her eyes and Addison relaxed, pressing her lips together to stop from smiling. "Call your brother over. Let's tell everyone."

What *were* they announcing?

When Fletcher and Olivia joined them, and Daniel had corralled a few other people, Harper clasped her hands together.

Addison knew she wasn't pregnant, going by the glass of champagne she'd been drinking moments before.

"What is it?" Fletcher asked.

"Harper and I have accepted your offer to get married at the Hamptons house," Daniel said.

"The invites go out tomorrow," Harper said, looking giddy.

"Oh, this is so exciting. The house is so beautiful," Olivia said, sighing.

Addison had heard all about the large sweeping waterfront property on Meadow Lane, or *Billionaire Lane* as it was known after Fletcher flew Liv there by helicopter for a romantic date.

As everyone around them began celebrating the news, Addison felt a little like an imposter sharing in their family announcement. She went to slip away when Harper caught her eye.

"You'll come, won't you Addy?"

What?

"Oh," she said, surprised. "Are you sure?"

"Yes. You're my friend now. I've stolen her." She winked at Olivia who laughed. "Please come."

"It would be good to have you there, Addy. You can stay at the house. We have tons of rooms," Olivia said. "Plus, Harper's friends are flying in from New Zealand but we're the girls in her life now."

Harper nodded. "Kristen is going to be my bridesmaid, but I would love both your help with choosing a dress and the bachelorette party."

"It would be an honor," Addison said, surprised but truly happy to be involved in her new friend's wedding activities.

"Me too," Olivia said. "You have a wedding planner, right Harper?"

"Hell yes," Harper said. "She's been waiting for us to decide on a venue. Everything else is *mostly* agreed upon."

Wow, the Hamptons.

It had been a long time, despite it only being a few hours' drive away from New York City, since Addison had been there.

"Plan to stay for the long weekend," Harper said. "We'll have the rehearsal on Saturday, wedding on Sunday then wedding lunch on Monday."

A weekend? With the Dufort's?

When she looked up, Hunter was watching her with an unreadable expression that unnerved her.

Was he thinking the same thing?

They were about to spend a weekend in the same location.

God help her.

It was one thing keeping her distance from him at an event. Quite the other when their rooms would be down the hall.

HUNTER watched Addison walk down the hall to, he assumed, the bathroom.

He smiled at the couple he'd been chatting to, placed his crystal tumbler on the side table, and went in the same direction.

The hallway turned to the right, and the bathroom was down the end. A woman he recognized walked toward him. He smiled and, just beyond her, Hunter watched Addison step inside and close the door behind her.

What was he doing? Stalking his prey?

Yes, that's exactly what he was doing. He leaned against the wall and plugged his hands into his pant pockets.

Four minutes later the door opened.

Addison gasped.

"God! What are you doing here?" Her hand flew to her chest.

"This is my brother's penthouse. Do you have amnesia?" he asked. "We met a month ago. We talked out in the living room."

"Ha-ha." She shook her head at him. "You just gave me a fright, that's all."

The door closed behind her, but she didn't walk away. He pushed away from the wall and pulled his hands out of his pockets.

One step.

That's all it took to move into her personal space.

He breathed in a subtle floral scent with hints of vanilla as his head dipped to the arch of her neck. "That's because your nerves are on fire."

Her eyes darted to his as he stood straight.

"No."

"No?" His mouth curled. He delighted in the little fight she was putting up.

More shaking of her head, as her lips pressed together. "No."

"So you aren't wondering if I'm going to touch you right now?" His fingers hovered over a bare patch of skin on her shoulder. "Or how my lips would feel on yours?"

Her mouth parted.

"Or whether I should offer you another ride home and this time there would be a different outcome?"

She was breathing faster now, but then again so was he. Except Hunter was more adept at hiding it.

Hers was a reaction borne of fear.

His was excitement.

The thrill of the chase.

"Run, Addison. You need to get far from me if you want to stay innocent."

She blinked.

"I'm a mother. I'm hardly a virgin." She laughed lightly but her eyes were rich with question.

He smiled widely.

"Oh, sweetheart. Your body I would pleasure. It's your mind I would corrupt."

As she began to swallow, Hunter moved an inch closer and let his finger fall to her skin and brush over her collarbone.

"Run, Addison. Before I take the choice from you."

Blue eyes sizzled in challenge as she drew in a breath. Then he saw her confidence fade. She quickly turned and walked away.

Hunter let out the breath he'd been holding.

The one she hadn't seen.

Then he walked into the bathroom and leaned on the counter, staring at himself in the mirror.

Fuck.

Letting her walk away had cost him.

His body needed this woman under him, surrendered to him.

And in that moment, he determined he would have her.

CHAPTER FIVE

Hunter left not long after his encounter with Addison. He watched her standing with a group of people, guzzling champagne and while a part of him wanted to see her home, if only to ensure she got there safely, he knew there was something he needed more.

So he'd slipped out and headed to Pendulum. His club was an exclusive members-only sex club for those with specific tastes and big bank accounts.

And while it was private, no one would ever know who he was because masquerade masks were mandatory.

His ownership was also so deeply buried it would take someone very clever to trace it back to him or the Dufort Dynasty.

While there, he took a submissive brunette to a private room, told her to strip and climb into the sex swing. Two minutes with the magic wand on her clit and she was wet and whimpering.

Then he'd taken it away for a moment before returning it. Over and over he tortured her until she was pleading.

It was such a beautiful sound.

Would Addison be a moaner or a screamer?

Hunter then had Ms. Brunette take his cock in her mouth and fucked her throat while she clung to the black harness of the swing.

As he'd come, his eyes clenched. All he could see in his vision were those cobalt blue eyes and long tanned legs of Addison Hill.

Hunter had been playing with both their minds.

He couldn't have her, and he knew it. She was an extension of his family now that Olivia was engaged to Fletcher.

If she was a club girl, they could have fun and it wouldn't be a problem. But women like Addison got attached. If he hurt her, and he would, his brothers would kick his ass.

So, he had a month to get her out of his system before they would be spending time together under the same roof. There was no way he was going to avoid her by not going to Daniel's wedding. He'd just take the chopper over in the morning and then leave later that night by the same form of transport.

Of course he could rent a property nearby to reduce the tension of being in close proximity to Addison, but he wouldn't.

The Hamptons home was special to all of them. He had his own room there, for God's sake. Fletcher had purchased it from his father years ago when Johnathan said he was selling it. As children they'd spent many happy vacations there—before things had gotten worse with his parents.

His brothers had been a little older than him when his father's philandering behavior began to surface, and his mother's drinking increased. Hunter had been somewhat sheltered from a lot of it.

Before that it had been summers of sunshine, riding bikes, flying kites on the beach, licking melting ice-creams and following his big brothers to midnight bonfires when they were supposed to be tucked up in bed.

Wonderful memories they all cherished.

Now it was a location they traveled to for adult fun. Friends would stay or they'd have the occasional weekend away together when they were all bachelors.

Those days were over now and a new chapter was starting.

Hunter might have different sexual interests than his brothers, but they were all very close and his family was important to him. Regardless of how imperfect it was.

Because it *was* imperfect.

Being in the Hamptons with Addison sleeping and showering close by was going to be a test of his willpower. Hopefully, by then he would lose interest in her.

Fortunately, the pre-wedding activities for Fletcher and his brothers excluded the women. There were wedding suit fittings—Daniel had asked Fletcher to be his best man, which was no surprise, but Hunter was also to wear the same suit as his brother.

And there was the bachelor party that the two of them would plan. It was crazy to think they were going to celebrate Daniel's last night as a single man.

Frankly, that night had well and truly passed the moment he met Harper, but this was the tradition.

TWO weeks later, Hunter was sitting in his office, the Manhattan skyline and a bright blue summer sky behind and all around him thanks to the floor-to-ceiling glass on his seventy-second-floor view, when Fletcher walked in and sat down.

"Please, don't knock. Help yourself. Would you like a pair of my spare underwear too?" Hunter leaned back in his leather executive chair.

"You don't wear underwear." Fletcher shrugged, then tilted his head. "And if you did, why would you have a spare

pair in your office? A shirt I get—I have them too—but...
ugh no, actually, don't answer that."

Hunter smirked.

He loved that the little knowledge his brothers had about
his kinks meant their imagination went into overdrive.
Especially when he dropped little comments. On purpose, of
course.

It helped to offset the natural bullying that came with
being the younger brother.

He may not be quite as big as Daniel, but he wasn't a
small man either. He'd always made up for size and being
the youngest, with cunning. Fletcher was the more laid back
of them all, but as the former *Playboy of Manhattan* he'd had
his own reputation to focus on.

"What are you getting Daniel for a wedding present?"
Fletch asked.

"Nothing. He has everything he needs and more."

"You can't *not* get him anything. It's his wedding day."

"And Harper's," Hunter reminded him. "Maybe they'll
do the no-gift rule. Or, and hear me out, how about a trip to
Machu Picchu?"

Fletcher choked on the coffee he was drinking and
laughed as he wiped his mouth. "He'd hate it."

Hunter grinned and slowly nodded. "But who *would* love
it?"

Together they both mouthed, *Harper.*

"Evil. I like it." Fletcher laughed. "But I might just go
with the *his and hers* Rolex set."

Hunter sat forward and grabbed his pen; fairly certain
Daniel wouldn't want gifts. Especially another Rolex. He
had three.

"More importantly, Best Man, is everything set for this
weekend's bachelor party?"

"All booked. I can't believe you wouldn't let me book
strippers. His face would have made my life," Fletcher said.

There was no way.

Daniel had been very specific. He didn't want strippers as it could leak to the media too easily and Harper would be upset.

Hunter didn't think she would mind.

It was more likely Daniel had promised her he wouldn't in the hope she wouldn't either. But if he knew Olivia, and he did a little, it was likely she would make sure Harper had a blast. One way or another.

"I probably saved your face. Oh, and did you book a meeting with the app guy?" Hunter asked.

"It's in your calendar for tomorrow," Fletcher said, then his expression turned thoughtful as he tilted his head. "He asked if Johnathan was going to join us. I thought that was weird."

Their father?

Hunter's brows twitched. "Clearly hasn't done his research. It's no secret we bought the majority of shares off Dad. It was all over the national media."

Fletcher tucked his shirt into his pants unnecessarily as he stood.

"Daniel has been CEO for years, but he didn't ask about him. Maybe he's working off an old database." Fletcher shook it off. "Anyway, I'm keen to see his presentation. Keep an open mind."

"I will," Hunter promised.

"You'd be surprised how much these memberships and the advertising on the app itself can generate. Read the attachment in the meeting appointment I sent."

Yeah, he hadn't gotten to that yet.

"I'll get to it. We've had contract renewals with all major suppliers this past quarter. These things take fucking forever."

And if he was being honest with himself, he'd been distracted lately. He'd even found himself taking a different turn—or ten—and driving past Addison's brownstone.

So now he was a stalker.

His brothers would love to know that.

"How are you traveling to the Hamptons?" Fletch asked, one foot out the door, his hand on the doorframe.

Oh, hell no.

Before he could answer, his brother continued.

"I've booked the big helicopter. Olivia, Addison, and I will be leaving on the Friday afternoon so if you want to jump aboard, you're welcome."

Nope.

"I'll just fly in on Sunday for the wedding." He stood to stretch his back. When there was silence, he lifted his eyes.

"What?" he asked.

"Don't."

"Don't what?" Hunter laughed with little humor. He knew exactly *what*, but he wasn't in the mood for the brotherly lecture.

But here it was in three, two...

"There is an entire weekend of activities. Pre-wedding dinner, day events, the wedding breakfast. You need to be there, Hunt." Fletcher frowned.

"Are these people trying to eat themselves to death? How many wedding meals do you need?"

Fletcher laughed. "Just be there on the Friday and Daniel won't kick your ass."

His brother gave him the *look* and then left.

"Fuck." He cursed quietly and walked over to the windows so he could stare out across the city. The sun was sinking into the Hudson River, burning orange and for some unbeknownst reason it made him think of Addison.

Where was she right now?

Had she been thinking about the way her body had shivered under his touch? Was she planning her lingerie for the wedding weekend, hoping he'd corrupt her as he'd promised?

Friday.

Saturday.

Sunday.

Monday.

Four goddamn days he would have to keep his hands off sexy blue-eyed Addison.

Impossible.

Even he could admit that.

CHAPTER SIX

Addison sat beside Olivia on the blush pink sofa. Their daughters Sammy and Sienna sat on the other side behind them, kicking their legs while playing on their iPads, and they waited.

And waited.

"Are you coming out or are you going to get married in there?" Olivia called out, grinning.

Silence.

The two of them glanced at each other, and Addison saw a knowing look in Olivia's eyes that probably matched her own. They both stood at the same time, dropped their glasses—Addy's a champagne, Olivia's grape juice—and shot across the room.

"Harper?" Addison asked, quietly.

Sniff.

Another glance at each other and Olivia gave her a sad face. "You want to open the door, honey?"

"I'll be out in a minute," Harper said, her Kiwi accent thick. "I'm just—"

"Emotional?" Addison asked.

There was a small moment of silence and then the door opened.

They all ignored the magnificent gown she was wearing as Harper wiped the tears falling down her face with the back of her hands.

They both enveloped her in a hug.

"I'm so stupid," Harper cried.

"No, you're not," Olivia said, pulling back. "You're miles from home and everything you know. And everyone you know."

"Trying on wedding gowns is a big deal. Trust me. We both cried," Addison said.

"You did?" Harper asked, and they both nodded.

"Oh yeah, it was ugly," Olivia said. "Especially Addy."

"Hey!" She laughed because it was true. "My mom died when I was little so there was all that to deal with."

Harper gripped her arm, and her eyes flew open. "Oh, God, Addy. Here I am crying because my people aren't yet here, but you *lost* your mom?"

She shot Sienna a glance, but the girls were in their own little digital worlds.

"I was little. Like five. So, its fine," Addison said, knowing that was a big fat lie. Losing your mom at any age was heartbreaking, but you learned to live with it and adapt as the years went by. It wasn't the same as losing a parent as an adult. She knew that too because her father had passed away last year. He had been a smoker all his life and, as everyone told him he would, he got lung cancer.

So she had divorced Rob and then found herself without any family, all within two years.

It was an odd feeling. She felt like her life had no footing some days.

Friends became more like family and while she and Rob were no longer married, keeping a good relationship was important.

He had been dating, so one day he'd remarry and have more children. The gap between them would be greater then.

Addison didn't know if she would marry again. Marriage hadn't been what she expected. Not that she had imagined it like a fairytale as some people did. She had hoped to build the family unit she'd never had.

Rob had three siblings and as they'd begun to have children, his family was growing in size.

She loved that Sienna had lots of cousins but for Addison, on the weeks she didn't have her daughter, it was just her.

On her own.

Not dating.

She loved spending time with Harper and Olivia, but they too were marrying and building their lives with amazing men.

Billionaire men.

At times it felt awkward. They both lived in these incredible penthouses and while neither of them had come from money anywhere near the level they now had, they were wealthy women.

Security. Designer clothing. Fabulous parties.

She faked it as best she could, then caught an Uber home to her brownstone at the end of the night.

Well, except that one time with Hunter, but she couldn't think about that right now. Or ever again.

He'd run his finger across her skin at Liv's engagement party and her body had imploded. His eyes had been sizzling like he was the damn devil.

Maybe he was?

In two weeks' time, she would be with him and his family for Harper's wedding.

It was going to be hell.

How appropriate then that he was the devil.

If Addison was ever going to marry again, it would be to a man with a big family or someone who wanted that. At only twenty-nine she had time. She'd choose wisely this time. Someone with passion, but a solid man who would grow with her.

Someone she could rely on and know he was her true partner in life.

Her person.

Like Olivia and Harper had.

So she'd never lose her footing in life again.

"But as you're finding out, when you put those damn dresses on, they open the floodgates." She smiled at Harper who nodded. "Plus, I heard you lost your dad?"

"Yeah. I've decided I'm going to walk down the aisle by myself. Daniel's dad offered but I don't know him."

Olivia rubbed her arm. "I think that sounds like a great idea for an independent woman. You are giving yourself away. You don't belong to anyone else."

"That's true. I never looked at it like that," Harper said. "Kristen said she would if I wanted."

Kristen was Harper's best friend who was flying over from New Zealand.

"You'll know what feels right. Now, let's take a look. Are you ready to come out?" Olivia asked.

When she nodded, they moved back into the private room, and she followed them out.

"Is it too much?" Harper asked, running her hands down the huge skirts of the rustling cream gown.

"If you have to ask, then it's not the one," Addy said. "You'll know. As soon as you look in the mirror, you'll know."

Seven gowns later, Harper plopped down on the seat beside them in her bra and panties and let out a long sigh. The girls giggled behind them, getting very excited about this game of (expensive) dress-up, calling Harper a Disney Princess.

"Jesus, I'm exhausted," Harper said, and they all laughed. "Am I allowed to ask about the bachelorette party?"

"No," Addy and Liv said in unison.

"Kristen and I are planning it remotely. She arrives Thursday, right?" Olivia asked.

"Yup," Harper said. "Can't wait. Then Mom arrives on Friday, and we fly straight to the Hamptons."

Addison smiled. Thursday was only a couple of days away and would help to lift the bride-to-be's spirits.

"Okay, one more," Harper said, bouncing up.

And wouldn't you know it, the water works started once again as Harper found her dress.

Liv and Addy clinked glasses as Harper said, *I'm saying yes to the dress.*

THE next day Addison got the official invite from Olivia for the bachelorette party as she was sitting at her desk procrastinating.

Liar.

You are thinking about him.

Cindy knocked on her office door which was open.

"Hey," her manager said. "Got a moment?"

"Of course. Come in."

"Did you see the results from the focus group we did?" Cindy asked, and Addison nearly winced. Normally she would have opened it eagerly, keen to know what the consumer panel had been thinking.

"No, not yet," she admitted, clicking to find the email.

"We need to revisit the new product development on the vodka line extension," Cindy said. "Our consumers are maturing and so are their tastes. Their responses are pretty clear. They found it sugary and said they wouldn't choose it over other options when shopping."

Addison nodded, thinking.

"Then let's go back to them with the herbal infusions and see what they say." She had always thought that was the better idea but a louder voice in the room, who was out of touch with trends, had pushed to go with the vanilla, raspberry, and boysenberry tones.

Addison had suspected this would be the outcome of their research so had patiently gone through the process and waited. Sometimes it was better to say nothing and let the data speak for itself.

"Go for it. I'll approve the additional budget for another panel," Cindy said. "And Addy, good job. You voiced your thoughts well during concept, and I wanted to let you know it didn't go unnoticed."

"Thank you," she said, nodding.

"I'll be reviewing who sits on the product development panel soon. It will save us thousands." Cindy winked.

"Sounds like a smart move to me," Addison said, affording herself a small grin. "I'll let you know what the results are."

"One last thing. I heard you were at the Dufort's engagement party recently," Cindy said, leaning her hip against the door.

Ah.

Cindy was the chief executive of Bridge&Co Wines and Spirits, so she knew what was coming next. If she was in her shoes, she'd do the same thing. The Dufort's were a huge global organization.

"Yes. Fletcher Dufort is marrying my best friend." She nodded.

Cindy held her gaze for a moment.

Please don't—

"Well, I think you know what I'm going to ask, so I'm just going to say, if there is an opportunity then I know you'll jump at it."

She wanted to jump at something, but it wasn't having a contract with Dufort for their liquor supply.

Although that would be a huge bonus for her.

"It wouldn't be appropriate, I'm sorry."

Cindy smiled and left.

CHAPTER SEVEN

Jackson Wiles stepped into the lobby of the Dufort Towers in New York City. He'd known it would be impressive. Hell, they were one of the top hotel chains in the world. But this was much fancier than he'd been expecting.

Not that he was a small-town guy from Idaho, or the like. Quite the opposite. He'd grown up in Los Angeles and was used to the glitz and glamor of Hollywood and all that came with living in the city of angels.

Or the city of dreams if you believed that drivel.

He didn't. Jackson had made his dreams come true with hard work and focus.

So no, Jackson wasn't new to the Dufort brand. Just like most Americans, he was very familiar with the quality hotel chain. Recently, however, he'd begun to look at the hotel chain differently.

Before him the enormous lobby was luxury personified and almost sparkled. The whole luxury look and feel was part of the Dufort brand, which he knew from doing his homework to pitch them his new app.

Actually, the place did sparkle.

An enormous chandelier hung from the center of the ceiling which had to be at least four stories high, and the walls were shiny and glistened as tiny crystals bounced off them.

The carpet was thick and on closer inspection, featured hundreds of little double Ds from their logo. His eyes followed the path around the circular waiting area which encompassed four sofas and behind it was the reception desk.

Across the large space there were two sets of elevators which led to each tower, and one private elevator which he knew led to the executive area where Daniel, Fletcher and Hunter Dufort had their offices.

That was who he was here to see.

His half-brothers.

CHAPTER EIGHT

"Please sit down," Fletcher said, shaking Jackson's hand. Hunter did the same before moving around the boardroom table.

He sat and watched the young tech guy from Appopolis LLC. In truth, the guy was probably only a few years younger than he was.

"Thanks for meeting with me," Jackson Wiles said, and then turned as several of their team members stepped into the room.

"Sorry, sorry," one of them said. "Daniel's presentation went on a few moments longer."

Ah, the monthly team CEO update. He'd skipped it to finish a few urgent things.

Fletcher introduced everyone and when all the handshakes and pleasantries were over, everyone sat.

Jackson seemed to be a confident young man, and he watched everyone in the room as if assessing them.

Including Hunter.

He inched his brows up a little when Jackson's gaze landed on him again and the man's lips stretched into a smile.

Faint, but there was something about it that sent a chill up his spine.

Odd.

"Let's get started," Fletcher said, clapping his hands. "The floor is yours, Jackson."

"Thank you. It's great to be here," he said. "The team and I at Appopolis have done a lot of research on Dufort Hotels so I hope you enjoy my presentation. Feel free to ask questions throughout."

He tapped on a tablet and the screen in front of them lit up with a slide.

Yawn.

Hunter was already bored. He'd seen enough PowerPoint presentations in his career already.

Jackson clicked through, presented slide after slide of information on Dufort which they clearly knew.

Cool. The guy had proved his point. He knew their business.

Next!

"We've called it LUXON," Jackson said, showing an image of a mobile phone with the name and their highly recognizable Dufort logo.

A few impressed murmurs filled the room.

Hunter only just held back the eye roll.

It wasn't that the proposal was bad, he just had a feeling about this guy that he couldn't put a finger on.

Still, he tried to keep an open mind.

As director of sales, numbers were his language and those were usually shown at the end. All the pretty images were more Fletcher's thing.

However, should they go ahead, Jackson would be dealing heavily with Hunter as they negotiated the cost of implementing such a system into the Dufort business.

"Let me show you one of our client apps in action," Jackson said, then smirked. "You'll have to excuse the fact it's a competitor of yours... and nothing I am showing you is confidential. Any one of you could search for it in your app store and sign up today."

Hunter tilted his head. "For free?"

Jackson's eyes darted to his and for a moment he felt a sense of familiarity.

Had he met this guy before?

Perhaps he'd seen him in *Forbes*? Fletcher had hinted at his fast success, and that well-known media company calling him a tech genius.

"Do we know each other?" he suddenly asked.

The room went quiet.

"No. We absolutely have never met before." Jackson replied with such certainty it sent another shiver through him.

Hunter glanced at his brother, who shrugged.

He dropped it, but the nagging feeling didn't go away. And while Jackson had sounded sure, a flicker in his eyes captured Hunter's attention.

Had Fletcher done a background check on this guy? A real one?

Well, they would be doing a deep dive before they progressed further. He rarely ignored his instincts, and something wasn't right.

Giving Jackson and his team access to their intellectual property, client and supplier data was not something they would do without intense scrutiny of the company and owners.

Appopolis would have access to every piece of data Dufort had.

So no, this guy wasn't getting access to anything until they'd swept through this life and knew every single thing about him.

"In answer to your question, yes. It is free. There are different levels to these products. When you pay, you open up tools and benefits that the free membership doesn't allow," Jackson said. "Let me demonstrate." The lights in the room dimmed as a video began to play.

Hunter felt like he was inside an Apple product launch. It was impressive even if he didn't want to admit it.

"As you can see, it takes pressure off the support team and puts control back into the hands of the corporate traveler. Making changes is quick and easy, and in real time so you can rest assured any booking changes are accurate."

Hunter pressed his lips together.

That assumed a hell of a lot about their tech systems. But he kept quiet.

"And it connects with the traveler's digital assets such as an Apple Watch, so he can use that to sign in rather than looking through emails or even the app itself after flying."

Fine, it had some merit.

Perhaps more than a little.

Feeling a bit more comfortable as the video continued, Hunter's mind drifted.

Tomorrow was Daniel's bachelor party, and Harper's bachelorette. What were the girls doing? Was Addison going?

Of course she would be.

A vision of Addison with a male stripping and forcing her to rub her hand up and down his cock suddenly flashed through his mind.

Jesus. His own cock twitched.

Down boy. I'm at work, for fuck's sake.

Plus, strippers weren't whores, so they didn't do that sort of thing. Performers at his club did, and he wondered if she would like that. Or would she be shy?

Would it excite her?

Was she someone who liked to watch, or be watched?

He found himself wondering a lot of things recently.

Did she date? *Was* she dating?

Fuck, what if she was?

He clenched his hand and the pen he was holding popped out of his fist into the air and landed loudly on the table.

Everyone in the room turned to him.

Hunter cleared his throat. "Apologies."

"He has the attention span of a three-year-old," Fletcher said, shaking his head. "But don't be mistaken, he's listened to every single word."

Not today I haven't.

"Yeah, he does." Jenny, one of his team members said, nodding, and Hunter laughed and gave her a wink. His team knew exactly what he was like, as did his brothers, but today they were all wrong.

He had been distracted with thoughts of Addison for too long. He had a week to get her out of his system before they left for the Hamptons and so far, that was looking unlikely.

Jackson laughed. "No worries. Look, I've taken up enough of your time today. I'll email you the presentation when I get back to my hotel later tonight and follow up next week."

Everyone stood, shook hands and Fletcher's PA, Scarlett, arrived to see Jackson out.

Before he left, Hunter called out to him. "Where is your business located?"

"Los Angeles," Jackson replied, glancing out the large glass windows and indicating the Manhattan skyline. "This is my first visit to the Big Apple."

Interesting.

"Are you staying in one of our hotels?" Scarlett asked.

"Yes, ma'am," he answered. "The new SoHo Dufort Hotel."

"Please provide Mr. Wiles with some vouchers for the SoHo Bar and Grill while he's here," Fletcher said.

"That's not necessary—"

"If you're going to do business with us, you need to know our product. Take them. Enjoy," Hunter said, crossing the room and shaking his hand.

Jackson shook it and nodded his thanks, then followed Scarlett out.

When the room emptied, Hunter turned to Fletcher who was frowning at him.

"We need to vet him," Hunter said.

"Of course, we fucking do. That's standard operating procedure. What's wrong? That was an impressive presentation. They clearly have cutting-edge technology," Fletcher growled.

"Instinct," Hunter replied.

Fletcher shook his head. "I'll get the report done but you need to lose the attitude. It was plainly obvious in there."

Hunter stared out at the empty hallway, wondering how he could know the guy. If Jackson hadn't been in Manhattan before he wouldn't have been to any of Hunter's clubs. It was rare he went to one outside of the city.

"Don't you think he looks familiar?" He ignored his brother's comment.

"I've never seen him before in my life," Fletcher said, collecting his laptop and slipping his phone into his pocket. "You okay?"

Hunter ran a hand through his hair.

He wasn't sure what he was feeling; why he was so untrusting of the guy. Yes, he trusted his instincts but there was something nagging in the back of his mind.

Maybe he was going through a damn mid-life crisis. At twenty-eight. Both his brothers were marrying—and it was sudden. He was happy for them but, because they'd all said they would never marry, Hunter had imagined them living the bachelor life forever.

Naïve perhaps.

But while they had their own homes, interests, and friends, the three of them were best friends.

Hunter was mature enough to know he hadn't lost his brothers, but there was still a feeling that his life was a little emptier than it had been just a few months ago.

Which was a little privileged of him, he realized. God, he was a major shareholder in their family dynasty which, along with other investments, made him a billionaire a handful of times over. He had a wonderful family–if you overlooked his philandering father and alcoholic mother— and he had some great friends.

He was healthy and fit, and had traveled the globe, fucked some of the most beautiful women in the world, and met kings, princes and dukes.

Yet the awareness that he'd never have what Fletcher and Daniel now had, was nudging at him.

Love.

Romantic love.

And for the first time in his life, it felt like a loss, rather than something he'd agreed to.

Then he'd met Addison and couldn't get her off his mind.

It was messing with him. Confusing him.

"I'm just distracted by a few things," Hunter said. "I could be wrong but something about him feels off. We should also look at a few other companies. Just do your due diligence and I'll do the numbers."

Yeah, that came out a little harsh.

Fletcher raised his brows.

"I'm going to let that fly because you clearly have some shit you're dealing with," Fletcher replied, and began to walk out. "Call me if you want to talk."

Damn it.

Hunter grabbed his coffee mug and laptop and stood staring out the window. He had been an asshole, but that didn't mean he was wrong. His instincts were still on fire.

Who the hell was Jackson Wiles?

CHAPTER NINE

Addison checked her dress in the mirror, twisting from side to side.

"Mommy, you look beautiful," Sienna said, from her cross-legged position on her bed.

"Thank you, darling." Addison turned to her daughter. She leaned down and kissed her forehead. "Do you have your bags packed for Daddy?"

Her little girl nodded.

"What time is Sammy coming?"

Sammy had her own driver and personal protection because she'd been abducted by her lunatic father and Fletcher had insisted on it.

He'd also briskly moved them into his penthouse on billionaire row, so they were no longer living a few blocks away.

"She's meeting you at Daddy's," Addison replied. "I want you to be good tonight. No treats after nine o'clock, okay?"

Rob kept giving in and letting Sienna have *just one more cookie* before bed. It meant she slept poorly and was a little monster the next day.

She nodded, but a smirk appeared. Addison stood up straight and put her hands on her hips.

"I mean it, Sienna. If you're grumpy tomorrow and want to come home early, the answer is no. You have to stay with Dad all weekend."

Which was a complete lie.

Every mother alive knew she'd never say no to her child, but damn it, for the past three weekends Rob had had Sienna, she'd called in a terrible mood and cried until Addy had given in. She was definitely the bad cop parent.

Rob only had her every second weekend, so it had been six long weeks since she'd had a weekend to herself. Single parenting was no joke.

Sienna's face looked horrified, and guilt set in.

Addison crouched. "I'm just saying you need to stop with the sneaky treats at night so you can have a good sleep and spend quality time with your dad."

Little nod.

"But what if I want to come home?" Sienna sniffed.

Heaven's above.

"You can *always* come home. Always. But your mummy is busy this weekend and your dad wants to spend time with you. You're his little princess." Addison brushed her thumb over Sienna's cheek.

God, she was going to kill Rob.

She shouldn't be telling her child not to eat treats. It was his job to teach her good habits too. This was half their problem during the marriage. He had no backbone.

He couldn't even say no to a nearly seven-year-old wanting a cookie, let alone throw his wife against the wall and kiss her passionately. Two sentences that shouldn't go together, but the point was, Rob was weak. He'd never been enough for her.

She *had* loved him, though. They'd met when they were younger and in hindsight, he'd been more of a friend to her while they were studying and learning how to be adults. Addison had thought he was what she wanted. Loyal, grounded, solid.

The sex hadn't been horrible. He had been her first and had some moves. He went down on her at least once a week and knew how to make her orgasm.

She hadn't really thought about if he was *the one,* then suddenly she'd found out she was pregnant.

They married quickly, which had been important to them both, before Sienna was born. They'd been together for years by then, so it was expected by their friends and families, and no one had been critical of the situation.

She had wondered from time to time, if she hadn't gotten pregnant, if they would have just drifted apart.

Then who would she have become?

Would she have discovered she had different desires than the average person? Perhaps she would have met someone who was a little more playful or risqué in the bedroom and enjoyed a more sexually adventurous life.

She'd never wish Sienna hadn't been born, but she still wondered.

After Addison had left Rob, and he'd made her feel like there was something wrong with her, she'd gone to a therapist.

There she was told to be open about her sexual interest and go explore. Safely. She was told there was nothing wrong with her.

But the damage had been done.

She'd lost ninety-five percent of her friends, her marriage and her father who had died thinking she was some kind of sexual deviant.

After leaving Rob, she'd only slept with a handful of men and never found the courage to ask about their sexual tastes.

How exactly did one bring it up? And when?

Date two or three? And say, *so, hey, any chance you'd like to tie me up? Or got any kinks you'd like to share?* So unless she got brave fast, she was going to die alone and unfulfilled.

The alternative was joining dating sites that catered to those into BDSM or sex clubs.

Nope.

No way.

She was not touching that world with a barge pole. That was not who she was. She couldn't be a respectful mother *and* step into that world.

Was she curious? Yes.

Did shame strike her down for even thinking about it? Fuck, yes!

So it was a hard no.

No, no, no, no, no.

TWO hours later, Addison clinked her flute against Olivia's less alcoholic one, inside one of the bars at Dufort SoHo at Harper's bachelorette party.

The gorgeous space had been closed to the public for the evening and filled with over fifty women, music, and an eternal flow of champagne.

"You guys, this is too much," Harper said, dancing over to them.

"It's amazing," Kristen, said, her arm looped around Harper's. "I'm never going home. I love New York."

They'd loved Harper's best friend from the moment she arrived. She was gorgeous, funny, and full of life.

The two were complete opposites, though. Harper was olive-skinned with long dark curly hair which she had inherited from her Hawaiian father. Kristen had creamy skin and long blonde waves. She was also a lot shorter. Five foot four at a push, Addison guessed.

But it was her eyes that captured you when you first met her. They were an emerald green. Before she could ask, Kristen had said, *yes they are real.*

Stunning was the best way to describe her with a very down-to-earth personality Addy was beginning to associate with New Zealanders.

"That's because you're dressed in Dolce and Gabbana and drinking Cristal. It's not like this every day," Harper said, laughing. "Plus there's snow."

Olivia laughed.

Addison arched a brow in question.

"Harper's a beach girl at heart. They met in Hawaii. Daniel has promised her multiple tropical island holidays between December and February."

"Can't he just buy an island?" Kristen asked.

Addison choked on her champagne. "I love her. And it's good to not be the only non-billionaire in the room."

"Hey, I'm—" Olivia started then stared into her drink. "Am I?"

They all nodded.

"It's not my money, though," Olivia said.

"You're his fiancée, honey. That's your life now," Harper said. They all glanced at the private security standing in the shadows.

"There are worse fates, ladies. Jeez, don't look so miserable about it." Kristen laughed.

Addison smirked. "Come on, the stripper will be here soon. Let's get some shots down so we can represent all the single ladies." She grabbed Kristen's arm and giggled when Harper's mouth fell open.

She'd be waiting all night for the stripper to arrive.

Because there was no way any of them were facing the wrath of Daniel by actually booking strippers.

"Are there really strippers?" Kristen asked as they walked to the bar.

"No," Addison laughed. "Pretty sure Daniel would kill someone if we tried that."

"He's pretty protective of her, isn't he?" Kristen said. "Still he's damn hot and hella rich."

"They all are."

"All? Oh right, there's a third brother. What's he like?" Kristen asked

Olivia joined them and ordered an iced water with lemon. "Hunter Dufort is sexy as hell. Except he's more likely to whip your ass before he licks it."

Addison nearly choked on her tequila shot and while her thighs clenched at the image of Hunter with a whip she still cried out, "Liv!"

"Nothing wrong with a whip or two." Kristen shrugged.

Addison grinned and dropped her eyes to her drink. She was always careful not to give anything away. She might crave some of what Hunter had to offer but she wasn't going to publicize it.

Not even to her friends.

Especially not her friends.

She finally had great people in her life and there was no way she was risking them finding out. The judgment was more than she could handle.

Again.

"Every night, though? It's not just a fantasy for him, that's his life. Sex clubs and whips and chains. No thanks," Olivia said, then tilted her head. "I can't help but be curious if he's a Dom or sub though."

"Definitely a Dom," Addison said before she could stop herself and both women looked at her.

Fuck.

"I mean, obviously." She shrugged.

"Obvious, how?" Olivia asked. "Although now you say it, yeah, I can't see him being submissive."

No way.

Hunter was the ultimate alpha male.

"I don't know," Kristen said. "I haven't met him but some men with power like being dominated. Crawling on the floor to a madam or some such thing."

Not Hunter.

He'd be the one telling her to crawl.

Not her... someone. Definitely not her.

"Well, you'll meet him at the wedding," Olivia said. "Just don't get attached. He's not the marrying kind. None of the brothers were but Fletcher says Hunter won't. Ever."

Addison picked up a shot glass and downed it.

Ever was a long time.

Why those words affected her, she didn't know. It had been weeks since she last saw Hunter at Harper's engagement party.

She touched her lips, the memory of his touch still there and if she was honest, the desire to feel him again was growing, not diminishing.

Sweetheart, it's not my dimples you should be afraid of. Trust me.

Night after night she had twisted and turned as this deep husky voice threaded into her sleep until she inevitably had to slide her fingers between her legs.

Run Addison. You need to get far from me if you want to stay innocent.

After the things she'd imagined, he'd do to her as she orgasmed, Addison wasn't sure she could ever look Hunter Dufort in the eye again.

Her vibrator had needed new batteries and as she'd replaced them, she imagined him leaning against her kitchen bench smirking.

That grin. Those words.

"Oh, sweetheart. Your body I would pleasure. It's your mind I would corrupt."

Did she want him to corrupt her?

At night, yes, she did. She craved it. She wanted him to pleasure her. She wanted *him*.

Then the light of day would arrive along with her shame for even thinking about it.

The memory of her father's expression and words sliced through any desire that may have lingered. It may be normal to some, but she'd been punished for desiring what most people didn't.

She had lost her father and her friends.

Except Liv.

Thank God.

There was also the small fact that Hunter Dufort had left the party without even a glance. He believed she was more innocent than she was.

Or was trying to be.

He'd told her to run.

If the opportunity came up again, would she run to him, or away?

Would he want her or was he just playing games?

A dangerous game given their common friends. Friends that were his family. No, Hunter Dufort wasn't going anywhere. He would be in her life forever.

There was no way she could risk her friends finding out she had slept with Hunter if he followed through with his flirtatious temptations. Olivia meant the world to her and after the rejection and judgment she endured after leaving Rob, it would destroy her if she had to go through that again.

Sienna would lose Sammy, and she would lose Liv and Harper.

No.

It wasn't worth it.

Clearly Hunter was a discreet man. She never saw anything about his personal preferences in the media. He was regularly photographed just like all his brothers, but the only headlines were about his investments or wondering who the next lucky young woman would be to snag a Dufort billionaire.

From what Olivia was saying, that would be no one.

He was busy corrupting women's souls, as he so aptly put it.

She doubted he had relationships, so if she did dare step into his deliciously depraved world, it would be a one-night affair.

Which she would never consider.

Again, not that it was on the table.

Addison wanted a relationship. One day. With someone who was willing to get their kink on in the bedroom from time to time. Hunter wasn't after monogamy so if the same wild hunger flared to life again when she saw him, and she knew it would, she had to remind herself of the risks.

She couldn't lose her friends or self-respect.

What he'd want to do was well outside her comfort zone. Wasn't it?

She tossed back a third shot.

"Strippers are here!" Kristen called out.

"What?" Harper cried from across the room, and they all laughed, and then piled onto the dancefloor.

CHAPTER TEN

"Harper is going to kill you," Daniel said, smirking at Hunter from across the body of the helicopter. He was still full of adrenaline, and Hunter enjoyed seeing his big brother so happy.

"She can try." Fletcher laughed from beside him. "You loved it."

"Fuck yeah." Daniel grinned widely.

In a decision that they would probably pay for later when the bride-to-be found out, he and Fletcher had arranged a sky dive for the groom as the first part of his bachelor party.

The sun had been sitting low in the sky as they were flown over the countryside with a view of northern New Jersey and the NYC skyline. The instructor had strapped Daniel to the front of him and edged to the open door while they were at fourteen thousand feet.

He had shot them a *fuck you* grin as the instructor had pushed out of the plane. Then Fletcher had followed.

"Though if she asks, I'm going to deny it," Daniel added.

"Sorry, but you're glowing like your bride." Hunter laughed.

"You could have jumped," Daniel pointed out.

"Nah. If all three of us had fallen to our deaths? Boom. Goodbye Dufort Dynasty."

Daniel nodded. "True."

It wasn't unusual for boards or executives to have guidelines around these sorts of thing. Many had to fly on different flights to conferences or overseas trips, in case of a disaster.

"We're heading to a Sky Bar next. All the boys are waiting for us," Fletcher said, stretching out his legs. "You don't have to confess until tomorrow."

Daniel twisted the cap on his water bottle and took a long swig. "Where are the women?"

Oh no he wasn't.

Hunter shook his head. "Nope. Forget about it. You are enjoying your last night as an unmarried man. Albeit a week out from the wedding. They are well looked after."

Daniel let out one of his impatient long sighs.

Hunter could only imagine how much his brother wanted to see his fiancée and share the jump with her. Harper would get over it quickly. She was pragmatic like that.

What was it like to be that in love? The draw to see Addison again was driving him insane and all he wanted to do was fuck her.

Slowly, while she begged for release.

God damn, he needed to touch her again.

"A thousand dollars says she's in his arms by midnight." Fletcher laughed. Daniel simply shrugged, smirked, then turned to the window.

Fletcher grinned at Hunter, and they shook their heads in shared humor.

While he was enjoying this brotherly banter, envy had begun to thread through him.

Hunter was beginning to wonder what it felt like to be so loved and so adored that it felt like returning home in the arms of that woman.

What did it feel like to know a woman's body so intimately over and over, and know how to pleasure her like no one else?

Perhaps he could claim that now even without knowing someone. But he suspected this was a different kind of pleasure.

One he would never know.

And yet, the thought of another man daring to touch the one woman he was trying to get out of his mind made him clench his jaw.

Some would say he was being possessive.

Which was ridiculous.

Because she wasn't his.

TWO hours, one cigar and seven whiskeys later... or maybe it was eight, the room was packed with some of the wealthiest men in New York City.

Some were friends, others were those you kept close for different reasons, and the rest business colleagues who Daniel had felt it appropriate to invite.

Within ten minutes of arriving, everyone had heard about Daniel's sky dive and were sharing their own adrenaline-filled adventures.

"I don't understand this tradition," Hunter said to Fletcher as they sat on a sofa a few yards from the bar. "If it's your last night of freedom from monogamy then why are there no other women?"

"Not sure the idea is to shag a dozen women just before you tie the knot," Fletcher said, laughing. "Traditions rarely make sense. It's just an excuse to get drunk."

"Then goal achieved," Hunter said, lifting his glass.

"You're not drunk."

It was true. Seven whiskeys may have loosened his lips, but it wasn't going to put him on his ass.

He grinned as Daniel flopped down beside them. "Bungy jumping. Boys' trip next year."

Oh God, they had created a monster.

"No, thanks," Fletcher said.

"Come on. We're heading to New Zealand to visit Harper's mom. Fly over and we can go to the South Island and jump there."

"I don't care if it's on the moon. I'm not bungy jumping." Fletcher's tone was firm.

"Hunt?" Daniel asked.

"Maybe," he replied.

"Knew you would." Daniel nodded.

"What does that mean?" Hunter asked.

"You're more daring than the rest of us," Daniel answered, as if this was fact.

Which it wasn't.

Hunter frowned. "Why? Because I like my women strapped in leather against the wall while I fuck them?"

Daniel's whiskey froze at his lips and his brows lowered. "Do you?"

"Do I?" He smirked.

"Fuck's sake," Daniel said, shaking his head as Hunter's lips spread into a slow smile.

Fletcher snorted, then jerked and pulled his phone out of his pocket.

"Shit." He jumped up. "Shit!"

"What?" Both he and Daniel spoke together.

"Shit," Fletcher repeated, staring at Daniel for a long second.

It was obvious from his expression Fletcher was looking for the right words.

Daniel stood, sobering instantly. "Where is she?"

"The police station."

CHAPTER ELEVEN

Addison paced the cell. When were they going to let them make a damn phone call?

"Do you know who my fiancé is?" Harper slammed her hands on the bars.

Olivia had her face in her hands half-crying, half-laughing.

"Harper, stop." Addison walked over to her. "They'll give us a phone call soon."

Hopefully.

"I'm not worried about me." She glared at the cop leaning against the wall. "He's going to get you all fired. Let us out of here. We didn't do anything."

The cop flinched.

Addison frowned. "She's right. This is Daniel Dufort's fiancée. You should let one of us make a phone call. The longer we stay in here without our rights, the more pissed he'll be."

The cop was young, but she could see his eyes darting around working out what he should do.

A minute later he spoke into his comms, then another officer came in and replaced him, and the first one disappeared. Hopefully to talk to someone who would give them access to a phone.

"Where's Kristen?" Harper asked a second time. She was really drunk.

"With that guy. The one who helped us," Olivia said. "Now come and sit down. We'll be out soon."

"Mother truckers," Harper said, flopping down on the bench beside her friend.

Finally.

Not that Addison blamed her for being angry but to be fair it had been Harper's idea to slip their security and sneak out of her own bachelorette party.

It had never occurred to her the seven-kabillion-dollars'-worth of engagement rings Harper and Olivia were collectively wearing would have attracted the wrong kind of attention.

Now she knew.

Still, things had gone downhill really fast once it was obvious…

It had been close to eleven when the party was in full swing. Kristen had been trying to chat up the personal security guys when one of them shook his head, picked her up off her feet and carried her back to the dancefloor.

Then turned and walked away.

That had set them all off giggling.

"Come on. I want to meet some sexy American boys. No offence Harp, I love you, and I know this is your hen's night—"

"A hens what?" one of the women near them asked.

"Hen's night. It's what we call it in New Zealand. Not bachelorette whatever. Probably a British thing," Kristen said. "Anyway, can we blow this popsicle stand?"

Harper and her Kiwi friend had bent over laughing. If only she had been sober enough to stop what happened next, but even sober pregnant Olivia had been pulled into their shenanigans.

"We're in so much trouble," Olivia said, still half laughing.

"So much," Harper said. "Daniel is going to kill me."

"Well, at least Kristen is safe with that guy," Addison said. "I can't believe you knew him."

"Weird, right? Such a coincidence he was there." Olivia leaned on the bars. "I need to pee."

All three of them began to laugh again.

"I can't believe we are in jail." Harper wiped her eyes. "On my bachelorette party. I am in so much trouble."

She was right. When Daniel arrived, there would be hell to pay.

But not Harper.

Some heads were going to roll though.

"This better stay out of the media or I will be working tomorrow," Olivia said. "So when we do get out of here, keep your heads low."

"Yes, ma'am," Harper replied, looking more sober as the reality of the possible long-term repercussions set in.

Two hours earlier

HOW they had successfully slipped all six of the personal security personnel, Addison wasn't sure, but she was confident of one thing: Daniel was going to be pissed. She hoped they didn't lose their jobs over it. Knowing Harper, she wouldn't let that happen.

Still, Addison had been drunk enough to find their shenanigans funny as they had run from the building, while poor Olivia had been trying to talk them out of it.

Yay for the sober pregnant one.

But she'd failed.

So in the end she just threw up her hands and joined them in their adventure.

The four of them were channeling their inner *Sex in the City* goddess as they looped arms and skipped down Sixth Avenue.

"I want a hotdog. And a pretzel," Kristen said.

"I thought you wanted a New York man?" Harper giggled as they stopped at a hotdog stand. "And don't get a pretzel, they're not nearly as good as they make out in the movies."

They weren't?

"Okay, one hotdog with all the things, please," Kristen ordered.

As they stood waiting for Kristen's order, Olivia stepped in closer to Addison and shivered. "Oh my God, I'm freezing. My coat is back at the hotel."

"Same." She pressed up against her friend. Then she glanced around them and noticed a bar she recognized. "Hey, let's go inside. Harper and Kristen will love this place."

Addison had been to *SoHo Social* a couple of times with other friends over the past few years. It never failed to disappoint with its patio out back, live music inside and the long dark oak bar.

"Let's do it," Kristen said as she finished off her hotdog and wiped her mouth.

They stepped inside and the golden lighting and chic rustic design made her smile. She loved this place.

"Cocktails," Harper declared, and in minutes they were surrounded by tall good-looking men who were flirting their pants off.

"Holy smokes. Hottie at six o'clock," Kristen said, nudging Addy with her elbow.

"He looks a little young," Addison said, studying him and wondering if he was an actor. There was a familiarity about him.

"My vagina isn't ageist," Kristen said, sending a wink his way, and Addison nearly spat her drink out in front of her.

"How very inclusive of it." She laughed, wiping her mouth with her arm.

Predictably he climbed off his stool and made his way over to them. He was well built, tall and had a quiet confidence about him. As he got closer, she reconsidered the *quiet*. There was a healthy dose of arrogance that could go either way.

"Good evening, ladies," he said, his eyes roaming all over Kristen. His accent gave away he was from California.

"Good evening," Kristen replied, suddenly shy, and Addison nearly giggled. Though she could hardly laugh the way Hunter got her all tongue-tied.

"Ah, you're an Aussie," the man said.

"What? No!" Kristen said, obviously offended. "What a shame. You had so much potential."

He smirked, unfazed by her directness and held out a hand. "Jackson Wiles."

She stared at it a long moment, then shook it. "Kristen."

"Please accept my apology. I haven't spent any time in Australasia yet," Jackson said. "But if all the women are as beautiful as you, I might just have to rectify that."

"They're not," Kristen said, smirking back and Addison figured he was now forgiven.

"Nor as direct, at least," Addison said, leaning in and offering her hand. "Addison Hill. Nice to meet you."

He laughed and shook her hand. "I'm from Los Angeles. I'm quite used to women asking for exactly what they want."

His eyes dropped back to Kristen's and Addison knew he was dying to ask about the stunning green.

Then Olivia joined them. "Jackson?"

"Olivia. Wow. Nice to see you again." He pulled his eyes from Kristen's.

Addison raised a brow at the coincidence of her friend knowing this man. Manhattan was small geographically but not by population. And he'd just said he lived in California.

"You know him?" Kristen asked, reading her mind. "Does everyone in New York know each other?"

They all stared at her for a second then burst out laughing.

"No. Jackson presented at Dufort this past week. He's an app developer," Olivia said, snorting. "Or should I say, tech genius?"

He groaned.

"You are?" Kristen asked, looking impressed.

"So *Forbes* said," Olivia added.

Addison watched Jackson look away and she could see he wasn't happy for the attention to be on his career.

"Don't believe all you read." His attention was back on Kristen. "Let me guess, you're in marketing."

Olivia and Addison shared a grin. If he'd been asking them, he would have been correct. But Kristen was a teacher.

"Not such a genius after all, I see," she replied. "You'll have to keep guessing."

"Can I buy you a drink and take you up on that offer?" Jackson asked, tilting his head, and Addison could see the blush appear on Kristen's cheeks.

Sigh.

It was very sweet watching two people dancing around an obvious attraction. She was trying hard to remain sassy, but Jackson was a very attractive man, so she didn't blame her new friend for melting under those eyes.

Hunter hadn't tried to woo her. He'd told her to run. And it had her panties wet in under two seconds.

Proving yet again that she was not normal.

"Where's our bride?" Olivia asked suddenly.

They all looked around and Harper was nowhere to be seen. After sharing a few nervous glances and checking their mobile phones, panic began to sink in.

No security and a missing bride.

This wasn't good at all.

"Shit," Kristen said and began moving through the crowd as Jackson followed.

Then they heard it.

"Hey!" Harper yelled, and they watched her push at a guy's chest. "Give that back!"

Addison darted back as the man tore away from Harper and zigzagged through the crowd past her, narrowly missing them.

"What did he do?" Kristen cried.

"He has my ring!" Harper screamed, chasing him.

Jesus.

That thing was worth ten times Addy's house.

"Fuck that." Jackson growled and ran after him.

All four of the women chased after him.

Just before they reached the door at the front of the bar, Jackson leaped and caught one of the thief's ankles.

Crash.

The two men went tumbling to the floor. Arms and legs went flying as people around them scrambled away, yelling. Jackson was having trouble holding the guy.

Next minute Addison saw Harper out of the corner of her eye with a wine glass.

Oh no.

In the split second that she realized what was about to happen, Harper had the glass raised and then smashed it over the guy's head.

Holy shit. Everyone went still. Except Harper, who grabbed the man's hand and yanked her engagement ring out of it.

"Fuck you!" she yelled and kicked him in the groin. Jackson jumped up and pulled Harper away from the man.

"I think we should just get out of here." Addison looked over to find Kristen rubbing her head and being comforted by Jackson. Had she been hurt?

"Holy shit," Olivia said, twisting her enormous diamond ring in a mindless way.

"You need to text Fletcher," Addison said quickly and her friend pulled out her phone, nodding.

The thief was curled into a ball holding his family jewels, moaning.

"I'll call Daniel," Harper said, but it was too late.

The cops burst through the door, guns down by their side.

"That woman attacked me," the thief yelled, his hand still at his groin, the other pointing in their direction.

All three of their jaws dropped. They glared at the man, then back at the cops, then everyone began yelling out what had happened.

"Which one of you assaulted him?" Cop One asked. None of them answered.

Cop Two helped the thief to his feet and glanced over.

"Either you tell me which one of you did it or you're all coming with me," Cop One said, shaking his head.

"He stole my ring," Harper said, holding up her hand.

"The one on your hand?" the cop asked with a raised brow.

"Well yes, but he took it." Harper crossed her arms. "So I took it back."

"By assaulting him?"

Silence.

"All right, you, you and you, you're coming with us," Cop One said, and when they began to argue he held up a hand. "Handcuffs are optional. Either come with me now or I will cuff each one of you and drag you into the cruiser."

Holy shit.

They were being arrested?

While Addison wouldn't mind being cuffed by a certain someone, this was not who or what she had in mind. She suspected he'd find this quite amusing when he found out.

As they were escorted out of the bar, she glanced over her shoulder and saw Kristen standing beside Jackson who mouthed, *I've got her.*

Well, there was no point all of them being locked up.

She gave him a quick nod of thanks and shot Kristen a small smile.

Welcome to New York City.

CHAPTER TWELVE

"You have ten seconds to bring my fiancée out here before I rain down holy hell over this precinct and the city." Daniel growled and rolled up his shirt sleeves.

Christ, this wasn't going to end well, Hunter thought, running his hand over his hair.

"Mr. Dufort, you do realize this is a police department and I am a police officer. You have just threatened me."

Daniel leaned in while Hunter shook his head.

"Today you are. If you want to keep your fucking job, you will go get Harper Kane right now and release her."

Fletcher ended the call he was on and stepped over to them. "Lawyer is on the way. Brent is calling the mayor."

The policeman stared at them, unimpressed, and crossed his arms.

Daniel shrugged. "It's your funeral. The longer I wait, the more people I call, and the quicker you lose your job."

The man raised a brow. "One more threat and I'll arrest you too, Mr. Dufort."

The two men glared at each other.

"At least tell us what they're being held for. And who is in there," Hunter said.

The police officer listed their names.

Fuck.

Addison was with them? Suddenly, he was feeling a little angry himself. The thought of her being in there and having no one to get her out killed him a little inside.

"They're being held for assault," the policeman said.

Daniel snorted and his brows shot to the roof of his head. "Have you seen the size of those women? Assault of what? A tequila bottle?"

Hunter and Fletcher both snorted.

"Are they hurt?" Fletcher asked.

The cop glanced back at the computer and tapped some keys. "It doesn't look like it."

"It doesn't... *look* like it?" Daniel asked slowly, his face turning an angry shade of red. "Look a little closer, my friend."

Jesus, where were their lawyers?

Fletcher ran a hand through his hair. "What the hell did they do? I've got messages from Olivia's security detail saying the women disappeared from the bachelorette party."

Hunter pulled off his suit jacket and tossed it on the bench seat behind him. "Is Kristen still there?"

"She's with Jackson," Fletcher answered.

What?

"Jackson Wiles?" he asked darkly. "From Appopolis?"

Fletcher nodded.

"Who?" Daniel asked.

"What the hell was he doing with our women?" Hunter growled.

"*Our* women?" Daniel asked.

Oops.

"Well, you know. Dufort women," he clarified.

"Who is this guy?" Daniel asked again.

"Tech guy. We might be going into partnership with him," Fletcher said. "All I know is he texted to say the girls were in jail and that Kristen is with him."

"So, he's the one who messaged you?" Hunter asked.

He hadn't known. They'd all just raced out to Daniel's car and were now inside the station. It had been a blur. Helped by all the fucking whiskey they'd drunk.

What the fuck had Jackson Wiles been doing with them? A chill ran down his spine.

"Can we argue about him later? We need to get Olivia out of jail. She's fucking pregnant," Fletcher said, and it was the first moment Hunter realized how stressed his brother was.

Rightly so.

His fiancée was growing a human inside her.

The doors banged open.

"Thank fuck!" Daniel said, following two of his lawyers up to the desk. "Get my fiancée out of there."

Brent nodded. "Yes, sir."

"Are there charges laid against these three women?" Luke, their second lawyer, asked.

The cop shook his head. "No, sir. The victim is not pressing charges." He glared at Daniel. "Unfortunately."

"Fucking *sir* him, but you threaten *me*. Fucker. I want this guy's badge," Daniel growled.

Hunter leaned his head back against the wall and was overcome with the urge to laugh. Not that he did. But it was tempting. This entire situation was crazy.

"Then why are they not being released?" Luke demanded.

"Where's the damn chief?" Brent said, his phone up against his ear. "Tell him the Dufort Foundation is eager to hear from him so they can process payment of Senator Le Croix's campaign. I'm sure he'd hate a call at this hour to learn his funding has vanished into thin air."

Hunter sat up and caught Daniel's eyes. He shrugged and slid his hands into his pockets. This was how things were done.

"They were drunk and disorderly," the cop said. "As you know, gentlemen, I have the right to hold them overnight."

"Like fuck—" Fletcher began to growl but stopped as the chief of police walked in.

"Mr. Dufort." He looked incredibly unimpressed about being here. "Mr. Dufort times three. I see you are *all* here."

They all turned to face him.

"I do not appreciate being woken up in the middle of the night because your girlfriends are out causing trouble."

Daniel raised a brow and crossed his arms. "Harper is not my girlfriend. She is about to become my wife, and you might want to check your tone."

Brent stepped forward. "Chief, I think we can all agree it's in everyone's best interest to let the three ladies out. It appears there has been a big misunderstanding."

"Has there?" he asked, slipping his hands into the pockets of his NYPD jacket.

"Yes," Daniel said. "A very, very big one. One that can be escalated and cause us *all* a lot more trouble if I don't see my *fiancée* in the next ten minutes!"

His voice had gotten darker and darker as he spoke.

"I'm dialing the senator," Brent said.

The chief took in the scene and then let out a sigh. It was nothing he hadn't seen before. There were a lot of powerful rich people in Manhattan.

"Oh, for fuck's sake. What are they in for?" the chief asked, walking into the secure area to speak to the policeman.

And they waited.

Seven minutes and fifty-five seconds later—he knew because Daniel was counting—three humble and bedraggled-looking women exited through the double security doors.

"Thank fucking God." Daniel went flying across the room. Harper burst into tears before slamming into his chest and being swallowed up by his huge arms.

Hunter cringed, imagining these people who were now his family behind bars.

"What the hell happened? Is the baby okay?" Fletcher asked, wrapping his arms around Olivia.

Of all of them, she was looking half humored by the situation. Surprising, given she was the sober one.

"I'm fine," Olivia replied, shooting the cop a dark look as he gave them all a lecture about behaving in the future.

Then the noise around him blurred as Addison stepped into focus.

And God, she was stunning.

Sure, she was drunk and just being let out of jail, but she was still as gorgeous as he remembered.

The blush-pink jumpsuit she wore finished mid-thigh showing off those long-tanned legs of hers and gave a hint of the firm breasts beyond the spaghetti straps. In her hands, she held her heels and a clutch purse.

Her eyes roamed the room, then froze when they found him. She blushed and he couldn't hold back his smirk.

"Hello, Addison."

"Hunter," she replied, her eyes full of nerves, which only added to the excitement in his pants.

Down, boy.

Not here.

"What happened?" Daniel demanded, looking around the group, then down at Harper.

"Someone stole my engagement ring. He yanked it off my hand. I didn't even know it could come off that easily," Harper said.

"Jesus, woman. I would have just bought you another one. I'll buy you ten of them, for goodness' sake. Don't go assaulting people or putting yourself in danger. Do you hear me?" Daniel said, taking her chin in his fingers.

Hunter watched Addison's eyes widen. Ten engagement rings that size would be a chunk of cash, that's for sure. Something not many people could do. But he knew Daniel would if it meant keeping Harper safe.

Addison glanced at him, and he slid on his poker face.

Hearing someone was a billionaire and seeing it in action was quite different. Addison was living that right now and he could see her discomfort.

He didn't use his wealth to impress women.

Most men did.

He had no need.

The women he met wanted his cock, not his money. His cock and his ability to pleasure them beyond their fantasies. Which is why he didn't date. He rarely fucked a woman outside of the club life.

While there were rumors about his sexual tastes in certain circles, no one could confirm them. And that was just the way he liked it.

If his proclivities hit the media, it would be a problem, so he was very, very discreet.

"I don't want ten. I want this one." Harper twisted her rock on her finger.

"Then don't ditch your fucking security team," Daniel growled.

"Don't tell me what to do, Daniel Dufort," Harper replied. "I'm a hardened criminal now. Don't mess with me."

"Jesus," Daniel said, shaking his head. "I'm too drunk for this. Let's go."

Fletcher shot Hunter an amused look. "I'm taking Olivia home. Addison, let's get you in a cab."

"I—" she began.

Hunter took a step toward her. "I'll see her home. Get Harper and Liv home."

Everyone stared at him for a long moment.

"Thanks Hunt," Daniel said, and everyone followed suit.

"You've been drinking. I can smell it," Addison said. "I'll jump in a cab."

"I'm not driving. My driver is outside." He placed a hand on the small of her back. "Come on."

"Wait," Harper said, staring at her phone. "Oh… Kristen is back at her hotel. Who is Jackson?"

Who indeed.

CHAPTER THIRTEEN

Addison slid onto the soft leather seat and tried not to breathe too deeply.

She stunk of jail.

She wasn't entirely sure, but she thought she'd sat in urine. Or vomit.

At least the front of her looked half decent.

When she got home, she was planning to drop her bag and phone, then step into the shower fully dressed. The fact that the clothing was made out of silk was beside the point. It was already destroyed.

A whole week's salary down the drain.

Fitting into the rich lifestyle of her friends was costing her a bomb. Not that they would care what she wore. But she did.

She couldn't afford to keep buying designer outfits, so she had to stop buying them. Except for maybe the wedding.

She wasn't wearing H&M in the Hamptons.

Or Banana Republic.

Not when the flaming hot man sitting in front of her, wearing her yearly mortgage payments in one suit, would be there. The same one whose eyes roamed over her body as if he had rights to it.

And damn if he didn't create desires within her, she'd been tamping down physically and mentally.

"Are you okay?" Hunter asked, his voice low and dark.

"Yes." She smiled, a little amused now by what had occurred.

Now they were free.

"Are you still drunk?"

"Trying to decide if you can take advantage of me?" she dared to tease.

"I'll take that as a yes." He glanced away.

Addison bit her lip. Yes, she still had a bit of alcohol in her system, giving her some Dutch courage, but perhaps it was time Hunter Dufort realized she wasn't some innocent schoolgirl.

"Why?"

His eyes darted back to her. "Why what?"

"Why would you assume I'm drunk?" she asked.

Hunter leaned forward and placed his forearms on his knees, studying her. His sleeves were rolled up, revealing strong muscular arms, free of tattoos but darkly tanned.

She swallowed at his piercing stare.

"I am not going to fuck you, Addison, so relax. I don't take advantage of drunk women."

"Then why is the car taking us to your place and not mine?" She crossed her legs.

He sat back and arched a brow. "You know where I live?"

"I know where I live, and it isn't billionaire row," she answered, indicating the high rises.

Instead of answering, he stared at her until the car pulled up outside his building. The door opened and Hunter climbed out first, holding a hand to her.

She took it and they walked to the private elevator, which seemed to magically ping open when they got close.

They stepped in.

Hunter's towering body stood far too close as they rode the seventy-two floors to his penthouse.

When the doors opened, she swallowed, but Hunter didn't delay in guiding her inside with his hand.

"Would you like a shower?" He walked ahead of her as she stopped in the middle of the sweeping room full of dark leather furniture.

Oddly, while it was masculine, it was also incredibly warm and stylish. The sofa itself blended well with the wooden coffee table, potted plants, and neutral cushions.

A large plush cream mat covered the polished floors and interesting prints hung from the walls.

But it was the vista beyond the home that was the highlight. Lights from the city sparkled, drawing her across the room.

"I love Manhattan," she said, and felt him step up behind her. "It's magical, you know." She turned and found him closer than she'd thought. "Oh!"

"Magical, dangerous, unique," Hunter said, his fingers reaching out to push her hair back behind her ear. "A little like you."

She tried to breathe naturally and failed. "Why am I here?"

Hunter drew in a long breath. "I needed to see that you were really okay."

He did?

Why?

Addison suddenly felt vulnerable. "I can't shower. I have no clothes to change into."

"I'll find you some."

No, you don't need to find any.

Was he really not going to fuck her?

She nodded, and he led her to a guest room which had its own bathroom.

"Everything you need is in there. I'll lay some clothes on the bed for you." He leaned on the door frame.

She tossed her bag on the bed. Confused didn't begin to describe how she felt. The alcohol still swirling through her body wasn't helping.

Did he really think she was that innocent?

She wasn't.

What she wanted was for him to touch her. Addison took the few steps toward him, stopping in front of him.

"Why don't you join me?" she said, in her best seductive voice. Which wasn't all that great but, in her mind, she pretended it was.

That was the benefit of being half drunk. You could pretend.

Deep golden eyes gazed down at her, his jaw tensing. Then he turned and walked away, calling over his shoulder. "Shower. Dress. Then come back out to the living room."

Gah.

She huffed and closed the door.

CHAPTER FOURTEEN

What the hell was he thinking, bringing Addison back to his penthouse? He wasn't fucking Addison while she was still half drunk and fresh out of jail.

She had been through enough tonight. She shouldn't have to deal with his sordid desires as well.

And wasn't he planning to *not* sleep with her?

Yeah, that's right.

He snorted quietly. The lies he told himself...

In truth, she was here because he'd had a raw need to make sure she was okay. To take care of her.

He was becoming confused about his feelings for her, which seemed to get more complicated every time he saw her.

But send her home alone after what she'd been through? No. He wasn't about to do that.

Her vodka-enhanced courage had been adorable but once showered and sobered up, he was pretty sure Addison would be a little embarrassed at her attempt to seduce him.

He shook his head and stepped under the spray of his own shower. If she knew about *the room* he had downstairs, Addison would be shocked. She would never come on to him like that, if she knew the truth.

He didn't bring many women home, but he was more than prepared when he did.

His hand reached for his cock, frustration pouring through him.

God damn her for being who she was.

If only she wasn't so close to his damn family, he'd take her innocence, squeeze it in the palm of his hands and watched the grains of dust sprinkle to the floor as she screamed in pain and pleasure.

Over and over.

But she was Olivia's best friend, so he couldn't.

And yet, she was here. In his house.

Currently naked.

Hunter palmed his cock and groaned. He wanted her legs spread, her limbs bound as he took complete control of her pleasure.

As he spilled onto the shower floor, he hoped the release was enough to take the edge off before he could get her home.

He dressed in a pair of jeans and a dark sweater, rubbed his hair with a towel and then ventured downstairs, praying for a lot more willpower than he knew he had.

TEN minutes later, Addison walked down the stairs in a pair of his gray sweatpants and a white long-sleeved t-shirt.

He groaned.

She had clearly not worn a bra underneath the pantsuit and her hardened nipples were pressing against the cotton.

"I made you a hot chocolate." He pushed the mug across the kitchen countertop and ignored the urge to lift her onto it, and ram deep inside her.

Her brows lifted. "Wow, that's kind of perfect."

He smirked. "It's not my first rodeo."

"Of bringing drunk women home to your place from jail?" She laughed.

He quirked a brow while she pulled out a stool and sat at the Italian marble counter.

"You know, this place suits you," she said, her eyes roaming around the large open space.

"How so?"

She tilted her head a little. "Hmm, it's masculine. Stylish."

His lips lifted at the corners.

"Dark and yet not," she continued.

Not?

"Like it's not sure what it is. But it's..."

Hunter's eyes narrowed in curiosity at the way she was assessing him and his home. Clearly, she had put a lot of thought into him. And that was pleasing.

Very pleasing.

"As if..." she looked at him, as if suddenly surprised by what she was saying.

"Carry on." His voice was low.

"Sorry."

"Say what you were going to say," he said, circling the counter as Addison swallowed, her eyes not leaving his until he was standing in front of her.

"As if it's hiding something. Waiting."

"For?" he asked, stepping in closer and breathing her in.

"I don't know," she answered. "It's not clear. Like you."

He let out a small, dark laugh. "Is it not clear to you what I want? That I want to touch you?"

She shook her head. Then nodded.

"See. I'm confused. One minute you tell me to run and then say you want to touch me. And yet, when I offer myself to you, you walk away."

He leaned his hip against the edge of the counter. "I'm not taking advantage of you when you're drunk. Come on. What kind of man do you think I am?"

She tsked him, as if his rejection annoyed her. He grinned.

Taking her chin in his fingers, he lifted her face to his. "Neither of us should be playing this dangerous game, beautiful. Our lives are too intertwined."

"Yes, I know."

"And I've warned you before I will corrupt your innocent soul."

She slapped him away. "Stop with that nonsense. I'm not as innocent as you think."

God damn her.

He spun her stool around and slapped his hands down on either side of her, leaning in close.

"Don't tempt me, Addison Hill. You have no idea the things I want to do to you. Things you will never be able to undo."

She drew in a breath. "Tell me. I want to know what you would do to me."

Fucking hell.

His cock stiffened in his jeans, as his mind fled to the options in his room down the hall.

"Tell me." She repeated the words softly, her hand squeezing one of his biceps.

Shit.

His body burst into flames at her touch. He had to stop this. She had no idea who she was playing with. He stood away from the counter, his eyes blazing back at her, then pulled her off the stool.

"Come with me," he ordered, tugging her and marching through the house.

"Where are we going?" Addison asked, her voice breathless, but he heard the wonder within it.

This would scare her off.

He needed her to be scared of him.

Because he wasn't sure he could stop himself if she remained here much longer.

HUNTER stopped outside a door, and Addison watched as he pressed his thumb against a black panel on the wall.

Click.

"What is this?" she asked, trying to peek inside.

"It's everything you need to know," he replied in a dark tone. "And why I told you to run."

He pushed open the door.

She froze, staring inside the room, and let out a gasp.

Then, just as suddenly, her body flared to life.

Holy shit.

She felt Hunter watching her for a long moment, then his hand guided her inside the space, which was decorated in the same colors as the rest of the penthouse.

And that was where the similarities ended.

To say the furniture was different was an understatement. Against the wall was a St. Andrew's cross, giving away immediately that Hunter Dufort had his very own sex dungeon.

A high quality one, but it was still a dungeon.

Oh, my fucking God.

On one side of the room there was a large black-framed bed with black sheets. Two pillows, no comforter.

She walked in further.

A cabinet against the wall was lined with sex toys. Heat flashed through her body as she slowly swallowed and took more of the room in.

Her eyes slowly adjusted in the low light, and she spotted a sofa on the other side with a fur-lined throw. The sofa was surrounded by dozens of unlit candles, and a handful of whips here and there.

A panel on another wall displayed a few lingerie outfits. Not in lace, but leather.

And then there was the range of ropes to select from in different colors.

She chewed her bottom lip at one piece of furniture. It was padded on top, and underneath was a cage.

Oh, my God.

Her eyes widened and suddenly she wasn't sure. About anything.

"You cage women?" she asked.

"If it turns them on."

She glanced at him, and whatever he read on her face wasn't to his liking. His mouth twisted. "See? This place is not for you," he said.

He cages women. Holy shit.

He took a step toward her, and she was torn between wanting to run, and stay and have Hunter touch her.

God, she needed him to touch her.

"I can see it's not something you would like."

"That's an assumption." She tried to appear more courageous than she felt.

"Not at all. It's my job is to read the signals women give out. The cage terrifies you, Addison."

There was no point denying it, so she nodded.

"Yes."

"But the ropes excite you." He watched her with that golden piercing gaze.

Addison swallowed. "Yes."

"You want me to strap you against the wall," he said, his fingers moving to her neck, finally touching her and guiding her eyes to his. "Spreading you wide, running the whip over you until you tremble with more desire than you've ever felt in your life."

Jesus.

"You want me to push my fingers inside your drenched pussy to give you relief?"

She gulped.

"And I would. Once."

Fucking hell.

His fingers tightened on her neck, and she let out a tiny gasp.

Her panties were wet.

"Then I'd slap it," he said. "Have you ever had your pussy slapped, Addison?"

"No," she whispered, in a tone that could only be described as begging.

"I would play for hours as your pussy creamed down your legs. Stopping to stroke myself as you screamed for relief."

Holy shit.

Hunter's eyes flared at her obvious arousal.

"And?" she asked, needing to know what would be next.

Hunter released her and took a step back.

"And it can never happen."

What?

He shook his head and turned away.

Addison stood there, feeling empty. Her pussy was burning with need and her pulse raced. Her hand flew to her throat where his fingers had just been and she stared longingly at his strong, wide back.

She had never felt this sort of craving for a man before. He knew what he'd done to her, and yet he'd torn himself away with seeming ease.

"Why are you doing this?" Her throat was dry.

He took deep breaths. Was he angry? Then, in a flash, Hunter spun around and was on her.

His mouth slammed down on hers, his hand on her back pressing her body against his, the other in her hair.

She gripped his arms and opened her mouth to him.

And holy fucking hell.

He was like fire and ice.

His tongue commanded hers as she completely lost herself in his total possession of her.

Then he ripped away.

"Because of *that*," he growled. "Because *this* can never happen."

His mouth came down on hers once more. Softer, but not soft. Then he released her again.

"It's time for you to leave."

THE car pulled up outside Addison's brownstone.

"Give me your phone," he ordered her.

"Why?" she asked, and from her tone and body language he knew she was mad at him. He held his hand out anyway, and she handed it to him. Then he plugged his phone number into it.

"Message me if you need me."

"But not for sex."

He raised a brow. "Is that what you want, Addison? For me to just fuck you?"

She stared at him.

Of course she did. He'd purposely shown her what he could offer her then taken it away. It had been cruel.

He'd been hoping to scare her. Instead, her curiosity and obvious arousal had surprised him.

Talk about a plan backfiring.

But he knew Addison was a woman who would want more than a simple fuck in the end. He'd met women like her. She wasn't someone he could just please and throw away. She was Olivia's best friend.

So he had to shut it down.

"That's not what you want. Trust me." He spoke in a heavy tone. "We'd both have to live with this afterwards at every fucking wedding, kids' birthday and God only knows what else."

"You're right." She glanced away, trying but failing to hide her disappointment.

Hunter shook his head. She was confusing him with his brothers. He wasn't like them, and couldn't give her the romance that her two friends had with Daniel and Fletcher.

That wasn't who he was.

Hunter's desires weren't suitable for monogamy.

There was no way he could drag Addison into his world and break her, without significant consequences for them both.

"There's nothing here for you. I'm not the man you think I am. I am *not* my brothers."

Addison shook her head, collected her purse from the seat beside her, and reached for her phone.

He held her hand tightly and their eyes met.

"There would be no giant diamond at the end of this for you if we did get involved, Addison."

She ripped the phone from his hand and climbed out of the car. "Goodnight, Hunter. Oh, and fuck you."

The door slammed in his face.

He let her go.

He had to let her go.

FUCKING idiot.

Hunter walked back into his penthouse after dropping Addison home and shook his head.

You complete fucking idiot.

Showing her his sex room was one level of stupid, and then he'd had to compound it and fucking *kiss* her. He knew she'd taste incredible, but he wasn't expecting his body to react quite as powerfully as it did when she was hard against him.

Hot? Yes. She was sexy as fuck.

But there had been something else. The way she had reacted to the room. Her curiosity and intrigue had triggered everything within him.

How he hadn't slammed her against the St. Andrews cross and ripped his sweats off her, he had no idea.

Perhaps his prayers had been answered because that kind of willpower was superhuman.

Now she was angry.

It was best. It would help them keep their lips and hands to themselves next weekend at the wedding.

Hunter knew Addison was mature enough to keep private what had, or rather *had not*, happened between them.

So why give her your phone number, asshole?

His phone beeped.

Fuck you. Number deleted.

He let out a little laugh.

That's my girl.

God, he wanted to fuck the fire right out of her. But she wasn't his and never would be.

CHAPTER FIFTEEN

Hunter looked up as Daniel walked into his office and stopped dead in the middle of the room.

He knew his brother well enough to know two things at that point in time.

One, Daniel had been looking for Fletcher and hadn't been able to find him. Whether it was the law of nature, he didn't know, but when Daniel was in this kind of mood, he always went to their middle brother first.

And two, he was incredibly stressed about something because his brows were scrunched.

And in three, two, one…

"Where's Fletcher?" Daniel demanded. "He's not in his office. Scarlett said he's not in a meeting and he's not answering his phone."

"Look for Olivia and you'll find him," Hunter replied calmly, leaning back in his seat and knowing his calmness would rile Daniel.

Because the thing about little brothers—not that anyone would ever call him little—is they were created to taunt the older ones.

Daniel frowned. "What do you mean by that?"

"Stationary cupboard, probably." Hunter shrugged as if it was obvious.

Daniel had been outvoted recently when it came to overturning the anti-fraternization policy at Dufort Hotels. It had allowed Fletcher and Olivia to be a couple and remain working together. Even though he wasn't a man to hold a grudge, Hunter knew it was still a sore spot for Daniel, and who was he to let an opportunity like this pass.

Also, it wasn't untrue.

The new couple were like rabbits.

Daniel narrowed his eyes and glared. "Tell me you are fucking kidding me?"

Yeah, he couldn't.

"I'm joking," Hunter said, picking up his pen. "Now that you're here—"

"I can't chat. I need to find Fletcher." Daniel began to walk out.

Hunter frowned.

"Daniel." He called out but his brother didn't stop. "Daniel!"

It was rare for Hunter to raise his voice.

His brother stopped and turned; his brows raised. "What is it?"

Thank God he finally had his attention.

"Would you stop? I've been trying to get a moment with you for days," he growled.

Daniel took a few steps back into his office. There was one thing you could never fault his big brother for, and that was being a formidable and excellent CEO.

"Talk to me." His demeanor completely changed.

"Jackson Wiles."

Daniel closed the door and walked closer to his desk, plugging his hands into his pockets. "I'm listening."

Hunter tilted his head. "Why?"

"Because I agree. There's something not right."

He frowned. "Right. Of course, you met him."

"Yes. He brought Kristen home the night the girls were arrested. When we got home, he was there, and we invited him inside. I wanted to thank the man who helped get Harper's ring back," Daniel said.

"He seems legit, but something about him bugs me and you know I listen to my gut."

"You do, and I am usually one to demand you back that up with facts and figures, but in this instance, I have the same feeling about him."

"Why?"

"I can't put my finger on it. He appears to be interested in Kristen, but I'm not sure it's authentic," Daniel said. "He asked me more questions than he did her."

"People are curious about billionaires," Hunter said, playing devil's advocate for a moment.

"True, but when you have a hot piece of ass sitting beside you, who would you give your attention to?" Then he shook his head. "Don't answer that."

Hunter laughed.

"I didn't like him in the penthouse, so I saw him out and told Kristen if she wanted to fuck the guy, she had to do it in his hotel."

"Wow, I bet that earned you some demerit points," Hunter said.

"Harper knows the stakes," he said. "Kristen doesn't. She'll get over it."

Hunter nodded. "So he wants our business and just happens across the girls on Friday night? Seems a little coincidental."

Daniel rubbed his jaw, something he did when he wasn't happy, as Hunter sat back down at his desk. "Unless he's really fucking clever, it turns out it was coincidence. The girls stopped at a random hotdog stand and then went into that bar without any plans. He couldn't have known."

"The one down the road from Dufort SoHo?" he asked. "SoHo Social?"

Daniel nodded.

So perhaps they were wrong about the guy.

"I don't know what his agenda is, or what I'm accusing him of, but while Fletcher is having the usual due diligence done, I've been doing my own digging," Hunter said.

"And?"

Hunter rubbed the back of his neck. "Nothing. No red flags, at least. He started his tech business straight out of college and quickly hit the *Forbes* list."

Jackson Wiles was already a multi-millionaire at only twenty-five years old. Without any assistance.

That he could see.

"What else do we know?" Daniel asked.

"He was born to a single mom in California twenty-five years ago. He has a sister and a younger brother. His mother married when he was ten. A loser with a record of domestic abuse," Hunter said. "Jackson went to Brown. No idea how the family paid for that."

Daniel nodded, staring out the window.

"Scholarship?"

"Couldn't find a record of it. Someone has helped him. Or he had some illegal funds to pay for it. He's a clever-as-fuck tech kid. It's possible."

"So..."

"So I'm saying the last thing we should do is open up our data to someone who is smarter than our own IT people."

Daniel nodded.

"Do we think that's what he's up to?" Daniel asked, turning to walk to the floor to ceiling windows. "Getting access to our data? Something isn't adding up."

Hunter stared at his eldest brother for a long moment.

"No. It isn't."

It wasn't that long ago their family had been blackmailed by a US senator. While Daniel had gotten them out of that mess, there was always a risk when you had the type of fortune their family did.

"Keep him away from Harper," Hunter said. "I don't trust him."

Daniel wiped his hand over his face as he turned. "I'm not her keeper. Harper's best friend likes this guy. And I can't deny that he actually helped them the other night."

They stared at each for a long moment until Daniel cursed. "You're right. I'm doubling her security."

"We need to speak to Fletcher about this," Hunter said.

"I'll talk to him," Daniel said. "Let me know what else you find, but unless my signature is on the agreement, we are not doing business with Jackson Wiles."

He nodded.

Hunter relaxed knowing Daniel and he were aligned on this matter. He'd been second-guessing himself for over a week.

"Tell him to come and see me if you see our brother first," Daniel said, walking out of his office. Then he popped his head back around the door. "And if Fletcher is fucking inside this office, you better damn well tell me."

Hell no.

He pressed his lips together, which was a waste of time, as he knew his eyes were full of laughter.

"Fuck's sake!" Daniel disappeared again.

CHAPTER SIXTEEN

Jackson tugged Kristen against his chest and grinned down at her. "Can I kiss you goodnight?"

"Do you usually ask your dates?" she replied in that sexy-as-hell Kiwi accent and flicked her long blonde waves over one shoulder.

No.

He usually took what he wanted, but this was a complicated situation.

"Not usually, but Harper's soon-to-be husband is bigger than me and ten times richer, so I value my life."

She laughed and slapped his chest. "Liar. There's a stupid amount of muscle under this shirt. You aren't hiding it very well."

Touché, gorgeous.

Those legs of hers were toned as hell and he could only imagine what she looked like naked. He was dying to find out and that was interfering with his plans. She was a little distracting.

In fact, since meeting Kristen on Friday night, Jackson had thought his luck couldn't get any better. He couldn't have known the women of the Dufort men were going to be in the SoHo Social bar the night all of them had shown up, but life had a funny sense of humor sometimes.

When he had spotted Olivia, well before she saw him, he'd recognized Harper, but not the other two women. Both of them were gorgeous, but it had been Kristen who had caught his eye.

Those emerald eyes of hers had shone like the gems they were and almost dragged him off his barstool.

Plus, who was he to look a gift horse in the mouth? The Dufort women had been handed to him on a silver platter.

When he'd introduced himself and heard her accent, his cock had sat up to say hello. Kristen was sassy with a delicious thread of shyness, which just made him want to drag her underneath him and pound it out of her.

For hours.

First things first. He had a plan to stick to.

When he heard Harper cry out, he'd chased the guy who'd stolen her engagement ring without a second thought. He may not know his family yet, but he wasn't letting some asshole steal from them.

When the girls had been arrested, he had stayed with Kristen to protect her. She was a foreigner, and it would have been far more complex to get her out of the slammer. Worse, she may have been sent back to New Zealand before attending her friend's wedding.

Yes, he'd known all about the upcoming nuptials. Not that it was a secret. It was all over the gossip columns.

Before the girls were released, he had taken Kristen to a coffeehouse near Daniel Dufort's penthouse while they both sobered up and waited.

He liked her, yes, but he'd seen an opportunity and run with it.

"When you return to Manhattan after the wedding, I want to see you again." He brushed her hair from her face.

"I live on the other side of the world, Jackson," she said, nervously chewing her lip.

"And I live in LA." He smirked, "We're both adults, Krissy. I'm sure it's clear I like you. If not, consider this your official notification."

She shook her head, laughing. "Would you stop that? It's Kristen."

"You're Krissy to me." He tugged her hair.

If he was being honest, opportunity aside, he did want to fuck her brains out. She was funny, smart, and incredibly sexy. But first he needed to get closer to the Dufort's, and she was the perfect door opener into their personal lives.

It was fifty-fifty if they went for the app idea, and it would be months before they did their due diligence and made a decision.

"Now, say yes, so I can kiss you."

"No," she said, pulling out of his arms and dancing away.

He laughed.

"But you can dream about it." She wiggled her fingers at him as she walked inside the pricy building on the billionaire's row.

He shook his head, watching her disappear inside. She didn't remember, but they had already kissed. She'd been drunk and pressed into him in the cab the night they'd met.

"I think you're really hot," she had said. "I think you should kiss me."

"Oh, yeah?" he had replied.

"Mmm mmm."

"I am not taking advantage of you like this."

"Please do," Kristen said in response. "Like really, really take advantage. It's been months."

Okay, that had freaked him out. He had definitely not planned to kiss her after that.

Jackson had leaned down with the full intention of whispering that a gorgeous woman like her should be in the arms of a man who loved and respected her, not an asshole like him, when she had taken his movement for something else, and met him halfway, planting her soft warm lips on his.

And well, he was a red-blooded man, with alcohol in his system too, and, yeah, he'd pulled her against him and plowed right in.

It had ended up being one of the hottest kisses he could remember.

So, now he wanted those beautiful lips on his again. While she paved the way and connected him with his half-brothers.

A win-win.

As long as she didn't find out.

He would reveal himself after she left.

CHAPTER SEVENTEEN

Hunter slid his sunglasses on and walked across the tarmac to the helicopter that was just starting to wind up.

No Addison.

He'd been working up to this moment all damn week, and she wasn't damn well here.

"I'll take that for you, sir." An employee spoke, taking his bags.

"Thank you."

A smaller helicopter to the left of him was being loaded with all their luggage.

He counted the bags.

Four, five, six. Way too many—

"The fuck, man. Did you tell Daniel we were fucking in the office?" Fletcher asked, shoving his shoulder.

Oh, that.

Hunter smirked. "Technically? No."

"Hunter!" Olivia cried. "Oh, my God."

He held up his hands. "Hey, you guys need to be more discreet."

Olivia groaned.

"What?" a sexy voice asked. He turned and his body tightened at the sight of the gorgeous blonde in front of him.

A floaty cream and red sundress whipped around her legs, and she wore flat beige sandals. On her arm hung a small woven handbag from which she pulled a pair of sunglasses that she popped over her eyes.

"Nothing." Olivia moaned, putting her face in her hands.

Fletcher glared at him, and he slapped his brother on the back. "Payback." He laughed, then glanced down at the woman he really wanted to kiss. Hell, he wanted to do significantly more than that. "Hello Addison."

"Hello," she said as impersonally as if he were a doorman, then walked off.

Olivia followed.

Fletcher frowned and turned to him with a raised brow. "What did you do?"

Hunter shrugged. "Don't look at me like that. Not every woman wants me, despite the rumors."

"Did you fuck her? Jesus, Hunter, tell me you did not fuck Addison," Fletcher growled.

Chop, chop, chop.

The helicopter was ready for them.

"I did not." He answered honestly.

The look in his brother's eyes, the one of shock and disgust, was the reason he could not touch her again.

Ever.

Addison was one woman he could never have.

Why did that bother him so much?

He climbed aboard, following Fletcher, who sat opposite Olivia, leaving him to sit facing Addison.

Excellent.

Nothing like forty minutes of torture.

The bird lifted into the air and tilted as the pilot directed them toward the Hamptons. With headphones on, the drone of the helicopter was mildly soothing as they all stared out their respective windows, watching Manhattan disappear below them.

Fletcher and Olivia began to chat across the channel, discussing the events and wedding preparations.

It was amazing to him how quickly Olivia had become part of their family. They'd all known her for years as she had been their PR manager, and in hindsight it was inevitable the two would end up together. Their chemistry as colleagues and lovers was clear.

They'd been able to overturn the anti-fraternization policy at Dufort Hotels, but Hunter believed the two would have found a way to be together one way or another.

When his eyes left them, he found Addison watching him. She held his gaze for a long moment, then turned to look out the windows once more.

But not before he saw the desire in her eyes.

And something softer.

But she sat with her lips pressed, contempt clearly still right at the surface.

As he'd planned, he reminded himself.

He'd left her unfulfilled.

Was she aware that's what was upsetting her? That what she wanted was his hands and mouth on her skin, and the release of an orgasm around his hard and hungry cock?

It was what he damn well wanted.

Fuck it all.

Hunter slid his glasses back over his eyes and rested his head against the seat. It was clear he had started something he needed to finish.

He knew he couldn't go four days without touching her again. Doing it without his brothers finding out was crucial.

The question now was, how?

And when?

"TAKE whichever room you want, Addison," Fletcher said as they walked up the stairs. Two employees carried most of the luggage ahead of them, with him and Fletcher carrying the rest.

Hunter had his own room, as did Daniel.

"Daniel and Harper have a room upstairs, correct?" Hunter asked.

Olivia nodded. "Yes, and her mom and Kristen will be on the lower floor."

The family estate was three stories high, with eight bedrooms and ten bathrooms. It also included a large chef's kitchen, one casual and one formal dining room, two living areas—one of which opened out to the outdoor area with a large pool, hot tub, tiki-style bar, barbeque and a dozen loungers and other outdoor furniture.

The garage housed five luxury vehicles and the front of the property faced the ocean and had a landing area for the chopper. It was how they usually traveled to and from the Hamptons.

Once the family arrived tonight, the wedding planners would begin the setup and it would turn into a fairytale. He had no doubt that was what Harper had in mind.

She was a romance author, after all.

Olivia directed Addison to the room across the hall from him.

Of course she had.

"Thank you," Addison said. "This place is absolutely stunning."

"I know, right? It's why I fell in love with Fletcher."

His brother snorted.

"Is that what it takes? A sweeping beachfront property to find the love of your life." Hunter smirked.

Fletcher barked out a laugh. "You looking to fall in love, Hunt?"

"Nope."

His eyes met Addison's, and she glanced away.

"Meet us downstairs when you're ready. The others will begin arriving in the next hour, so I say we greet them with cocktails," Olivia said, clapping her hands in excitement. "Oh, I love weddings."

Groan.

"You. Come here," Fletcher said, and pulled his fiancée into their bedroom.

When he turned, Addison had disappeared.

Hunter walked the few feet to his bedroom and dumped his bags. He stared through his open door at Addison's closed one, and considered his next move.

CHAPTER EIGHTEEN

Four damn days.

Four.

Addison's thighs burned from squeezing them together. And her jaw ached from being angry at the gorgeous, stupid man.

Why had Hunter looked at her when he told them he didn't want to fall in love? She hadn't been asking for a wedding ring. Just a goddamn orgasm would be nice.

And yeah, it had been nice of him to clarify there would be no ring at the end of an affair with him.

What an assumption on his behalf.

And what a damn jerk.

Still, he'd left her on fire, and nothing seemed to satisfy her cravings. Now she had to spend days with him.

Ugh.

Addison had decided to just ignore him as much as she could and even be a little rude. Because she was a grownup.

Clearly not behaving like one, but what other options did she have?

He was someone who loved to play games.

She had to be stronger.

Unfortunately, she didn't trust her body to say no.

Not that he was offering anything. He was simply messing with her mind and trying to control her.

Perhaps Hunter just liked being desired?

Well, she would show him she wasn't a woman who would be played with. She would find a way to distract herself.

It was all just bad timing. She'd been denying her sexual needs for a long time. Hunter Dufort had cracked her open just enough that her body wanted more than the little taste she'd had.

Walking around with sensitive nipples and constant arousal was uncomfortable and a little embarrassing.

But she would have to find it elsewhere.

He was right. The two of them getting involved for a night or any length of time was a bad idea.

If her friends got wind of it, she'd be horrified.

The risk was too great for her after what she had lost.

Addison lifted her bag onto the bed and began to unpack. She didn't need to change, happy with the sundress she was wearing, so she walked into the bathroom off the bedroom and set up her makeup and toiletries.

A knock sounded at the door.

She smiled.

She knew Olivia would be back. Her friend was so excited about the wedding. They'd been discussing outfits and plans all week.

"Come in," she said as she walked back into the room, sliding lip gloss on her lips.

The door opened.

She froze.

"We need to talk."

"NO, we don't." She turned away from Hunter, walking further into the bedroom as he closed the door.

"Stop," he commanded, and her body did as he asked.

God damn it. How was he able to do that to her?

She felt him come up behind her and his hands slid down her arms.

"I shouldn't have left you like that the other night." Hunter swiveled her around to face him. He palmed her cheek. "You need release."

Fuck.

Say no.

"Don't be so arrogant." She breathed hard. "I am fine."

Damn it, why did her voice have to give her away?

"It's not arrogant when you can see the truth in someone's eyes. You may be angry with me, but you need me. You need what I can give you."

Addison groaned and shook her head. She tried to move away, but he held her firm.

"Fine. I want you to fuck me. Happy?" She seethed.

"No," Hunter said.

Her brows shot up. "No? Is that your favorite word?"

How dare he?

She pulled out of his arms, successfully this time, taking a step backwards. He followed, pressing her legs against the back of the bed.

"I'm not happy, because I want to fuck you just as damn much, Addison. But my brothers would string me up if I touched you. And they're right. I am not someone you should go near."

"Does Fletcher know?"

Hunter shrugged. "He asked if I'd fucked you and I said no."

"Oh, thank God." She let out the air she didn't know she'd been holding in.

God, that had been close. She had to be more careful.

Hunter frowned at her.

"Why are you so worried?" he asked.

"None of your business," she said. "But you're right. This can't happen."

His eyes roamed her lips, and she swallowed.

"Then we are both fooling ourselves because I can't work out how to stop desiring this." He swept his thumb over her bottom lip. "So it's going to be hell until we do."

She hated that he was right.

Her body was pulsing with just the feel of his fingers on her mouth. When had a man set fire to her body with so little touch before?

Never.

That's when.

"So I propose we do this discreetly. You can say no, but I would rather taste your sweet pussy and give you the release your body seeks."

Holy hell.

Even his words sent shocks of pleasure through her.

"Don't."

"Don't what, Addison? Tell you how satisfying it's going to be when I finally sink deep inside you?"

She clenched her eyes closed as her core burned with the need to be touched and relieved of this ache.

"How?"

She hated herself as the word fell out, but felt no regret. She needed this.

Then she could forget about Hunter Dufort.

He smirked.

"That's where the fun comes in, Addy." He leaned in and licked her lips as she drew in a jolty breath. "Say yes now and then do as I say. No matter when, or what the situation is."

She rolled her lips together, tasting him.

"Those are the rules. I am in charge of your body. It's mine all weekend. Agree, and I will ensure you are pleasured beyond your wildest dreams."

Before she could overthink this, she nodded.

"Good girl," he said, and pulled her against him. His thick hard member pressed into her belly, promising her the relief she was seeking. "Now part these lips and kiss me."

CHAPTER NINETEEN

*K*nock, knock.

Hunter released Addison's lips and took a couple of steps away from her, then faced the window.

Calming his breathing, he counted.

"Hey," Olivia said as she opened the door. "Oh!"

With his back to her, Hunter smirked, then turned to Addison, who was looking like a deer in the headlights.

"That should open freely now." He gave the latch on the window a nudge. "Let me know if it doesn't and we'll get someone to look at it."

She blinked at him.

Come on gorgeous, work with me here.

Hunter suspected her brain was a little fried from their kiss. He was surprised his wasn't.

It wasn't far off.

God, she was fire and ice, this gorgeous woman.

With Olivia standing over them waiting for the confirmation he wasn't in there doing… well, exactly what he had been doing, his heart was thumping.

The last thing he needed was Olivia going to Fletcher, concerned Hunter was having his devious way with her innocent friend.

"Thank you," Addison finally said, and he had no doubt her gratitude had double meaning.

He winked and then smiled at Olivia as he walked out. "My pleasure. See you ladies downstairs."

CHAPTER TWENTY

Two hours later, the chopper had returned from picking up Daniel, Harper, Kristen, and Mrs. Kane from Dufort Towers.

Now the house was bustling with people sipping cocktails and nibbling on Hors d'oeuvres which were being handed around by servers.

"This house is so beautiful. Harper, wouldn't you rather be in a house like this?" Alice Kane, Harper's mom, had flown in from New Zealand. "It's so much nicer than being inside a box."

Also known as a multi-million-dollar penthouse, Hunter thought. But, semantics.

Fletcher nearly choked while Hunter pressed his lips together and slapped him on the back. Out of the corner of his eye, he saw Addison hide a smile behind her drink.

"Mom!" Harper cried. "Don't be rude. Daniel's penthouse is one of the most desirable pieces of real estate in New York City."

Kristen shook her head and mumbled. "Lord, here we go."

Hunter had heard Harper's mother was outspoken, but seeing her in action was something else. Entertaining, at the very least.

"If she wants a house, I will buy her a house," Daniel said, not fazed in the least by her comments. He was used to dealing with difficult and demanding personalities as a CEO, so Harper's mother had been, he'd told his brothers, a challenge to win over, but nothing he'd not been willing to do or incapable of.

They'd left New Zealand, after their short visit, with her blessing.

"Also, it's not *my* penthouse, sweetheart. It's *ours*," Daniel added.

"Well, on Sunday it will be," Alice said.

Daniel brushed Harper's hair off her shoulder and leaned down to kiss her. "It belongs to Harper already. I don't need a wedding or marriage license to know this is the woman I love and will spend my life with."

A round of feminine sighs filled the room as Harper leaned into him. She gazed back at him adoringly.

Hunter watched Addison. Did she have that kind of love with her ex-husband once?

Did she want it again?

"You're a good man, Daniel," Harper's mother said quietly, then smiled at him and Fletcher. "I guess not all of you are monsters."

Olivia coughed.

He'd heard a little about how Harper's father had had a secret family, so her cynicism was to be expected. And not unreasonable.

"I don't want a house... or maybe I do, but I also love our home in Manhattan," Harper said.

"She wants a house on Oahu," Kristen said, then shrugged when Harper glared at her. "What? You do."

"Okay, can everyone please stop spending Daniel's money?" Harper cried, rubbing her forehead.

Daniel placed his cocktail down on the coffee table.

"Okay, first..." Daniel started.

Oh boy, he'd seen that look on his brother's face before.

Addison glanced over at him, and he could see how uncomfortable she was. He picked up a tiny cracker with God only knows what on it and walked over to her.

"Another drink?" She nodded and followed him into the kitchen as Daniel continued.

"It's *our* money and if you want a house in Hawaii, choose one and we'll buy it."

Hunter laughed as he dropped their glasses on the counter and requested fresh ones from the staff who had been hired for the weekend while they were at the estate.

"Yes, sir." One server replied and began pouring a peachy colored liquid into both glasses. It was some type of cocktail both Addison and Olivia had been gushing over. It was delicious, even though he'd made a fuss about preferring whiskey.

He turned and leaned his hip against the countertop to gain some privacy and smiled down at her.

"Wow, she's direct, huh," Addison said, referring to Harper's mom.

"There's always one in the family."

"Where are your parents?" she asked.

"Johnathan is staying a few blocks away at a house he's leased for the weekend," Hunter said. "Mom will arrive on Sunday for the ceremony."

Probably drunk.

Addison nodded and didn't ask anything more. But for some reason Hunter wanted to tell her. He wanted her to know more about him.

"They divorced when we were teens. Dad cheated. A lot. She drank as a result. And still does." He took their topped-up glasses and led them a few steps away, toward a set of open French doors.

"I'm sorry," Addison said, taking her glass from him.

"It will be the first time both of them are in the same room as each other since the divorce, so we're hoping for a miracle." He laughed, leaning a hand on the doorframe, and staring out into the front yard. "Or at least that she doesn't make a scene. It's anyone's guess how it will go."

"Let me know what I can do to help," Addison said, her voice full of kindness. "Not that I have any clue what I could possibly do, but I want Harper to have a happy day."

Hunter nodded and stared at the helicopter sitting in the distance. Their pilot was taking a rest before heading back to the city.

"Daniel would do anything for her. Its great seeing him so happy and in love. I never thought any of us would get married." He wondered what the hell was wrong with him. He never shared these kinds of thoughts with a woman.

Or anyone except his brothers.

"And now Fletcher," she said.

He turned and gazed down, his eyes flickering over her head to check his brothers weren't paying attention to them.

They weren't.

"Yes. Another wedding the two of us will attend, Addison."

A blush hit her cheeks. "I know."

Her eyes met his. "We need to be cognizant of that. What we share this weekend… it has to be discreet."

"It will be." She replied too fast.

He nodded.

"When we return to Manhattan, we go back to being family acquaintances," Hunter said.

"I'm not going to fall in love with you, Hunter," Addison replied, and the sound of his name on her lips sent a flash of electricity through him.

His cock jerked, causing him to stand up straight, drop his arm and clear his throat. But what was more alarming was her statement. It felt like a challenge. One he most certainly would not take up.

And yet he hadn't liked hearing those words from her.

Focusing back, his eyes slid over her silky shoulders. It sounded like they were on the same page. She was more eager than he'd anticipated in keeping their attraction for one another discreet.

So… game on.

"Are you wearing panties?" He kept his voice low as those cheeks of hers heated once more.

"Yes."

"I want you to excuse yourself and go take them off."

Addison's eyes slowly slid to his as she chewed her lip. They were glistening with nerves and excitement. Hell, he wanted to scoop the sexy vixen up into his arms and take her upstairs right fucking now.

But that wasn't how these games worked.

Out of the corner of his eye, he saw Fletcher making his way over to them. Hunter leaned an inch closer to her.

"Slip your fingers inside your pussy until you are wet, then come back downstairs." He straightened. "Fletch."

Addison cleared her throat and then lifted her drink to her lips.

"What are you two planning over here?" Fletcher grinned.

Addison choked on her drink, coughing.

"Ah, excuse me a moment." She wiped her mouth, then handed Hunter her drink and left the room.

Great, now he had to stand talking to his brother knowing she was about to touch herself. He loved how good she was at this already.

He grinned.

"We were thinking of spiking Harper's mom's drink with some tequila and really getting this party started."

Fletcher nodded. "She's something, all right. But she won't ruffle Daniel."

Not in a million years.

"Only I can do that." Hunter shrugged.

"That's what little brothers are for," Fletcher said. "He spoke to me about Jackson Wiles."

Oh.

"We can talk about this next week, Fletch."

"No, I want to clear the air. I dismissed your instincts and while they may not be backed up by anything solid, that was unfair of me."

Because Daniel felt the same?

Was there an unspoken rule in the universe that age equaled wisdom? Because he didn't think that was correct. There were some dumb-ass old people in the world.

"I appreciate it," he said instead.

"So, was Addy okay? She looked flustered."

No, she was aroused.

But he wasn't going to share that little detail.

"I just noticed she was a little uncomfortable with all the talk about money. It's happened a few times," Hunter said.

"You seem to notice a lot about Addison," Fletcher said, a brow raised.

Here we go…

"Just because I like to chain women up, doesn't mean I want to fuck every single one I meet."

Lies.

He wanted very much to fuck Addison Hill.

"Seriously, bro. Keep your fetishes to yourself."

He sniggered. He'd been hoping to divert the conversation away from Addison and it had worked.

"Why do you like it?" Fletch then asked. "The BDSM stuff."

Um, what?

Neither of his brothers had ever directly asked him that question. They may have expressed their distaste, but never asked *why*.

"Control," he answered, honestly, turning away to face the yard again. "Power and control."

"You don't think your wealth and the fact that you're six foot three and two hundred and ten pounds gives you that?"

He shrugged. "Yes, but it's more than that. It's total control of another and watching their surrender to their pleasure. Come on, Fletch, you don't want to know any of this."

His brother tossed back his drink. "No, probably not. I just don't understand it."

He slowly turned.

"You can't tell me you're not dominant with Olivia."

"Careful." Fletcher growled, narrowing his eyes.

Hunter shrugged. "I'm just saying it's no different. My needs are just more extreme. All three of us are alpha males. You understand the need to take control and possess your woman. I know you do."

Fletcher swirled his drink.

"Dominate. Not hurt her."

"Ah, see, that's just a misunderstanding. There is a fine line between pleasure and pain. Trust me. It's a very fine line," Hunter replied.

This is what his brothers didn't understand. They thought his sexual choices were depraved and wrong. Instead, they brought untold pleasure to all his sexual partners.

Had his brothers stated their beliefs in so many words?

No.

So this conversation was a surprise. And not all that unwelcome.

"That's where we're different. The last thing I want Liv to feel is pain. Nor does she desire it."

"And I don't like chocolate chip ice-cream. It's just a preference." Hunter shrugged.

"Well," Fletcher said, turning back toward the room as a panty-free blonde with blue eyes walked in. "Make sure you add Addy to that list. She's Olivia's best friend and not that type of woman."

Hunter slowly turned to face his brother as a flash of irritation spread through his body. He wanted to say so many things he knew he'd regret. And not for the first time. She wasn't the first woman he'd been told to keep away from. And likely wouldn't be the last.

He swallowed down his anger and planted a fake smirk on his face. "What makes you think I am interested in Addison? She's a little vanilla inexperienced for my tastes."

Fletcher turned to him. "Let's keep it that way."

Fucker.

His brother slapped him on the shoulder and walked off. His eyes moved from Fletcher's broad muscular back and found Addison watching him from across the room.

All his fury melted away as he read the arousal on her face.

No.

He wasn't staying away. Not for anything.

Addison Hill was his.

At least for the weekend.

CHAPTER TWENTY-ONE

"My mother is driving me mad. She's been here for less than forty-eight hours, and I want to kill her already." Harper joined Addy and Olivia out on the deck.

Addison had walked outside for some fresh air after dinner. Hunter's fiery gaze was on her constantly and while her body had been in a state of need before, now it was screaming.

She'd done as he asked, slipping her fingers inside herself after removing her panties. It had felt naughty and exciting. Her nipples hardened as she made her way downstairs.

Then nothing.

Over the past four hours, she thought he would've snuck them away or slid a hand between her legs at the dinner table.

But no.

Oh, he'd watched her all right. Lust was thick in his gaze when she dared look up. He'd also placed a hand on her back as they walked to the table, his fingers pressing into her flesh and sliding an inch lower.

That one inch had felt more erotic than anything she could remember.

Her body was burning for something.

Anything.

Then his fingers had grazed her shoulder as he used the back of her chair to stand at one point.

God, it was hell.

She was aching. Wet. Frustrated.

Her nipples were so erect, it was painful. She needed to touch herself and find release instead of standing here squeezing her thighs together.

"She just doesn't understand," Olivia said. "It's a different world here. And she seems to really like Daniel."

Harper nodded. "She loves him. He seems to be the only person able to manage her."

"It's amazing what a man will do for the woman he loves." Addison smiled, and they all sighed like the hopeless romantics they were.

"I'm so lucky, aren't I?" Harper said.

"Me too," Olivia said, bumping her hip into Harper's. "I was going to wait to ask, but... I want you both to be my bridesmaids when we get married."

Addison and Harper gasped and threw their arms around her and cried out *yes.*

"Am I interrupting?" Daniel asked, and Harper tucked herself under his arm and updated him.

"Any idea where you are getting married?" he asked Olivia.

She patted her stomach. "We haven't decided yet. But after this one arrives."

"Get married in Hawaii," Harper said.

"That's your answer to everything," Daniel said, planting a kiss on her forehead.

"Well, it's a good answer." Harper shrugged and Addison laughed.

"I'm going for a walk on the beach while it's still light enough," she said, noting the sun sinking into the horizon.

"Want some company?" Liv asked as Fletcher stepped up behind her, wrapping his arms around her middle.

"No, I won't be long." She put her drink down. "Back soon."

Fletcher had given them the codes to the property, so she punched the code into the keypad and stepped out of the gate and down onto the beach.

ADDISON kicked off her sandals and carried them as she walked slowly down to the shoreline and let the breeze flick through her hair. She rarely got out of the hustle of the city, so the hum of the ocean was both welcome and foreign.

It nearly dulled the arousal racing through her body.

Nearly.

The water kissed her toes as a wave crept up the beach further than expected. She lifted her skirt despite it being short enough, giggling at the coolness on her feet and backed up... into a solid wall.

Large hands gripped her arms. She knew who they belonged to by the way her body exploded into awareness.

"It's nearly dark," Hunter said.

"I'm a big girl." She turned, giving him a cheeky grin.

"No. You're not. While you're here with us, you need to be mindful of wandering off on your own."

"That feels a little dramatic." She frowned.

"Trust me. People will do anything to get money," he said. "Let's walk."

His hand pressed into her lower back as they continued the path along the beach.

"I don't have any money." She laughed.

"There are a lot of people in that house who care about you and do have a lot of money. Anyone looking for an opportunity could tap into that. Just be smart, please," Hunter said, his tone more serious than she was used to hearing from him. "Daniel shouldn't have let you walk out here alone."

She pursed her lips and nodded. "Fine."

Around them a few late-night dog walkers strolled the beach as their canine friends darted in and out of the water, chasing balls and sticks. A couple of young kids squealed in the distance.

But while Addison was taking in her surroundings, her focus was on the large handsome man walking beside her.

Still not touching her.

Finally, she spun.

She couldn't take it anymore.

"I did what you said."

Hunter's lips stretched into a smile.

CHAPTER TWENTY-TWO

"And?" Hunter asked, knowing every second was a delicious form of torture.

"And what? I took my panties off and all you've done is ignore me all evening. I don't like this game." She glared at him.

His smile broadened. "Liar."

Addison huffed and began to walk off. Then she spun around again and, because he had started to follow, she slammed into his chest.

"Whoa there." She slapped at his chest, but he grabbed her wrists. "Stop."

Her body did as he instructed.

On instinct.

And that pleased him.

Hunter glanced around. It was dark now. The only light came from the quarter moon in the sky and flickers from surrounding properties.

Letting go of one wrist, he slipped the strap of her sundress off her shoulder. "I think this tiger inside you needs taming. I told you your body was mine, Addison, and that means I will play when I am ready."

"No. I get to decide." She said the words with a little shake of her head.

"You decided when you conceded earlier. We both agreed. If you say no, then our agreement is off." He nudged at the material of her dress, all but exposing one of her nipples.

As his finger ran across her skin, teasing the needy nipple, he lifted his eyes to hers.

"Do I continue or stop?" Her body pressed into his and he knew it was involuntary. "Because I know you're wet, your pussy throbbing, wanting my touch."

"Asshole." She moaned.

He watched her as the need to retain control fought with her desire for pleasure. It was the same with every sub when they first stepped into this world. They resisted until they broke.

And when they did, it was a beautiful thing.

"You gave me full control and in return, I have promised you complete pleasure." His fingers lightly brushed her nipple.

Finally, he gave her a taste of what he knew she craved.

Touch.

His touch.

Her gasp was as powerful as if he'd entered her.

"This is not pleasure, it's pain." She groaned.

Hunter leaned closer. "Patience, gorgeous."

He pushed the fabric away and pinched her nipple.

"Oh, God." She cried out.

He continued working her, thumbing the nipple and rolling it around in his fingers.

"Look at me," he ordered and when she did, he found wet globes full of lust begging for more. "Imagine my mouth on your breast. My tongue lolling around then sucking hard. The other one begging for attention."

He squeezed her nipple hard, and her mouth parted. "Yes, God. Do it."

"I'm in charge here, Addison. One more instruction from you and I will stop." Fletcher slapped her nipple.

"Please," she cried softly.

"That's better," he said, releasing her other wrist. Tugging the other strap of her dress down, he quickly took the other nipple.

"Oh, God, how can this feel so good?" she groaned. Flick after flick, the other pressed harshly between his thumb and finger as he held her eyes, watching her begin to pant.

"You pussy is burning, isn't it?" Hunter asked.

She nodded.

"Words, Addy. Tell me."

"Yes. I... please."

He smiled as she only just stopped herself from giving him an instruction again. "Good girl. You're learning. For that, I have a gift for you."

He released a nipple and reached into his pocket.

"What is that?" Addison asked when the silver shiny objects appeared in his hand.

"These are nipple clips. You will wear them every day we're here. I'm going to put them on you now and unless you're asleep, you do not remove them. Do you understand?"

She shook her head. "I can't. Not in a bikini."

"Then our deal is off. If you say no, this ends. All of it."

"Hunter, be reasonable," she cried.

"You're right." He nodded. "When you sleep, you should wear them too. I want you aroused constantly."

She groaned as the first one clipped onto her nipple. The second one went on and she bit her lip.

"Your pleasure is mine. This body is mine." He ran his hand down between her breasts. "Are you starting to understand?"

He lifted the straps of her dress back onto her shoulders and one side of his mouth lifted at the disappointment on her face.

He was tempted to leave it at that, but they only had a few days and, in all honesty, he wanted more of her.

"Come here." He tugged her against him and bunched the fabric of her dress as he slid his hand underneath it. "Widen your legs."

Holy hell.

She was dripping.

Hunter's fingers slid between the hot wet folds, and he had to suppress his own groan. Addison didn't and his cock lurched at the sound she let out.

"Jesus fucking Christ." He moaned, wishing they were somewhere less private so he could see her pussy.

"Oh God, Hunter, fuck me."

Shit. Just when he'd been enjoying it, she had to go and instruct him again. Damn it all.

"Stop," he said, freezing his hand. "Order me one more time and I will walk away. And Addison, I *really* want to pleasure you right now."

"I didn't. I..."

"You're learning. That is your last warning." Without warning, he plunged a finger inside her. Deep.

"Fuck," she cried, wobbly on her feet.

Holy hell, she was tight, hot and dripping.

Another finger.

"I'm going to come. Oh, shit." She began to cry.

No.

He couldn't allow that.

"Do not come." He growled and pulled out.

"What are you doing?" she gasped, almost collapsing in his arms.

"I tell you when you can come." He slipped one finger in again. "Not before and not after."

She let out a groan and her body began to tremble. "Hunter, please."

He loved to hear her beg. The sound shot straight to his cock and tightened his balls.

"Good girl, more of that and you will get what you need." He pressed two fingers in and thrust fast, his thumb tapping on her clit.

"Oh, God, oh, God."

With her nipples clamped, and his fingers fucking her, her clit stimulated, he had her at his mercy. It wasn't complete and utter compliance, but it would do for tonight.

"Is this what you need, Addison?"

"Yes, fuck, oh God let me come," she cried.

God damn it.

Hunter shook his head. She had been so close but couldn't help but take control. He had to be strict, or this wouldn't work.

For either of them.

His fingers slipped out, and he stepped away.

She gasped and stared at him with her mouth wide open. Panting.

He didn't say a word, just lifted his fingers to his mouth and licked them.

"I hate you," she sobbed "And fuck you. I will finish myself." Then she lifted her dress and began to rub her clit.

Fucking hell.

His cock, which was already hard, twitched angrily at his fly.

"I don't think you understand, Addison." He took a step toward her and grabbed her wrist. "I have not given you permission to touch yourself. If you are looking for a subservient man, you have come to the wrong place. These are my rules."

"I hate your rules," she said. "I don't—"

"There is only one chance to say no. If you voice it, be sure." Hunter stared down at her with intensity. "Beg for your orgasm right now and I will give it to you."

Normally he would make his sexual partner wait, but given their situation out here on the beach and how new she was to these dynamics, Hunter was willing to compromise.

Just this once.

Plus, Addison needed to come. The risk was she could lose her damn mind and give something away to those around her. A pity as twenty-four hours of torture would mean one hell of an orgasm when she finally claimed it.

"Fuck you." She growled, even as she stared at him with a mix of rage and need. "Please, can I come?"

"Lift your skirt," he ordered, and as she did, he found her wetness. "Let the dress go and I want you to tug on those nipple clips."

She followed his instructions and lifted her eyes to his. Hunter leaned down. "Open those lips for me."

His tongue swept in and, as he claimed her mouth, his fingers slammed into her pussy. He felt the moment her muscles clenched and began to spasm around him.

"You may come." He growled against her lips and moved back a few inches so he could watch the pleasure as she did.

The pain, relief, and pleasure.

After he had fucked her pussy until her body collapsed against him, Hunter scooped her up and found a patch of grass up the beach and sat with her in his arms.

Something he never recalled doing with another lover.

Yet with Addison, it felt right.

"I still hate you," Addison whispered into his chest.

He nodded. "Good."

It would be better if she did. Because she felt way too good and those eyes of hers were bewitching him.

When she finally lifted her head, she asked. "What about you?"

Hunter raised his brows and smirked. "Do you want to suck me off right now or bask in that orgasm?"

"Fine. I want to bask." Her head rested back on his chest.

He let out a thick, quiet laugh. "Good girl."

CHAPTER TWENTY-THREE

Addison woke the next morning surprised that Hunter hadn't snuck into her room during the night.

She had been hoping he might.

The orgasm on the beach had been incredible. She'd never come with such intensity. She would have collapsed on the sand if he hadn't caught her. Which had been an unexpected cherry on top. There was something far too nice about being held by Hunter Dufort in his strong, muscular arms.

An experience she was trying to forget.

The games, however, were creating a love-hate relationship. She craved them and wished he'd just take her to his bed.

Giving up total control didn't come naturally to her. Not as an independent woman. Yet he'd played her body like a fiddle, dominating her mind and manipulating her at just the right times.

A well-orchestrated act.

One in which he was clearly an expert.

She knew she wanted a night with him, but at what price? How many other women did he have dying for his touch right now?

She had told him she wouldn't fall for him, and she'd meant it. She still meant it. Except she hadn't expected to feel like an addict wanting more of him.

Sex with Hunter would be pure carnal bliss.

And yet, she had felt cared for by him afterwards, which was unexpected. Even, she realized now, when he'd been guiding her, teaching her, she had felt his strength and care.

And always he had reminded her the choice was hers.

The boundaries were clear.

The rules were clear.

And he'd been strong and unbending in defending them.

It was intoxicating.

She realized that what she had been wanting all this time was a powerful man to take control. With Hunter, she may have bitten off more than she could chew, but she was committed to following this through.

Finding a truly masculine man who possessed such personal power was not something done easily came across every day. Her cheeks heated just thinking about what was to come.

One day, she would look back on this experience and be grateful for it. For now, she was still incredibly frustrated. She wanted his cock inside her. She wanted her thighs wrapped around him.

She wanted his mouth on every inch of her.

He'd carried her back to the house, or at least until they got close, then lowered her to the ground. He had cupped her cheek, given her a slow but delicious kiss, and then guided her inside.

Only Harper, Daniel, and Kristen had still been up. She had excused herself and headed upstairs, leaving Hunter to join his family.

Now she lay there, her nipple clamps on, the pain sending slivers of pleasure through her.

One night.

She needed one pleasure-filled night with him and then she would walk away.

And hopefully, no one would find out.

Because that was a terrifying thought.

"HERE she is," Kristen said, her hand on Hunter's biceps as the two stood close.

Addison forced her brows to stay in place as the nipple clamps rubbed against her cotton bra, reminding her of his claim. And yet he remained in place, his gaze casual as she walked into the dining room.

"Good morning," she said, and nodded as coffee was poured when she sat.

"Morning Addison." His deep voice skated along the surface of her skin. She hid her shiver and added milk to her coffee.

Kristen sat opposite her. "We've got the wedding rehearsal this morning at The Meadows Club. Did you want to come along?"

She felt Hunter's eyes burning into hers. Did she? She wasn't family or even extended family. She was here because she was Olivia's best friend and now Harper's friend. This felt like more of a family occasion.

"Oh—"

Harper walked in and sat next to her. "It's up to you. The wedding party is officially just Fletcher and Kristen, but Mum and Liv are joining us. Hunter, what about you?"

His eyes slid to Addison's, and she saw the tiny flames flickering within the golden hue. "I have some things to tie up, so I will meet you afterwards."

Addison began to cough on the sip of coffee she had just taken. Harper slapped her back. When she looked up, the corners of Hunter's mouth were curled.

"Sorry,"—*cough*—"I'll stay around here and have a swim. Relax by the pool." If this was an opportunity for her and Hunter to have sex, then she was taking it.

She wasn't sure she could make it through another day of his slow torture.

He better not be playing with her.

Beep beep.

"Oh heck," Harper said, tossing back her coffee and grabbing a piece of toast. "Daniel! The wedding planner is stressing me out. We have to go."

Addison smiled at Kristen, who giggled. "I better go. Bridesmaid duty. Enjoy the pool. I am so going out there before we leave. This place is like something from a romance film," Kristen said, then began to leave. "Thanks again, Hunt."

Hunt?

A slice of jealousy speared through her as a plate of poached eggs and toast was placed in front of her. She picked up her utensils and began to cut everything into little pieces. Placing a piece of egg on some bread, she lifted it to her mouth and her eyes connected with *Hunt's*.

He smirked.

She chewed and swallowed. "What?"

His smile grew. "Such a mom thing to do."

She raised a brow. "Eat?"

"Cut it into tiny pieces. My mom called them soldiers," Hunter replied.

"That's sweet," she said, then couldn't help herself. "*Hunt.*"

His smile disappeared.

As she continued to chew, and she found herself unable to read him, a sense of fear—no, excitement—struck her.

Hunter stood, wiped his mouth with his napkin, and walked around the table. Then he leaned into her hair. "I expect those clamps to stay on under the bikini. When you head upstairs to change, there will be another one on your dresser. Put it on your clit."

Then he left.

Jesus.

Now she was sitting eating breakfast alone.

Wet.

And angry. Because if he was playing with Kristen or anyone else this weekend, she was out.

Hunter would hear her resounding *no.*

CHAPTER TWENTY-FOUR

Hunter placed the little box on Addison's dresser and went to his room to shower and change. Slipping on his swimming trunks, he heard the vehicles leave the property.

He had a decision to make.

He was enjoying the slow torment he was putting Addison through. His cock was so hard it was like a goddamn baseball bat.

Yet, they had limited free time together.

His father would arrive today and their mother tomorrow morning. His attention would be torn.

Away from Addison.

With limited toys to play with at the Hamptons house—well, let's face it, they called it a house, but it was an estate—he would have to make do.

Hunter stepped out into the back section and found Addison laying on one of the sun loungers in a white bikini and floppy sunhat. The bikini contrasted nicely with her golden tan and was very *Hamptons*.

Hunter's life was filled with sexy, wealthy women, but none of them were as gorgeous as this blonde-haired beauty.

"Sir, would you like some refreshments?" a young man asked.

Ah, shit. The house staff.

"No. Thank you." He looked around. "Can you ensure we have some privacy, please?"

"Of course. Everyone is out front setting up the marquees for the nuptials tomorrow," the young staffer said. "I'll go assist them. Let me know if you need anything else."

"Thank you."

He grabbed a towel from the shelf and made his way down to the pool, dropping it on the lounger next to Addison. She lifted her head from her book.

"Hunter, I'm not—"

"Are you wearing it?" he asked.

She nodded.

"Good."

He turned and took a running jump into the pool.

It was probably the five hundredth time he'd done it in his life, so it was like riding a bike. Still, when he broke through the water and threw back his head, wiping the wetness from his face, he couldn't help but grin at the surprise on Addison's face.

"Get in."

ADDISON was going to lose her damn mind over this beautiful-looking man. Seeing him with no shirt and all those ripples of muscle was one thing, but his raw masculine sexual prowess had her wet in two seconds flat.

How was that possible?

Or it could be the clamps she now had on her nipples *and* clit. The latter was driving her insane, keeping her in a constant state of arousal which was both delicious and frustrating.

She stood and dropped her book and hat on the lounger, pulling her hair tie from her wrist and twisting up her hair.

"I like your hair off your face," Hunter said as she slid into the water, one slow step at a time. "But I like the flush on your cheeks more."

He swam closer, now just a few feet from her.

"Who's fault is that?" she mock-frowned at him. His lips stretched into a half smile. One full of danger and promise.

"You can say no," Hunter said. "But it looks to me like you are deliciously compliant."

"And that turns you on."

She submerged to her shoulders, and somehow their bodies found each other. Hunter grabbed her hips, and all the air left her body.

Addison glanced up at the huge house.

"No one is here," he said, and she nodded as his fingers dug into her hips, their legs gently moving to keep them afloat, and his breath warm on her face.

"Why does such a powerful man like you desire submission?" she asked, as her palms flattened on his chest. Her tummy did a little dance at the feel of his round, muscular pecs.

Water dotted his face, and his hair was mussed, giving him a more youthful and carefree appearance than when he was in his business attire. She liked him like this. Even the dark hair on his face after a day of not shaving was sexy as hell.

"Would you rather I carry you out of the pool and just lick your pussy until you come? Then fuck you?"

She blushed. "I wouldn't complain."

He smirked. "You would."

She tipped her head and narrowed her eyes in question.

"Addison, you need more than that. I can see it. You want me to take you to the edge. You want to be out of control."

She drew in a bumpy breath. "How?"

"How will I do it? Or how do I know?"

The latter.

She hated that it was obvious. How many other people saw the truth of what she needed so much? Her heart thumped. Suddenly, she felt as if the whole world could see what she was.

"How do you know?" she clarified, her fingers digging into his skin.

"Relax," Hunter replied, one of his hands moving up her body in a soothing manner. "This is our secret. Your body calls to me. It knows I can give you what you need. Only a Dom would recognize a sub. And then, not always."

Addison nodded, chewing her bottom lip.

"Are you ashamed?"

She shrugged. "A little. It's all new to me. My ex... never mind."

"Let's leave other people out of this." His fingers slid over the back of her neck, sending shivers through her body. "We have a small window this morning, Addy. Do you want to play?"

His fingers dipped inside her bikini bottoms, and his eyes blazed as he found the clip. Fire shot through her core and she let slip a guttural moan.

"I would like to take that as a yes, but I need to hear you say it," Hunter said, his eyes roaming her face.

Yes?

No?

This was it. She was diving into the deep end with a man who had desires and fantasies much darker than hers.

"Nervous?"

"Yes."

He cupped her face. "You do not need to be. All you have to do is say no, and I will stop. Until then, you are mine to do with as I please."

Fucking hell.

Yes, yes, yes.

"Two seconds to say no." He released her face.

"Yes." The word fell out of her mouth.

Holy shit.

Hunter nodded and his hand slipped back under her bikini, and two fingers slid through her silky, wet flesh. Then he entered her. Dark, determined eyes full of control held her in place.

"Slide your hand inside my shorts and grab my cock," he commanded. "Now."

Addison had felt him against her body a few times, but until she wrapped her hand around it, she had no idea how long and thick it was. Her eyes widened slightly.

Hunter's lips twitched.

"That's going inside you. Every fucking inch," Hunter said. "Wrap your legs around me and don't make a sound."

CHAPTER TWENTY-FIVE

Did he want to fuck her right there in the pool, with the sun beaming down on her golden skin and blonde curls?

Fuck yes.

But he had promised her his kind of pleasure and while they didn't have his dungeon or a club to play in right now, he had enough toys with him to give Addison what she craved.

What *he* craved.

With her wrapped around his body, Hunter walked up the pool steps, grabbed a towel, and walked through the house.

"Keep hold of my cock." His voice was gravel-rough, and low.

"What if—"

"No one is here," he repeated, walking up the stairs and kicking open his bedroom door.

Then closed it.

Hunter slid her down his body until her feet hit the floor. He cupped her face and claimed her mouth.

Soft, compliant, and needy lips.

She opened to him with eagerness, her tongue sweeping in hungrily. He gripped her hips and tugged her against him.

Usually, he kept these types of intimate moments to a minimum, but he wanted more of her. All of her. Addison fit him perfectly from her toes to her nose.

It was a moment of weakness. A moment he couldn't and wouldn't entertain again.

He had to remember who he was and what he could never have.

Hunter let her lips go more abruptly than he meant to, and large blue eyes shot to his in question.

Shit.

He had to focus.

"Remove your bikini and go lie down." He spoke too softly. Much too fucking softly.

She blinked.

What was wrong with him?

"Inaction is as good as a no, Addison. Consider this your last warning." He growled lightly, leaning closer. "Go."

She touched her lips and nodded. Then began to remove her bikini as he walked to a small cupboard and unlocked it.

Toys.

There weren't many. A whip, a couple of vibrators, chains, a number of butt plugs and silk ropes.

He grabbed the latter first.

When he turned, his cock leaped to attention. Lying on his black linen was a very naked Addison. On her tits were his clamps, and while her thighs were closed, he could see the little silver chain from the clamp on her clit. Little did she know the bling on the end was a two-carat diamond.

She was all his for the next few hours and damn, he was going to wipe that fear and desire from her face and replace it with utter pleasure.

"Are you just going to stare at me?" she asked, a hint of confidence in her challenge.

Oh, she was a slow learner.

"If I choose to. Yes, I will." Alas, time was not on his side, or he would have, as a punishment for her cheekiness, made her wait. He slapped the silk ropes against his thigh and her eyes widened. Slowly, he walked around the bed to her head and took an arm. "Move up the bed."

Addison moaned quietly, and he smiled. When he had her tied to all four of the posts, he walked back to the cupboard and brought some of the other items with him to the bed.

Then dropped his shorts to the floor.

He stared at her pussy, spread wide for him, and couldn't wait to taste her.

"I don't need to touch you to see how wet you are for me, Addison. You are glistening. You are beautiful."

Hunter picked up the black leather whip and began to slowly run it over her thighs. Gently. Then up her torso, and over her hard, clamped nipples. He continued this over and over for a few minutes and began to stroke his cock.

"Hunter, please." She begged.

"We're just getting started, sweetheart," he said, slapping the whip on the inside of her thighs.

Gasp.

He whipped the other one.

Gasp.

"Oh, mphhf."

He grabbed a pillow and lifted her hips, tucking it under them.

"That's it. Now I can access this gorgeous pussy."

With a skillful flick of the wrist, the black straps of leather reached out and kissed her pussy. She cried out from what he knew was both pleasure and pain.

Hunter's entire body was on fire watching her. His cock was swollen and twitching to get inside her.

He flicked the whip again.

And again.

"Please."

"Please what?" His voice was thick. Heavy eyes, thick with desire, pleaded with his as he stared down at her. "What do you want, Addy?"

He gripped her chin, licked her lips slowly and asked her again. "Tell me."

"I… I want it all."

He lifted a vibrator from the side table, the type with the big fat end that looked like a microphone. "I'm going to need you to be a little quieter," he said, turning it on and running it along the inside of her leg.

She panted out sexy little sounds.

He turned her head. "Take me in your mouth, but just the head." As she opened and leaned into him, he gripped her face. "Just the head, greedy girl. You take more, I stop."

Big eyes held his as she nodded. He let her face go and pressed the head of his cock inside her hot, wet mouth.

Holy fuck.

Her tongue swirled around the end of him desperately, as if she was sucking on a popsicle on a steaming hot day. And damn, she had some skills. If he wasn't careful, he would come.

He had more control than this, but this woman, fuck, she was sexy as hell.

Hunter turned his attention to the buzzing vibrator and moved it along the inside of her thigh and the outside of her shaved pussy. Teasing, taunting.

She moaned around his head, licking, sucking, as if by doing so she could direct the vibrator. Her body arched off the pillow eagerly and then he pressed it against the metal of the clit clamp.

"Oh my God," Addison cried around his cock as her body jolted up.

He grinned, knowing the vibration on the metal was enormously pleasurable. He wanted to feel how moist she was, but it was important he stretch this for as long as possible.

Her pain was his.

Her pleasure was his.

She tugged on the restraints and arched, crying out again, his cock leaving her mouth this time.

"Back on my cock or I stop." She clamped back around him, big eyes pleading. He moved the vibrator to her nipples, delivering the same shot of sensation through the metal clips on her breasts.

He swapped hands, freeing his fingers to delve elsewhere.

"Take me deeper." He pushed his cock further into her mouth. His fingers spread through her pink glistening folds and then sunk inside her.

She arched.

Then he removed them.

She released his cock.

"Bad girl, Addison." He removed the vibrator and turned it off.

She panted at him. "No, don't—"

He raised a brow. "No?"

She shook her head. "More. I'm sorry."

He gripped his cock. Usually he was more patient than this, but the sight before him was so fucking hot and erotic he was losing control.

Something he never did.

Stroking himself up and down, he stared down at her. He leaned between her legs and gripped her hips, blowing on her core.

"Shitshitshit." Addison moaned.

He reached out his tongue and slowly licked her from her asshole to her clit and then sucked the clamp between his lips.

"Oh, fuck." She cried out as her body began to tremble.

Again he stood and ran the black whip over her body, knowing she was on the edge. He stopped at her head, slipping his cock into her mouth, pressing deep down her throat.

"Mine. All mine to fuck how I want." He tugged on a nipple. How he'd love to have her strapped to his bed for more than just these few hours so he could fuck every hole over and over.

Hunter slipped out of her mouth and undid the silk ropes.

"What are you doing?" she asked.

"Wrists together," he said, re-tying them. "Now on your knees and ass in the air. And this time I want to hear a *yes, sir.*"

She raised a brow at him.

He raised one back.

"Yeah, yeah, or you will stop." She got into position. He remained standing, watching her, and she looked over her shoulder.

"Oh, for fuck's sake, yes sir!" she muttered.

Hunter lifted the whip and let it slam down on her tanned, golden ass.

"Mother fucker." She cried out, throwing her head back. "What was that—"

He had her neck in his hands. "Yes, sir. Without the attitude. Do you understand?"

She paled.

His fingers slid between her legs and swept the creamy moisture up over her ass. "Want to stop?"

"No," she growled, and his balls tightened, sending a buzz up his goddamn spine.

He reached around her to slam his lips on hers. "Head down."

Another flick of his wrist and the whip swept over her ass and pussy. Again, he let the leather kiss her flesh as she cried out. And he continued until her ass was as pink as her cunt.

They were running out of time.

Hunter leaned in, lapping at the juices flowing out of her as she cried into the pillows.

"Good girl," he said. "You've been very good."

Hunter removed the clamp from her clit, then grabbed the vibrator and climbed behind her.

"I'm going to fuck this pussy of yours now, Addison. Do you want that?" He ran his hand up over her ass and along her back.

God, she was so primed and ready.

Submissive.

So fuckable.

"Yes," she said, barely able to lift her head. Her need was so great.

He ripped open a condom, slid it on, and with his hands on her hips, lined his cock up. "Then relax for me, sweetheart."

The head of his red, swollen cock disappeared inside her. Her body reacted, clenching, trying to pull him faster inside.

Inch by inch, he pushed as Addison pressed back into him. She was wet, but Hunter knew he was a big man.

She was tight.

"Relax more." His patience was as thin as hers.

Another few inches and he was deep within.

And it felt way too fucking good.

CHAPTER TWENTY-SIX

Addison gasped at the pain-pleasure.

Had he torn her in two? Frankly she didn't care. She just needed him to move. God, the feeling of Hunter Dufort inside her was more than she could have imagined.

The fucking torturer.

He'd tied her up, whipped her, licked her, shoved his (fine, delicious) cock in her mouth and retained complete and utter control over her.

And she hated it.

But she also loved it.

So she hated him for that.

Finally, he was fully inside her. She wanted to scream for him to move, to thrust or to do something, but if she said a word, he would stop.

Because Hunter was in control.

She was at his absolute mercy.

"Fuck, Addison." He cried, out his hand on the small of her back, the other gripping her hip.

She moaned.

That was all she could do, it seemed.

Her arms were tied, her knees spread and her pussy filled with him.

Slowly he began to move and oh my fucking God, he felt amazing. She threw her head back, sucking in a long lungful of air.

Then he began to speed up, the grip on her hips tightening.

Would he come fast?

He hadn't let her come yet and while she usually needed clitoral stimulation, she was close.

Really damn close.

Was she allowed? Should she ask?

Irritation laced with heat shot through her. She hated how much she was enjoying the lack of control.

The buzzing began, and she felt the vibrator on her clit once more.

"Oh, God. Hunter, please." She cried.

"Not yet," he growled, and lifted her body so it was flush against his back. "There you are."

The vibrator lifted to her nipples once more, and she flung her head against his chest. "Jesus, I'm going to die."

Hunter let out a sexually charged, short laugh.

"If you want to come, you will need to beg for it, sweetheart." He growled in her ear as his cock thrust in and out.

Well, if that was all it took, she would have begged hours ago.

"Please, Hunter. I need to come," she cried.

The vibrator lowered to her clit and began to circle.

"Then come, little Addison. Come around my cock," he ordered.

And she did.

More powerfully than ever in her goddamn life. And then moments later, so did he.

HUNTER released her arms, and they both flopped down onto the black duvet, catching their breath.

She was speechless.

And a little unsure what to say.

"I need to take these off." She removed the nipple clamps.

Addison wasn't sure, but now they had done the deed, she was pretty sure the game was over. She popped them on the bedside table and glanced at him.

Hunter nodded. "You may keep them if you like."

She smiled. "Thank you."

Then he did something unexpected. He lifted his arm in that way guys did, and she curled into his chest.

"You don't have to do this," she said.

"What? It's a gift."

"I mean this. Cuddle," Addison replied.

When he didn't respond, she lifted her head and found him staring at the ceiling. His face was unreadable.

"You think I'm incapable of cuddling?" he asked, dark eyes lowering to hers.

She leaned up on one elbow. "No, I just didn't think you would want to."

He sat and pressed her back onto the bed. "There are lots of things I want to do, Addison Hill." His mouth lowered and sucked harshly on a nipple. She flinched. "Some too painful and pleasurable for a woman like you."

"What the hell does that mean?" she asked, offended.

His gaze pierced hers. "You're right. I am not a cuddler. Let's write it off as a weak moment."

Hunter got off the bed and walked into the bathroom. "Get dressed. The others will be home soon."

As the door closed behind him, Addison let her mouth fall open.

How dare he?

She had known this wasn't going to be the most romantic experience of her life, but Hunter had gone from snuggle bunny to asshole in three-point-two seconds.

She gathered her bikini, left the stupid nipple clamps and the clit clamp, and grabbed the towel that was on the floor. Covering herself, she went across to her bedroom and locked the door.

Asshole.

A tear slid down her face.

She had never been more vulnerable with another human being, and he'd just dismissed her.

As far as she was concerned, Hunter Dufort was dead to her.

CHAPTER TWENTY-SEVEN

Hunter heard Addison's shower running after he had changed and left his room. Being the coward he was, he decided to head out. The others weren't too far away from arriving home to change for lunch and God knows what other damn wedding things were on the agenda.

But he needed a break.

He headed to the garage and selected one of the vehicles: a black Audi SQ8. The engine roared to life. He pressed the button to open the garage doors and the gates to the property.

Hunter steered the Audi out to the gates and when he cleared them, pressed the button to close them and then hit the gas.

Lowering the windows, he let fresh air into the car and took a long draw.

It was like he couldn't breathe around her.

Addison.

His cock reacted.

Jesus, dude. You just fucked her.

Yeah, and he wanted more. A lot more.

But it was worse than that. He had pulled her into his body, wanting to feel her pleasure and warmth afterwards.

And she had fucking called him on it.

Even *she* knew he wasn't boyfriend material. Not even suitable for a quick snuggle afterwards. What had he been thinking, letting his guard down?

He should have fucked her, then patted that pink ass back across the hall.

Addison Hill wasn't his.

And she had been the one to remind him.

He turned the car onto the highway and pressed the gas down harder until Hunter realized this was for the best.

Still, he needed space.

And a fucking whiskey.

He parked the Audi and walked into the familiar establishment. Taking a seat at the bar, a tall brunette made her way over to him. She wore a sleeveless tank top which revealed darkly tanned skin, and a pair of black pants he knew slid off easily.

"Hunter Dufort," she drawled, grinning as she leaned against the other side of the bar. "What can I get you?"

"Whiskey. Neat."

She smirked at him. "Coming right up."

When she placed the glass in front of him, she asked another question. "How long are you here for?"

"Long enough," he answered. "When do you finish?"

"When do you want me to finish?" she replied, her eyes shifting to one of the submissions he'd seen before.

"Not yet."

She, also known as Sandy, nodded and served another patron who had just walked in.

What the hell was he doing here?

Was he going to fuck her after being with Addison?

That had never stopped him before. Some nights, he had multiple lovers.

Monogamy wasn't his flavor.

Yet, here he was, drinking his sad-ass whiskey, staring at Sandy's tits knowing she was already wet just from their short conversation. She had the ability to take away the vulnerable feeling that was wrapped around him like a prison.

Why did he care that Addison didn't see him as a man worthy of a relationship or something more than just a really great fuck? Hadn't he been that to hundreds of women over the years?

Wasn't that what he wanted?

He'd told her there was nothing more at the end of this for her. He meant that.

So why the fuck was he here sulking?

She had left his gift on the table. The set of diamond clamps.

A loud message that it was over.

Game over.

Now he had to get through two more days of his brother's wedding with her across the table, hall, and every goddamn where else.

Sinking deep into Sandy could help ease his wounded ego.

"WHERE the hell have you been?" Daniel asked when he walked into the living room.

Hunter let out a laugh thick with whiskey.

"Sorry Dad."

"That would be me." Johnathan Dufort said from his seat on the other side of the room.

"Hey Dad," Hunter said, flopping onto the sofa.

Addison sat across from him and lifted her bottle of water to her lips.

"Hello, Addison." He smirked, and her eyes widened. Okay, so he was a little drunk.

"Where's my fucking car?" Fletcher asked. "At least you didn't drive it home, I guess."

Hunter waved his arm around. "Sandy's."

Daniel shook his head. "You went to Sandy's and got trashed?"

He shrugged and glared at Addison. "Sure. She was very accommodating."

"Who is Sandy, dear?" Alice, Harper's mom, asked.

Addison glanced away, and he immediately felt regret. His eyes roamed over her body. The one he'd had in his arms earlier today.

Now she felt like a cold stranger.

"Oh my God," Harper said. "Get him some coffee and painkillers. You cannot be hungover for the wedding photos, Hunter."

Addison got up and left the room. His eyes followed her. Fletcher unwittingly walked in between them. "Bro, what the fuck?"

Hunter tipped his head back. "For crying out loud. Three dads!"

Kristen snorted across the room. "What? It's kinda funny."

Then his father stood over him. "Come on, son. Let's get you up to bed."

Bed did sound good. Really good. Even if Addison wasn't in it this time.

"Okay, Daddy." He stood and winked at Kristen.

His father took his arm. "Jesus. Can you walk?"

"Are you blind? I just walked in here." He laughed. "Has no one seen a drunk guy before? Carry on. As you were. *Ce la vie.*"

Kristen was now laughing her head off.

He liked her.

"That makes no sense," Daniel said.

Kristen burst out laughing again, and Harper joined her. "Fine. He's a hilarious drunk."

When they reached his room, his father kicked the door closed behind them. Hunter flopped on the bed and shut his eyes. "Night."

But he knew his father was still there.

Great.

"What's going on?" Johnathan asked.

"You mean aside from us buying you out of the business?"

"Yes. Aside from that," Johnathan said.

He opened one eye. "Aren't you mad?"

His father pulled out a chair and sat down. "Yes. But also proud. It means I taught my boys well. I had put the Dufort Dynasty at risk. Daniel made the right decision, and you and Fletcher backed him."

Ugh.

That was a dumb week.

He needed sleep.

And Addison.

He would cuddle her now.

"Cuddle who?" Johnathan asked.

Crap. He'd said that out loud.

"Nothing. No one. I cuddle no one. I'm like you," he said. "Sleeping now."

"Hunter, you are not like me," Johnathan said, his voice becoming a distant noise. "Let's talk when you sober up. If you like that girl…"

"Nope. Don't tell anyone I fucked her. They'll hate me."

Actually.

Crap.

Had he said that out loud, too?

"I think the secret is safe as long as you stay in this room and sleep it off. We're heading out to dinner. See you in the morning," he heard his father say.

Then the world faded to black.

CHAPTER TWENTY-EIGHT

"Are you being a good girl for Daddy?" Addison asked, the phone on speaker as she sat on the edge of the bed doing up her shoes.

She'd opted for gold heels that wrapped around her ankle and matched her solid orange cocktail dress perfectly.

She was feeling a lot more daring the day she'd purchased it than she did now. The flared skirt finished a smidgeon above mid-thigh and had three-quarter balloon sleeves with a V-neck that ended nicely but eloquently between her breasts.

It was stunning and thankfully her time in the sun had darkened her tan even more.

"Yes, and he's taking us to the park today for ice-creams," Sienna said. "Sammy's friend is coming too."

Addison bit her lip to stop from giggling.

Sammy's friend was her bodyguard.

"That's lovely, darling. What else have you been doing?"

She heard a little sigh. "Just school."

"And homework?"

"All done. We weren't allowed ice-cream until we did it all yesterday," Sienna said.

Well done, Rob. It sounded like their little chat had sunk in.

She stood and wriggled her toes, getting comfortable in the new shoes. She'd spent too much on outfits for this weekend and if she was honest with herself, it had been to impress Hunter.

Waste of time, that was.

Asshole.

Well, no. That was unfair. She'd had the most explosive orgasms of her life. And it wasn't just the orgasms; it was the entire experience. Every touch, every sensation, every breath on her skin. Hunter had taken her places she hadn't believed possible.

Then crushed her.

"Darling, Mommy has to go to the wedding now. Have fun at the park and listen to Daddy and Sammy's friend, okay?"

"When are you coming home?"

"I will pick you up from school on Monday," she said, her heart aching.

It was rare for her to be away from Sienna this long. Her father had her every second weekend, but other than those two days a fortnight, she was always home. And even then, she was only a few blocks away, so often dropped things off.

Four days felt like an eternity.

Even with the distractions in her life right now.

"Okay," the little voice said.

"Love you, monkey." She heard Rob calling to her in the background. "Go. Tell Daddy to call me tomorrow."

"'K. Love you Mommy."

Click.

She smiled.

Six years would soon be sixteen, so she was going to spend as much time keeping her little girl close as she could.

This was what she should focus on. Not some man who obviously had intimacy issues and couldn't even lay beside her for five minutes after sex.

All afternoon she had felt raw, hurt, and stupid for giving her body to a man who hadn't respected her. Then she'd heard he was missing and not answering his phone.

Daniel had been furious. Boy, that man was scary when he was mad, but Harper had just patted his chest like he was some house lion.

Then Hunter had come swooning in.

Drunk.

And looked her straight in the eye as he told the room he'd spent the afternoon fucking some woman named Sandy. Hours after he'd had his dick inside her.

What an asshole.

Pain had sliced through her chest as he'd stared arrogantly at her. She hadn't been able to stay a second longer, so she'd left the room.

This morning she'd woken up feeling flat. What had started as a sexy game had not ended well. Had she really expected it would?

Well, she wasn't giving him another second of her time. She was here for Harper. To celebrate her friend marrying the love of her life.

Hunter had been right.

They should never have crossed the line.

Hopefully she wouldn't see him again for months, or years. Fletcher and Olivia's wedding would be an occasion they'd have to endure each other's company, but by then, both of them would have all but forgotten yesterday's events.

Right?

She topped up her lipstick and grabbed her purse. Opening the door to her room, she stepped out and walked straight into… Hunter.

Bang.

"Jesus. What the hell?" she cried as he grabbed her arms.

"Sorry. I was about to knock," his deep, sexy voice said.

She shook him off. "Get your hands off me," she whisper-growled.

He took a step back. "Can we talk?"

Addison frowned at him. "No, we can't talk. The wedding is starting in ten minutes."

"I want to explain," he said.

"Yeah, I think I am quite clear on everything. So, no thanks."

"Addison." Hunter growled, taking a step closer once more. She held up a hand, and he glared at it, then his eyes returned to hers.

"No. No. No. No. Is that enough *no's* for you? The game is off. It is over. I am not obeying another word out of your mouth," she said. "Now, please step aside so I can head down to the ceremony."

Dark eyes stared down at her, and dammit if she didn't want to know what he was thinking. And feeling.

"I didn't leave for the reasons you think," he said. She dropped her eyes to the floor, but a strong finger lifted her chin. "Don't look away from me."

"Stop bossing me around," she muttered.

"Your body likes it," he said, a dimple appearing on one cheek as that side of his lips smiled.

God damn him.

"I'm sure Sandy likes it too, so go boss her around." Anger rose within her.

"Th—"

"Hunter," Fletcher called as he ran up the stairs.

"Fuck," Hunter cursed, and stepped away. "This conversation isn't over."

Yes.

It.

Is.

Addison slipped away and ran past Fletcher, giving him a smile.

"What's up?" Hunter asked his brother.

"Mom's here." They both heard the chopper as it lowered to the landing pad next door. Their long-time neighbors, the Roberts, had offered their pad so guests could land now that their entire front section had been transformed into a wedding wonderland.

"I'll go get her," he said.

If Fletcher had seen anything, he didn't say anything.

The last thing his head needed today was to deal with that. But he really wanted a chance to explain things to Addison.

The image of her hurt eyes had haunted him when he woke up this morning. He shouldn't have cared, but he did.

CHAPTER TWENTY-NINE

By the time he arrived back with his mother, more guests had turned up. In total, there were over two hundred and fifty people attending the ceremony.

Afterwards, they were heading to The Meadow Club for the reception.

"You look nice, Mom," Hunter said, taking in her navy and silver slip dress with matching jacket and hat.

"Thank you, darling," Marie Dufort said, running her hands along her side. "Harper helped me choose it. She is a nice girl."

Hunter smiled.

"She is. Daniel has lucked out."

"As you will one day." She tucked her arm through his.

"No thanks. I'm not going through this circus." He stopped as she half-tripped on a step. "Mom, I thought you weren't going to drink this morning."

She frowned at him. "It was one glass, darling. Hardly a big deal. You know I don't like flying."

Jesus.

He led her down the aisle to her seat at the front.

"Where's your father?" she asked, and he could hear the tension in her voice.

"I don't know. He's around," Hunter replied and wondered how the fuck he had been landed with this damn job.

Olivia joined them.

Thank God.

"Hello, Mrs. Dufort." She leaned in to kiss his mom's cheek.

"Oh, Olivia darling. Thank goodness. Here. You sit on the other side of me so that monster cannot come near me."

Hunter and Olivia shared a look, knowing exactly who she was referring to. Hunter couldn't blame her. Johnathan had cheated on his mom with dozens, if not more, women over the course of their marriage. She had turned to the bottle and eventually snapped.

"Sure, let's sit," Olivia said. "What a beautiful day. Isn't this gorgeous?"

Hunter took in the transformation. Hundreds of seats sat on either side of a wide grass aisle scattered with white rose petals. Potted white roses had been brought in and white lanterns hung over the entire space.

Ahead of them stood a tall archway in the same green and white style with a podium and the marriage officiant standing awaiting the wedding party.

"Hey," Olivia said, and he turned. Addison had sat down behind them.

"I wasn't sure where to sit. Is this okay?" she whispered.

Hunter turned. "Yes."

Then, before he could say anything else, familiar faces caught his attention. He stood.

"Hunter, look at you," one of the men said.

He laughed, knowing where this was going. "Come on, I was two years younger. Hardly the little brother."

He shook Trent's hand.

"No, but you aren't little now."

The guy slapped his other arm with his spare hand. And it wasn't a soft slap. The guy was nearly as big as he was.

"Do you remember Clint?" Trent said.

"Yes. You ran track with Daniel," he said, holding out his hand.

"And beat him," Clint said, smirking.

They made small talk, conscious the wedding could start any minute. Addison was leaning forward, chatting to his mother and Olivia. When Daniel walked out, the room began to settle.

"We should find a seat," Trent said, then glanced down at Addison. "Can we squeeze in here?"

"Of course. Please do." A little blush hit her cheeks.

Oh, no fucking way.

But there was nothing he could say as Trent reached out his hand and introduced himself to Addison. Clint did the same, and Hunter was left with one option. To sit down with his back to them and listen.

"Friend of the family?" Trent asked.

"It's complicated," she replied.

You bet it's fucking complicated. My cock has been inside you.

"That sounds intriguing. I'm going to get that story out of you before the end of the night." Trent laughed.

And. She. Giggled.

Hunter stood and walked over to his brothers at the front of the reception before he turned around and punched Trent.

"What's up?" Daniel asked, immediately picking up his vibe.

"Nothing." He shook his head. He got the big brother *bullshit* look.

"Where's Dad? Mom is stressing out."

Was she? Or was *he*?

He turned and watched Addison tuck her hair behind her ear as Trent turned his body toward hers.

She laughed some more.

Fuck.

His fists clenched at his sides.

"He was finishing a call, then coming out," Daniel said, "If it's that big of a deal for her, he can sit on the other side. He said he didn't care."

Fletcher lay a hand on his shoulder. "Here he is. I'll come with you."

Hunter took a moment to calm, and turned to Daniel. "Hey. Congratulations, big brother. I'm really happy for you."

Daniel lowered his head an inch in acknowledgment. "Thank you, Hunter."

They hugged and did the back slap thing.

When he turned, Fletcher had walked with their father to the seats.

"Marie," his father said, and there was warmth in his voice.

"Johnathan."

"Our son is getting married."

Marie's eyes glossed over. "Yes. Yes, he is."

Jesus, Hunter could barely breathe. Neither of them had talked in over fifteen years.

His father then did the smartest thing a man could do. He sat the fuck down and didn't say another word.

"Right," Fletcher said, clearing his voice. "I'll just go and... yeah."

Yeah. He felt the same. They glanced at each other as if a miracle had happened.

And it probably just had.

Then the music started.

"Oh my God, I can't wait to see her," Addison said as they all stood.

"Do you cry at weddings?" Trent asked.

Do you cry at weddings? Hunter repeated in his head in a squeaky voice, like he was a ten-year-old.

What an ass.

"No. Well maybe," Addison whispered.

She did?

Kristen walked down the aisle first and made her way past them all in a silver gown. She stood opposite Daniel and glanced back. The crowd gave an audible gasp as Harper appeared at the end of the aisle.

God, she *did* look beautiful.

Hunter glanced back at his brother and *fuck me*. He thought he might tear up a bit himself. He'd never seen Daniel look so emotional.

And the most incredible thing was, when he looked back at Harper, she never took her eyes off Daniel.

Hunter watched as she lifted her full white skirt and navigated the train flowing behind as she carried a bouquet of white roses.

Harper really liked white roses.

Daniel took a step forward, obviously mesmerized by his bride, and Kristen took the bouquet from Harper.

"Don't kiss the bride yet," Fletcher said, and the room laughed.

"Fuck that," Daniel said, ignoring the rules and slamming his mouth down on hers. "You look so fucking gorgeous."

Women everywhere gasped, their hands going to their mouth or chest.

"Oh, my God." Addison said, and he turned to see a tear fall down her face.

Trent handed her a handkerchief.

Hunter wanted to do that. He wanted to be the one to…

Fuck.

Stop. He had to stop it.

Clearly, all this wedding stuff was getting to him.

The marriage officiant asked everyone to sit and then the vows were exchanged. "I now pronounce you man and wife. *Now* you may kiss your bride."

And he did. Like only a Dufort man could. Daniel wrapped his arms around her and lifted Harper off her feet, kissing the life out of her.

For like ages.

Uncomfortably ages.

When he dropped her to the ground, Daniel went with her, leaning in. "I love you, Harper Dufort."

"Me too," Harper said, then turned. "Oh my God, we're married!"

The crowd *whooped* and stood, clapping.

Hunter saw the pride and happiness on his brother's face. He'd never seen him look so happy in all his life.

"Oh, my little boy is married." His mother cried beside them.

There was nothing little about Daniel.

Across from them, Harper's mother was wiping her eyes.

Hunter had to admit it was an incredible moment. But he was still never getting married.

CHAPTER THIRTY

The next hour and a half were a blur as they were whisked to a handful of venues for the wedding photos while guests were shuttled to The Meadow Club for cocktails.

Their mother and father were as well behaved as could be and surprised them all. Marie appeared to get along with Alice Kane well. The two women were distracted by all the dresses and rings, and talk of babies, in between photos.

Before long, they were walking into the grounds of The Meadow Club, which even Hunter had to acknowledge was like something out of a fairytale.

The circular space surrounded in trees was scattered with thousands of fairy lights which were already visible and would sparkle much more as the sun continued to drop. Tables were draped in white linen, silverware, crystal glasses and white and blush roses.

Guests milled around, clearly on their second or third glass of what he knew to be very expensive champagne, looking merry.

Fletcher took the mic and introduced the happy couple. The guests cheered and clapped as Harper and Daniel walked in and took their place at the head table.

If he wasn't mistaken, Daniel was looking a little over everything, but his eyes were still on his blushing bride.

Hunter glanced around for Addison.

Olivia, as Fletcher's fiancée, had been with them for the photos, and Kristen as the bridesmaid, so it was the first time Addison had been on her own this weekend.

Then he found her.

Sandwiched between Trent and Clint, who had also found a handful of other friends they'd gone to school with.

Hunter sat at the family table with Olivia, his mother, father, Alice Kane, and the spare seat was for Addison.

"Addy," Olivia waved out to her.

"Hey. How were the photos?" she asked, sitting down in the seat beside him, and completely ignoring him. Yet, for the first time in what felt like hours, his body relaxed.

"Good. My face hurts from smiling," Olivia said, rubbing her jaw.

Immediately, their first dish was placed before them, and more liquor poured.

"Are you enjoying yourself?" Hunter asked her quietly. Addison turned her head a little, but didn't make eye contact.

And that fucked him off.

"Yes. It's so beautiful," she answered politely.

Fucking politely.

"You?" she then asked, and then a grin hit her lips.

He took a deep breath, let it out, and lifted his eyes. Trent fucking Michaels.

The guy was winking at Addison.

Hunter glanced back and saw her blush.

He stabbed at his chicken and shoveled it into his mouth. His tense jaw struggled to chew. When that did nothing to relieve his growing anger, he threw back his champagne.

"Whoa there, tiger. Wasn't one hangover enough for you?" Olivia asked, teasing.

His eyes shot to hers, then dropped to Addison.

"And when are you and Fletcher going to tie the knot, darling?" Marie asked.

"Oh…" Olivia began, and Hunter tuned them all out, focusing back on the woman beside him.

But what did he say?

What could he say?

He knew he'd reacted poorly yesterday, and yet his feelings for her were out of proportion.

Weren't they?

It's not that he hadn't ever held a woman after sex. A few times he'd even fallen asleep. He had no issues with intimacy or emotion. It was that she had called him on it. As if it was something someone *like him* didn't do.

Sure, cuddling and pillow talk were the actions of a man wanting to form a loving relationship. That wasn't what he wanted, nor could he offer it. But he'd wanted that moment with her.

She obviously hadn't.

But was that true?

Was it really impossible for him to one day have a loving relationship?

It wasn't like he could come home after a hard day at the office and chime, '*honey I'm home, but I'll be heading off to the sex club after dinner*', and then curl up in their bed when he returned.

He watched Trent's eyes on Addison.

Hunter leaned his forearm on the table and tossed another mouthful of champagne down his dry throat.

Addison glanced at him.

"Are you okay?" she asked.

"No, I'm not fucking okay." He growled low in his throat so only she could hear. "If Trent keeps fucking you with his eyes, I'm likely to commit murder."

She blinked at him, her eyes darting around the table. "Stop it."

"Then keep away from him." Hunter's arm draped over the back of Addison's chair in a possessive move and slowly his dark gaze drifted back to Trent's. *She's mine*, screamed from his body language.

Trent held his gaze for a moment and then slid to Addison again. She pushed her chair back and nudged him away.

Fuck.

"Excuse me." She stood and walked away. The desire to go after her was so unnatural to him that he had to force his feet to stay the hell put.

Olivia was watching him, her eyes narrowed a little. Enough that he knew their interactions had caught her attention.

Shit, shit, shit.

He had to be more careful.

"Is Addy okay?" she asked.

He shrugged, like he didn't care half as much as he did. "Not sure. I guess she went to the restroom."

Olivia dabbed her lips on her napkin and stood.

Shit.

Would she tell her best friend what he had done? If so, it wouldn't be long until Fletcher knew, and soon Daniel.

He'd fucked up.

He should have stayed away from Addison.

Hunter let out a groan and leaned back in his chair. A glance at the Rolex on his arm told him there were still hours of this goddamn event—also known as his brother's wedding—to go.

"Everything all right?" his father asked from his other side.

"Sure. And hey, thanks for last night," he replied.

"It's been a long time since I've tucked you in," Johnathan said.

Hunter let out a small laugh.

When his eyes drifted across the room, he saw Trent pushing his chair in and making his way toward the bar. Which was set up near the hallway to the bathrooms.

How handy.

Given there was still table service underway and there were enough servers for three times the amount of guests they had, there was only one reason Trent had headed that way.

Hunter ran a hand through his hair.

"You going to let that Michaels boy get your girl?" his father asked.

His eyes darted to his dad's.

"What? She's not mine."

Johnathan lifted his brows, then his glass to his lips, taking a healthy sip. Don't bullshit a bullshitter, his father had always said.

He lifted his own glass, took a drink, and dropped it back on the table. "Look, she's... fuck, Dad. I can't. She's a mom. She has a kid. And I'm—"

"So does Olivia. It didn't stop Fletcher," Johnathan said.

It wasn't the same.

He wasn't the same.

"I'm not Fletch. And you know what I mean by that." He shook his head. "That's not my life."

His father stared at him.

"Do you think I haven't heard you boys over the years swearing off marriage because of your mother and me? Well, look how that turned out," he said, gesturing to their surroundings.

Hunter let out a snort.

They sat in silence for a long moment, the music around them picking up as people finished their meals and began to move about.

"You said something to me last night," Johnathan said.

"Oh God, Dad. I was drunk as a skunk. Ignore whatever I said."

Johnathan placed his arm on the back of Hunter's chair and leaned a little closer.

"You said you were like me. After you confessed to fucking her." Hunter raised a brow.

The hell?

If he was planning on a lecture right here, Hunter was not going to sit and listen to it.

"What did you mean by that?"

"For fuck's sake, we're at Daniel's goddamn wedding. Can't the pep talk wait?" He growled and glanced around the table. His mother was still in a cheerful-looking conversation with Alice, and Olivia had still not returned. "I told you she's not mine. I'm staying away. End of story. Now drop it."

Hunter pushed his seat back and stood.

"Hunter—" Johnathan called, but he walked away. The last thing he wanted to hear was a lecture from his father about how they were alike, and it was best if he kept his hands off her.

He damn well knew that.

He found his feet weaving through the tables to the bar. And if he was being honest with himself, it wasn't for a drink.

He was thirsty for only one thing.

The one thing he was being reminded of over and over that he could not have.

CHAPTER THIRTY-ONE

Addison leaned into the mirror and slid her gloss over her lips. Her heart still pounded at Hunter's show of possession.

How dare he after what he'd done?

If they had been anywhere else, she would have confronted him. Instead, she had done the other thing available to her. Got up and left.

Of course, Olivia had followed. She now came out of the stall and washed her hands in the marble sink. Then reached for one of the five-million-thread-count hand towel and dried her hands, tossing it in the ten-million-dollar wicker basket on the floor.

Okay fine, she was exaggerating, but everywhere she went with the Dufort's, there was opulence, and she wasn't used to it. Not at this level.

The Dufort's now consisted of her two friends.

"It's a lot, isn't it?" Liv said, leaning her hip against the bench.

Addison stood straight and mirrored her stance as she nodded. They'd known each other a long time, so she didn't need to ask what Liv meant.

"I know you love Fletcher and have worked for them for years, but do you ever stop and look at your life and just go, wow?"

"Every day." Olivia said, nodding. "Look at me. Wearing a Prada dress that would have covered two mortgage payments just a few months ago."

Addy smiled. "Big bank accounts and big hearts."

Olivia smiled and tilted her head. "What do you mean?"

She shrugged. "Just that those Dufort men love big. The way Fletcher looks at you. And my God, Daniel looks like he would die for Harper."

Pink heated her friend's cheeks.

"You're right. I've never been loved like this before. Some days it's so overwhelming I can't believe it's real. Then he'll grab my face and kiss me, bringing me back to earth and I can see in his eyes he's mine."

Addison felt her eyes fill.

"Liv, that's so beautiful." She took her friend's hand and squeezed it. "You deserve it. After what you have been through. Truly, I am happy for you."

They both smiled at each other.

"Thanks, but that's not why I came in here," Olivia said.

Damn, she'd been hoping to distract her from any questions, but she should've known Olivia wouldn't drop it. Not if she thought something was up with her friend.

Olivia tilted her head. "Hunter."

Shit. Please tell me she didn't see or hear anything.

Addison's heart began to slam in her chest.

"You will probably find him in the men's room," she said, turning to put her lipstick in her purse and feigning humor.

"What?" Olivia said, then clicked and laughed. "Very funny. No, I wanted to check if he had upset you?"

Addison forced her eyes to meet Olivia's. "Hurt me?"

"Yes."

Aside from fucking Sandy just hours after having his dick inside me? Or dismissing me after demanding complete submission with not an ounce of care? No, he hasn't hurt me. Not at all.

"Why would you ask that?"

Olivia crossed her arms. "You left the table a little abruptly. Did he say something?"

Ah, yes. He was threatening to murder another man for looking at me. A man who is far more suitable to get involved with and might actually like cuddling after fucking my brains out.

"No. I am on my period. I felt... well you know. Leakage." She laughed. "False alarm, thank goodness."

"Oh good. I was so worried. I thought there was something going on between you," Olivia said, looking relieved. "I mean, he is gorgeous."

Addison looked in the mirror. Her gaze clouded as she pictured those golden eyes of his fixated on her as she cried out his name. That strong jawline, and dusting of hair which had deliciously scratched her inner thighs.

It was those same eyes which had hardened and dismissed her moments after when she was at her most vulnerable. She had opened to him like no other man.

And for that, she could never forgive him.

"He is, but I am not interested in him like that." She answered honestly.

Hunter was everything she wanted in the bedroom and everything she didn't want out of it.

Despite the lie beneath it, that was the truth.

"I'LL meet you back there," Addison said to Olivia as she spotted Trent at the bar. They could both see the cheeky smirk on his face as they walked down the hall.

"Have fun," Olivia said, nudging her arm and giving her a grin before heading back to the table.

Trent was a good-looking man, that was for sure. He was obviously confident and wealthy, like everyone else in attendance. Which made sense. Rich people socialized with like-minded people.

Still, Addison had to admit, none of them had ever made her feel that her slightly different bank balance was an issue.

She stepped up beside him. While the bridal party had been away, having photos done, Trent had kept her entertained. He seemed to know a few people and introduced her as a friend of the bride.

If he had noticed Hunter's unhappiness at his interest in her during the ceremony, he hadn't said anything or stopped flirting with her.

Because he *had* been flirting.

Addison wasn't interested in making Hunter jealous. She liked Trent and wanted to talk to him again.

Anything between her and Hunter was over. She didn't belong to him. Not now and not for the weekend. He had destroyed whatever trust she had in him the moment he had climbed out of the bed and dismissed her.

Then Sandy...

"Hey there, gorgeous," Trent said, half leaning on the bar.

She smiled, feeling her cheeks heat.

"Hi. Are you enjoying yourself?" she asked, taking the flute of champagne he handed her.

"I am now." He winked, sipping his drink.

Addison glanced around the party, taking in the darkening sky as the sun sunk low, and the sparkles from the fairy lights began to shine brightly.

"It's so beautiful, isn't it?" She sighed.

Her own wedding had been lovely, but very basic. They hadn't had the budget to do very much. At the time, she had been pregnant and thought she'd been in love.

She had loved Rob. She hadn't been *in love* with him.

"Ah, you're a romantic," Trent said, tilting his head.

"And you're not?"

He shrugged. "I can be. With the right woman."

"Why does that feel like a cheesy pickup line?" Addison laughed.

Trent grinned, then lifted his drink to his lips again. He stood to his full height and glanced to his right. Her eyes followed his and her body flushed with electricity as she found Hunter watching them from across the bar.

His jaw was tense, his eyes dark. Yet his expression was blank. Addison looked away and turned her back on him.

Why was he angry with her?

She hadn't raced out and spread her legs for another man the same afternoon he'd been between them.

"Ah, I see what's happening here," Trent said, and she lifted her eyes to his.

"What?"

He tilted his head at her. "Are you sleeping with Hunter Dufort?"

She choked on her champagne and began coughing. He patted her back. When she'd recovered, she let out a small laugh. "Wow, that's direct."

"Am I wrong? I need to know before I make a move."

Addison took a small sip and let out another cough. "Were you? Going to make a move?" They were dancing around this, and they both knew it.

Trent placed a hand on his chest. "Well, I'm mid-move, so if you aren't aware, I'm very offended."

She giggled.

The attention was nice. Addison couldn't deny that. Trent was fun, and his bright blue eyes and short dark hair certainly weren't horrible to look at. He was the perfect height for stretching up on your tiptoes and kissing. And clearly, he was successful. His tailored black suit hugged his wide shoulders and tight ass.

Her brain was telling her to go for it while her body was tugging at her to turn around and meet the golden eyes burning into her back.

For what purpose?

Another extremely hot few hours in his bed, or even better, his dungeon, where she would be his submissive? So he could walk away and tell her to see herself out?

No thanks.

Where was her self-worth?

"Hey," Trent said, leaning into her and lifting her chin. "Why the sad eyes? I usually get a much better response from women."

Her mouth curved up and her lashes fluttered before she could stop them.

Smash.

They both looked up.

"Fuck!" Hunter cursed.

Glass had exploded everywhere.

Holy shit.

He'd just crushed the glass in his hand.

Addison's mouth fell open as the bartender grabbed a cloth and helped cleaned up the mess. Hunter wrapped a serviette around his hand as he continued cursing.

"You better tell me now if there is something going on between the two of you. Getting on the wrong side of a Dufort is not my goal. Today or ever," Trent said, his tone serious.

She shook her head.

"I'm not. We're not." She spoke adamantly, because it could never happen. Not again. And they had agreed not to tell anyone.

Trent nodded. "Good. I am sure you've heard about his tastes. Keep away from him. And I don't just mean that for my benefit."

God, she hated how people kept saying that. What was wrong with having kinks or fantasies?

"Nothing wrong with a little spice in the bedroom," she said a bit defensively.

Trent's smile stretched across his face as he looked down at her. "I totally agree. Is that what you like, Addison?"

Her cheeks warmed. Oh. Was he…

"God, you are gorgeous. I can see what Hunter likes about you."

She swallowed.

"Dance with me." He took the flute from her hand as the music picked up.

Perhaps Trent was someone she could have the type of relationship she was looking for. Spicier, but also with loyalty and commitment.

Hope sprung in her chest.

Addison let him lead her onto the dancefloor. It was refreshing to have a man want to be seen with her instead of hiding and playing games.

Just normal open flirting and fun. And maybe it would lead to something more serious.

Trent pulled her closer and placed his hand on the small of her back, the other taking her hand and spinning them around.

"You are very charming." She laughed.

"You wanted romantic." He smiled, pulling her closer again. "And if I wanted to wine and dine you, milady, where is your castle?"

She couldn't help it. She giggled.

Again.

"My wee castle is in Manhattan," she said. "And you should know, I have a wee princess who resides with me."

It was best to just lay her cards on the table. She was pretty sure Trent would lose interest when he learned more about her.

"Does the princess have any issues with her queen dating?" He moved them to the music.

She liked that he had asked that instead of cringing at her being a single mom. It was surprising how many men did that.

Those men were tossed away immediately.

Still, there was something else she wanted to clear up.

"Trent, you should know I don't really belong in this world." His eyes narrowed. "Olivia is my best friend."

"Fletcher's fiancée." His eyes darted over to their table.

"Yes." She nodded.

"I'm confused," he said. "That makes you very much part of their world."

Her eyes darted away. "I'm a marketing manager for Brown&Co Wines and Spirits. I… well let's just say I spent a month's salary on this dress."

"You think I want you for your money?" A cheeky smile formed on his lips.

"No. I'm just letting you know I'm not a billionaire." She let out a laugh.

Trent shook his head. "Well, neither am I. Yet. So you should know that."

Her mouth fell open. Oh God, she had never stopped to think he would take her words the wrong way. That was not at all what she had meant. She wanted him to know she wasn't some celebrity, model, artist, or socialite.

"That's not where I was going with this," she spluttered.

"I know. But it was as stupid as what you said, so I wanted to let you know." He winked at her.

She shook her head, smiling at him.

Addison liked Trent a lot. He had a confidence and strength about him that was very attractive. What woman didn't like that? And yet, while it was playful and fun, her panties were dry as a bone.

Not that she expected a man to physically excite her just by talking and dancing.

Hunter would.

She groaned inwardly.

She had to forget about that damn Dufort man. Comparing him to any other man was a path to disaster.

And then, as if on cue, a tall figure appeared behind Trent and tapped him on the shoulder. They stopped dancing and Trent turned.

"May I interrupt?" Hunter's dark voice asked.

Trent cleared his throat and glanced down at her. "Lady's choice."

Oh great.

Addison swallowed and smiled at Trent. Then more tightly at Hunter. "Of course."

She wasn't going to make a scene. And she was curious about his hand and if he had truly hurt himself. One glance and she could see a couple of band-aids.

"Thank you for the dance, Addison." Trent winked again and released her. "Come and find me when you're free."

She drew in a deep breath as the raging male in front of her took possession of her body once more.

CHAPTER THIRTY-TWO

Hunter was afraid to speak.

He was likely to say the wrong thing if the fury and dominating need to control Addison flowing through his veins was anything to go on. So he simply placed his hands on her hips and drew her to him. His eyes locked on hers.

You are mine.

No, she damn well wasn't. Yet he hadn't been able to stand watching her dance with Trent Michaels a minute more.

The man was perfect for her.

He'd seen him at the clubs once or twice. His tastes were a little milder than Hunter's, and that would suit her.

Probably.

He was rich and his portfolio thriving. And Hunter knew he was the marrying kind. He would provide a happy life for Addison and her daughter.

Those eyes glanced up at him in question. A healthy dose of anger still fizzled within them. He wanted to smile, now that she was back in his arms, but knew it would come across as condescending.

She *should* be angry with him. He had acted like a complete asshole. Yet, he had no words to apologize and nothing more to offer. So he stayed silent and pulled her against him closer as the music slowed.

"I hate you." She spoke against his chest.

"I know," he replied into her hair.

A long moment later, her eyes lifted to his. "How is your hand?"

Hurting like a motherfucker.

"It's fine."

I don't want you near Trent.

"Aren't you worried your brothers will see us dancing?" she said, and he heard the cynicism in her voice.

He was worried, but he was beginning to not give a fuck.

"Unless I push you over that table and lift your skirt, I think we will be fine." He felt her body react, sending a spark along the length of his cock.

"God damn you, Hunter." She moaned.

Again, he stopped from smiling. Only just.

"I didn't fuck her." He leaned down into her hair. "I want you to know I didn't fuck her."

Addison finally locked her eyes on his. They gave nothing away and suddenly he worried. He didn't want her to think this could be anything, but he'd wanted her to know the truth.

And for Trent to get his hands off her.

"Why not?" she asked, surprising him. He had no answer for her. At least not one he wanted to acknowledge.

She wasn't you.

Shut up, brain.

"I was drunk. And my mouth had just been on you." He replied quietly, wondering if she knew her fingers were making little dents in his biceps.

Her eyes dropped.

"Addison, I shouldn't have left as I did. Or said what I did," he admitted. "Being with you was... more than I expected. I suppose you could say I was taken by surprise."

"So you kicked me out?" she said, meeting him eye for eye.

"I'm sorry," he said, realizing this could be it. Their last moment together. Now that he had apologized, she would head back to Trent.

Or some other man.

His chest tightened.

He couldn't let her go.

"I want more of you." He wondered what the hell he was saying as her breath hitched.

"I can't," she whispered.

Oh yes, she could. He could feel her body leaning into him in places only a woman interested would lean. He was a master at the subtle nuances, and Addison Hill still wanted him.

Just as he still wanted her.

"So if I slide my hands up your dress, I wouldn't find you wet?" Wild eyes met his. "Where it was dry only moments ago."

There was no way he was going to let her lie and say it had been another man who had created the desire building within her. He may have been furious watching her dance with Trent, but there was no fire in her eyes or arch of her back. Not like she had now.

Hunter knew what pleasure and desire looked like on Addison, and it had been missing in Trent's arms.

Now she was mad, frustrated and sexually charged. For him.

And yes, he was fucking happy about that.

"Stop it," she snapped, but her body leaned further into his.

"You can lie to yourself if you want, but you submitted to me for the weekend, and I own this body." He tightened his grip as the song wrapped up. "Come with me."

She tugged on him a second, then like a good sub she followed. Arousal roared within him as he placed a hand on her back and led them inside the club house.

Staff milled around, paying them no attention as they made their way through the building. He had grown up here. He knew this club inside and out.

They walked up the stairs and slowed by a door. He opened it and they stepped into a private dining room.

"Hunter." She gasped, turning. He closed the door. "I don't—"

He pressed her hard against the wall and leaned his forearm next to her head. His body was hard against her as he gripped her hip.

"If you are wearing panties, I am going to be very mad at you."

Her lips parted, and he slammed down on them, sliding his tongue inside with complete possession. Addison responded with the same passion and eagerness. Her hands gripped his shirt, and her hips tilted into his.

Hunter clutched the fabric of her dress and began to gather it until he could reach underneath. He released her lips and smiled.

"Shut up." She shook her head. "It wasn't for you."

"Oh yes, it was." He grinned. "Spread your legs and let me feel you."

He may have been cocky, but he didn't take what she was offering—or what he was taking—for granted.

As the gap between her legs widened, Hunter slid his hands through her flesh and moaned.

"Fuck, baby. You are very wet," he said. "Now you get to decide. Do you want my mouth or my cock?"

She glanced across his shoulders. "Here?"

"Yes. Now. Two seconds, Addison." His tone demanded. "Or I decide."

She hesitated.

"Time's up." He whipped her around, face-planting her on the large dining table.

"Oh God." She cried out as he nudged her legs apart with his foot.

"Now you will remember who you belong to," he said, unzipping and lining his cock up with her wet pussy. Sliding through her flesh coating the head with her creamy moisture, he pressed against her entrance. "Tell me who, Addison."

She mumbled against the polished wood.

"Tell me." He growled.

"Oh fuck," she cried as he pressed in further.

He slammed deep inside her. "Answer me."

"You! Damn it. I belong to you," she cried, and he began to thrust.

Fuck, it felt good to be back inside her. His cock was clenched by her tight, eager pussy. Where he felt he belonged.

No.

Fucking no.

He palmed her back as his cock slid in and out, her cries pulsing with their moment. Reaching under her, Hunter found her clit and pinched hard.

"Oh, shit." She arched. "Ow."

He stilled.

"The table," Addison said.

Hunter kicked out a chair and slid out of her. "Come here."

He spun her around as he sat on the chair and pulled her over him. She sunk back down on his cock.

"Now ride me, little Addison. Ride my cock and I want you to come," he ordered as he shoved her dress away and thumbed her clit. Her eyes bored into his as her body clenched around him and began to tremble.

"I still hate you."

"That's good. Now do as you are told, my Addison. Come. Now." He watched as her face changed and pleasure hit. His cock reacted and he came too, releasing his seed into her.

Fuck.

No condom. But right now, he didn't care. Not about anything but filling this woman with all he felt for her.

Which was more than he had expected. Much damn more.

She collapsed against his chest, panting. His own chest beat like a drum. When she began to sit up, he held her in place. "Stay."

This time, he wanted to hold her for a moment. For him. And for her.

"Good girl." He ran his hand over her hair. "Such a good girl."

CHAPTER THIRTY-THREE

Addison hated that she'd let Hunter control her again. Yet her body buzzed with delight.

Where was her self-respect?

At least he had not slept with that Sandy woman. Except that wasn't why she had fucked him. She'd literally had no choice. Her body had taken over, and when he ordered her, she just submitted.

She turned as Hunter pulled out her chair back at the wedding table, and sat down, hoping like hell her face didn't give away what they'd just done.

Olivia was sitting on Fletcher's knee, giggling and kissing him.

"Hey, where did you go?" her friend said when she finally noticed her.

"I found her dancing," Hunter said, saving her from fumbling with an answer. She was still coming down from that enormous orgasm and wasn't sure she could talk.

It had all happened so quickly.

He'd been worried about not using a condom, but she was on the pill. She was less concerned about pregnancy than whether they had transmitted anything nasty. Hunter had reassured her he was always very strict about using protection and getting checked.

Except this once, clearly.

"Tell me about your job," he suddenly asked.

"What? My job?" she asked, obviously surprised. "It's not overly exciting. I'm a marketing manager for Brown&Co Wines and Spirits."

He shrugged. "I want to know. Tell me more."

She blinked at him.

What was he doing?

"Is this about Trent?" she asked, leaning in to whisper, even though the music was loud enough to give them a little privacy.

His eyes darkened.

"No Addison, I want to know more about you because I just had my cock inside you."

Her eyes widened, and she glanced around. Was he insane? Someone might hear them. His family was sitting on either side of them.

"Can you stop saying that stuff?" She snapped behind her glass.

He smirked.

"No. I like the way you react." His hand slid over her thigh and between her legs.

Addison stared across the table and Harper's mum caught her gaze and smiled at her. Just as Hunter's fingers found her clit.

She coughed. Then slapped his hand.

"Fine. What do you want to know?" She turned to him.

"Do you enjoy it? How long have you been there?" He topped up their glasses with a bottle of the champagne sitting on the table.

She glanced around, looking for Trent. Had he seen her disappear with Hunter?

Did she care?

Hunter had been right about her body reacting to him just from dancing. It hadn't felt like that with Trent. She had to admit that.

The truth was, she was always aroused in Hunter's presence. The command of his body. The way he surrounded her entire being and took control.

Challenging her senses.

Stimulating her senses.

Hunter Dufort was a walking sex god.

Fine, if he wanted to know more about her, she would tell him. And bore him. Then he could give up this act.

"I wouldn't say I love my job, but I enjoy it enough. This is my fifth year. I started after Sienna was born." She dropped in a reminder that she was a mother with a daughter.

Hunter didn't look away.

"Do you manage people?" he asked.

Addison sighed. "Yes, Hunter, I have a team of twelve people. You don't need to know any of this stuff because you just fucked me. Stop pretending you care."

His eyes flared.

Someone cleared their voice over a microphone, interrupting them. She turned to face the front of the venue and felt Hunter lean into her neck.

"This conversation isn't over."

Yes, it was.

As was the weekend. At least it nearly was. Tomorrow she was flying home and while Hunter would be on board, Addison couldn't wait to run, not walk, away from the tall, muscular man with golden eyes who made her lose control.

CHAPTER THIRTY-FOUR

Hunter climbed out of the chopper the next day and reached his hand in to help Addison out.

"For fuck's sake, Hunt, move," Fletcher said, waiting to get out of the big bird. "Addison is able-bodied and can climb out herself."

He didn't miss the smirk on her face as she lifted her bag over her head to cross her body. Ignoring his hand.

God damn her.

She flicked between sub and independent far too quickly. In moments, she would be out of his life and...

And *what?*

He wanted these last few minutes with her. To touch her. He kept his hand out and because no one was as rude as him, Fletcher shut his damn mouth and Addison finally reached out and took it.

"Good girl," he said quietly as she brushed closer to his body.

When they reached the lobby where the elevator would take them down into the offices of the Dufort building, they waited for the staff to unload their bags.

"Wow, what a wedding," Olivia said. "Harper looked beautiful."

"So beautiful." Addison sighed, and he shared an eye roll with Fletcher.

Olivia nudged her fiancé after catching the look out of the corner of her eye and Fletch feigned pain by curling in on himself.

"Ow. Call our lawyer, Hunter. My woman is violent."

"You wish." Olivia laughed.

"Nah, that's Hunter's thing, not mine." He spoke casually, nipping at her lips.

Addison caught Hunter's gaze as he shook his head. The familiar irritation laced through his body.

"BDSM isn't violent." She suddenly spoke out, surprising him. Not just him. All of them.

Everyone went quiet.

Addison looked shocked herself and glanced away, shrugging.

"I'm just saying. Calling someone violent is a little harsh because they like it... um..."

Hunter pressed his lips together. It was either smile or kiss her. He wasn't sure which he wanted to do more.

"Dominant," he offered.

"Nothing wrong with dominant," Olivia said, nudging Fletcher. "You're dominant."

"Of course I am. I'm the man," Fletcher said.

"Yeah, that's not really how it works." Hunter started to explain and then waved his hand. "Anyway, change of subject. Addy, do you need a ride home?"

Now he really wanted to speak to her.

She shook her head.

"No. I'm picking Sienna up," she replied, taking her bag from the waiting Dufort employee. She glanced at him. "But thank you. And... thank you all for a wonderful weekend. Your house is just beautiful, Fletch. And Liv."

Olivia threw her arms around Addy.

"It was so nice to hang out. I've missed Sammy so much, but it was nice to be kid-free for a bit."

"Me too. I rarely get time to myself and do fun things like this."

Interesting. Why not? Didn't the father take her daughter every second weekend or whatever their agreement was?

Fletcher stared at him. "You going to the office?"

"No." He shook his head as the elevator doors opened. They all stepped in. "Heading home. You?"

They began to descend and then suddenly Olivia began to push the buttons rapidly. "Oh, shit, shit, shit. I left my phone on the chopper."

"Okay, well, don't blow up the elevator. We will just go back up and get it. It's not going to fly away." Fletcher grabbed her hand.

Addison laughed, tugging her luggage up. Every bone in his body wanted to carry it for her.

The doors opened and the two of them stepped out, leaving Fletcher and a dancing Olivia inside.

"Quick, go. What if it does take off?" she cried.

"I own it, so we'll just ask them to fly bac—" Fletcher's voice shut off as the doors closed.

Addison glanced up at him.

"Give me that," he said, taking her bag.

"I had it," she said, glancing around at the few employees in the lobby.

They walked to the entrance, and he was glad his hands were full of luggage as he doubted he'd be able to keep them off her. She looked relaxed and sun-kissed, and he had no doubt those orgasms had contributed to her glow.

The revolving doors led them outside onto the sidewalk where his car and driver waited. Fletcher's car sat behind his.

"Let me give you a ride." He stood way too close, deliberately.

"No, I have to pick up my daughter from her dad's." Addison took her bag from him. "This would be a little hard to explain."

Why?

"I can wait inside the car."

"I'm not worried about Rob. I don't want Sienna meeting you," she said, then blanched.

Ouch.

"Sorry, that came out much harsher than I meant."

"But no less true." His brow rose.

"No."

"Because you don't date?" Hunter asked, and when she hesitated, he nodded. "Right. Because you don't date someone like me."

Addison's mouth parted. "That's not fair. I heard you don't date either."

"Who said that?"

"You. You said you don't want to fall in love." She snapped the words at him.

"Love and dating are two different things, Addison."

She huffed.

"I have to go." She started to walk away, but he grabbed her arm.

"Stop. I want to see you again," he said. "I want more of you. I want…" he stepped closer, "…to pleasure you more. I think you want that too."

Her face softened. "We shouldn't."

"I'm standing outside my building where the media could photograph us together. Asking you to let me see you again. I think that tells you how much I want you, Ms. Hill."

"Hunter."

"Your name on my lips does things to my cock. Now say yes."

"Maybe."

It was a start. He led her to his car.

"What are you doing?" she asked, attempting to pull away from him.

"Take my car. I will head up to the office until Trevor returns. I have some emails to send, anyway."

He didn't.

"Seriously?" she asked.

"I don't want you in a damn cab or on the subway, Addy. Get in the car." He opened the door. When she climbed in, the look she gave him was so fucking feminine and sexy he wanted to climb in and smash those soft lips against his.

"I'll call you." Suddenly everything in his world began to right itself again.

And what that meant, he didn't know. And didn't care. He just had to see her again.

A FEW hours later, he walked into his penthouse, showered, and changed. Addison had been on his mind constantly since the car had pulled away.

This wasn't good.

He never thought about a woman this long. Or at all, if he was being honest.

He wanted to know if she got home safely—which he already knew as Trevor had confirmed—and he wanted to know if she was thinking about him. What was she having for dinner?

Was she looking forward to going back to work tomorrow? Was she okay after he'd pounded her so hard yesterday in the club?

Fuck, was she pregnant despite being on the pill? Not that they would know this early.

All of that was bullshit, of course.

What he wanted was to have her in his apartment, in his arms, in his bed. Hell, even on his sofa, just talking.

That last was the most surprising thing of all.

Hunter stood staring out his floor-to-ceiling windows at the view of Central Park below him.

What if she was pregnant?

Addison swollen with his babe. His stomach did somersaults. Why was the image of that so fucking sexy?

How would she feel?

Would she get rid of it?

Fury irrationally spread through his body. There was no damn way he would allow that. He'd make her marry him.

Christ, now he had her pregnant and walking down the aisle.

"Fucking hell, I am losing it," Hunter said aloud, as he ran his hand through his hair.

After dinner, he lounged on the sofa with his feet on the coffee table, scrolling messages on his phone as the TV quietly played in the background.

His mind was unable to focus on much of anything.

Daniel had sent a bunch of photos and *thank you's* to him and Fletch, so he replied to those texts and then found himself on Instagram.

Stalking Addison's account.

His face spread into a smile.

There was one of her with Harper and Olivia outside by the pool earlier today. All of them *not* in their bikinis.

He knew the exact moment it had been taken.

He'd been outside with Daniel contemplating a swim when his brother's voice had gone all high-pitched.

"What are you doing?" Daniel asked as Harper began to undo her bikini. "Wha—"

Hunter's eyes widened, and he broke out into a grin.

"Tanning my boobs," Harper had replied, and he watched as Addison pressed her lips together to stop from laughing.

"Same," Olivia said, and began undoing her strings.

"I'm out," Daniel said, and began to march back into the house, then he stopped and glared at Hunter. "And so are you."

Yeah, he wasn't going to risk the wrath of Daniel if he saw Harper's breasts. He was brave, but not that fucking brave. He winked at Addison and followed Daniel inside the house, nearly plowing into his back when the guy stopped and planted his hands on his hips.

"No one is going outside this door," Daniel declared.

"The fuck? Yes, I am. It's my damn house," Fletcher said. "And that is *my* damn pool. It's hot and I want a swim."

Their father looked up.

"Harper is topless sunbathing," Daniel said, crossing his arms.

"Ah." They all nodded.

"They all are," Hunter added.

"You saw my fiancée's tits?" Fletcher growled.

"Settle down. We hightailed it out of there as soon as they began to strip," Daniel said and glanced at Hunter. "I dragged him inside with me."

"Dragged is a little bit of an exaggeration." He rolled his eyes. "Anyway, are we sure the neighbors can't see in?"

They stood staring at each other, testosterone swirling in the air.

"They can't," Johnathan said. "Trust me."

And no one asked any more questions. His father would know after his past and the less asked, the better.

Hunter stared down at the photo on Addison's Instagram. The cheeky grins clearly showed how proud they were at getting one over on the men.

They had sat in that damn house drinking iced tea for over an hour, knowing those women were out there with their gorgeous boobs out.

He double-clicked the photo and the little red heart appeared.

CHAPTER THIRTY-FIVE

Hunter Dufort, or rather *Hunter_Dufort3452* had just hearted her photo on Instagram.

Addison stared at the notification on her phone.

She wanted to call him, but she knew it was the wrong thing to do. She couldn't see him again.

Trent had given her his business card before leaving the wedding and said he hoped to hear from her. On paper, he was the man she should be giving her attention to, not Hunter.

Yet one stupid little heart on Instagram had her chest beating like a teenager.

"Mommy?" Sienna asked.

"Oh, sorry. One more page and then lights out." She turned the page and then read two, because that's what moms did. She kissed her daughter on the forehead and felt her heart burst open when little arms wrapped around her neck. "Love you."

Oh, man.

"Me too, munchkin," Addison said, tweaking Sienna's nose and turning out the light. "To the moon and back."

It was a reminder of who she was and what her priority was. A love affair with a billionaire who frequented sex clubs? That wasn't exactly the sensible path for her to take. Even if she had stood up for him earlier today.

Addison walked out into the living room and flopped onto the sofa, her eyes quickly closing.

She was tired.

The weekend had been both fun and exhausting.

Hunter wanted to see her again, and she knew he wouldn't let her hide for long.

But it was impossible. She had Sienna ninety percent of the time and while it was theoretically possible, sending her daughter away so she could get involved with a man she had no future with, for a few really damn great orgasms, didn't sit right with her.

It felt irresponsible.

But on the other hand she could be setting up a date with Trent who was perfect, and that would be a good use of her time.

That could lead somewhere.

He could be the man she fell in love with. Married. Had more children with.

Hunter would meet someone else he desired and lose interest in her, she was sure of it.

It was just time.

They needed time to forget each other.

CHAPTER THIRTY-SIX

Friday afternoon, Addison stepped out of her downtown office, and found Hunter Dufort leaning against his car, dark sunglasses on. He looked so damn sexy, her knees nearly weakened.

His hands were tucked into his pants pockets, and he was ignoring all the looks from women passing by.

His eyes locked on her.

Her lips pressed together, and she marched over to him. "What are you doing here?"

"I'm taking you out," he said, like it was obvious.

She fish-mouthed it for a second. "Were you going to ask me?"

"No," he said, standing away from the car and opening the door. "After you."

Addison looked around, wondering if she was on some TV show. "Are you abducting me?"

"Would that turn you on?" he asked, his voice low.

She swallowed.

Jesus.

Yes, probably. Damn him.

She climbed into the back seat and when he did the same, sitting beside her, she turned to ask him a question, but his mouth slammed onto hers.

Fire flared through her body, vanishing all thought. His hands gripped her face, her body crushing into his.

As the kiss softened, his tongue swept inside, not letting up the passion or heat, claiming her. She felt the car move and her entire being surrender to him.

Yet again.

When he finally released her, they sat panting, staring at each other.

"Thank fuck," Hunter said, leaning back, pulling her against him.

"How do you know I don't have Sienna tonight?" she asked, knowing he wouldn't have *abducted* her unless he did. Hunter might be dominant, but he respected family. She knew that about him.

"I overheard Olivia talking to you on the phone yesterday."

"You didn't think to call or text?"

He shrugged. "I was waiting for you, remember? But I ran out of patience."

She shook her head. "Where are we going?"

"I figured you'd want to get changed so we are heading to your place, then I have a surprise for you."

Oh boy.

When the car stopped outside her house, Hunter said he'd wait in the car. "Wear something sexy."

Addison gulped, then headed upstairs.

CHAPTER THIRTY-SEVEN

This was either going to scare Addison off or tell him everything he wanted to know about her. He just wasn't sure which he was hoping for.

All he'd known was he'd spent every day looking at his phone, waiting for her message.

And she hadn't sent one.

Then, when he overheard Olivia, he'd known what he needed to do.

He was a Dom. An alpha. He didn't wait or ask.

He took.

And Addison wanted—needed—that.

But tonight would be the test. He wanted to see her in his world, and it would give them both the answers they needed.

When she stepped out of her house, his cock sprung to life.

Fucking hell.

The tight black dress clung to her tanned thighs, taking all the attention from the pair of stiletto heels strapped to her feet. The top of her dress was a halter style which hung low between her breasts.

Her fine gold chain with the small cross dangled just between them.

Holy smokes. He'd clearly died and gone to heaven.

Trevor opened the door, and she climbed in, dropping her black clutch on the seat between them. Hunter tossed it on the seat in front of them and pulled her to him.

Rich floral perfume filled the vehicle, as his gaze dropped to her glossy red lips.

"You are fucking beautiful." His fingers ran over her collarbone.

"Are you going to tell me where we're going yet?" she asked, her voice husky.

That he couldn't do. If he did, she would jump out of the car right now. But he had a strong suspicion that once they arrived, curiosity would get the better of her.

Hunter shook his head. "No. But I'm asking you to trust me. Can you do that?"

"Do I have a choice?" she asked, a brow raised.

"Always." He took her hand and stared out the window. "Always."

The car pulled up outside Pendulum and Trevor opened the door for them. Hunter removed his jacket and tossed it onto the seat, rolling up the sleeves of his black shirt.

The light bounced off his large watch and he noticed her stare at it. He knew she wasn't comfortable with his level of wealth. Not entirely.

Not many people were.

"Are you preparing for surgery?" Addison asked, a cheeky gleam in her eyes.

"Possibly." He laughed as he opened a small cupboard and pulled out two black masks.

"Turn around," Hunter said and put one of the masks over her eyes.

Addison's fingers lifted to it and those red lips of hers looked even more fucking sexy under the sparkling edge of the mask.

She blinked at him.

"Trust."

"Good girl." His fingers gently brushed her nipples. Then he put his own mask on and pulled her out of the car with him.

A man stood outside the discreet black door and nodded to him. "Evening, sir."

"Evening," Hunter replied, knowing the security man knew exactly who he was, and that he had a guest with him this evening.

The door opened and a long set of stairs, lightly lit, greeted them. He glanced at Addison, and they began climbing. His hand did not let go of hers.

Addison slowed halfway up.

"I know what this is." Her voice was quiet. "This is a sex club."

He stopped and glanced down at her. "You can say no at any point, and I will take you straight out of here."

Hunter watched as her eyes darted around, showcasing the thoughts in her mind.

She nodded. "Okay."

His cock twitched.

"Don't leave my side," he ordered.

The door at the top opened as soon as they reached it. Every step of the experience in his exclusive club was well orchestrated for the ultimate pleasure.

Warmth hit them as they stepped inside. The light was dark but still allowed good visibility. The walls were black, as was the décor, with hints of red, silver, and glass. The place screamed wealth and sexuality.

Everyone was fully dressed, and it felt like a normal bar except for the fact that people were openly making out.

"Oh," Addison said as she spotted a man having his cock sucked by a woman in a business dress on her knees in front of him.

Hunter tugged her up to the bar.

"Whiskey. Neat." He glanced at Addison, who was staring over her shoulder. "And a Cosmo. Double."

He wasn't trying to get her drunk, but taking the edge off would help her relax.

"Thank you," she said when he handed it to her. She took a large gulp. "So, what do we do?"

He smiled.

"Whatever we want. Do you want me to show you around?" Hunter asked.

"There's more?" Her eyes widened.

Oh yes.

There was a lot more.

ADDISON followed Hunter through the room as she tried to keep her eyes off people's private parts. While also wanting to see everything.

Her body was buzzing, even though it felt wrong. And yet right.

Basically, her brain was jelly.

He pushed a code into a panel, and it clicked open a door.

"Are we allowed through here?" she asked, and he smirked.

"Yes. Remember sweetheart, if you want to leave or you're not comfortable, tell me."

She nodded as they walked through a short dusky lit hallway that led to another large room much like the other, except this was vastly different.

The décor was the same.

But nobody was clothed.

With the exception of leather and rope attire. She wasn't a complete novice. She knew some stuff.

Holy shit.

She squeezed Hunter's hand, and he slowed, pulling her closer. She threw back her drink and dropped it on the bar. "Another one, please."

"Make that two. One whiskey," Hunter said to the bartender, then glanced down at her. "Look around, Addy. Take it in. Learn what you like and don't like."

Oh God.

Her nipples were already hard against the cowl neck of her dress and fortunately, they were hidden because of it. Her core was warm.

How could she not be turned on? But it felt naughty.

As her eyes roamed, she saw a group of people pleasuring each other. A man had his arms spread, fondling two women's breasts, his cock being sucked by another man. One of the women had her legs spread as another man finger-fucked her.

There was no shame, just complete pleasure on their faces.

Another couple sat watching, much like she was, but as she looked closer, she noticed the woman was stroking the man's cock.

"Voyeurs," Hunter said in her ear.

"Oh," she said, nodding.

"Would you like to be watched, Addy? Or to watch?" His hand slid behind her and ran over her hips. Her body stiffened. Not from his touch, but she wasn't sure about being as exhibitionist as the others in this room.

Hunter let out a small laugh.

"Let's try something else."

He led her to another set of doors and this one opened up to a space with about eight deep windows. Until you got closer, you couldn't see what was in them.

The light was a lot dimmer in this room and Addison spotted a few people standing, watching.

Then it hit her what she was looking at.

Literally.

Inside the rooms, which were softly lit, people were having sex. Hunter led her around the room, taking in the different couples and groups. And one woman on her own.

"They like being watched."

"Yes," Hunter said, and then indicated the woman to their right who had her hand between her legs. "And watching."

The almost unnoticeable music around them provided a decorum of privacy, but it nearly seemed irrelevant given the situation.

She cast her gaze inside one room, and it captured her attention. The young woman was strapped to the same kind of cross Hunter had in his room. A man and a woman were in there with her.

Hunter stepped behind her, pressing his body into hers. "Watch."

The woman ran her fingers over the other's breasts and flicked her nipples. The woman cried out.

This close to the window there was sound. Her pleasure sliced through Addison's body, and she tried to push down her own arousal.

Reacting to someone else's pleasure was strange and yet powerful.

The man got to his knees and began licking her from her toes, all the way up the inside of her thighs. Addison could see the woman tremble with need. How long had they been doing this?

Her tiny pleas were the answer.

Then the man plunged his fingers inside her, and she arched out in a cry.

Oh God.

Addison's panties became wet.

Hunter ran a finger along her arm.

She shivered.

"You like to watch." His voice was thick on her skin.

"I—" she began, but had no words as the other woman wrapped her mouth around one of her breasts as the man lifted a vibrator and began stimulating the tied-up woman's clit while his fingers kept sliding in and out.

Addison's lips rubbed together, and she tried to maintain composure.

"Touch yourself," Hunter said, pressing his hard cock against her.

She shook her head. "I can't."

"That was an instruction." His hand slid the fabric of her dress up. "Fingers inside your panties, Addy."

Oh fuck.

They were standing in a room with other people.

"Can they see us? The people in there," she asked thickly.

"Do you want them to?" Hunter asked. "Press the red button on your right if you do."

She didn't know.

No. Not this time. Addison wasn't even sure she could do this, but then the woman got to her knees and began to lick the other woman while the man entered her from behind.

Holy fuck.

He had the vibrator and was holding it to the woman's clit as the other woman on the cross cried out.

Hunter slid Addy's panties down.

"Now Addison," he said, and her hand flew to her pussy.

Then he stepped away.

"What are you doing?" she said, turning.

"Watching you." He rubbed his hand up and down his cock. "Keep going. I want to taste you when you come."

Oh God.

The sounds from the room, the knowledge he was watching as she slid her fingers through her wet folds, and that anyone inside this room could be—and probably was—watching her, sent her body into a spin.

She found her clit, and her eyes turned back to the display in front of her.

The woman's nipples had been clamped, and the man was slipping a vibrator inside her, but only the tip, as the other woman now sucked his cock. She could see the pain on the strapped woman's face as she arched and craved release.

Her moans and pleas filled the air as the man demanded her to beg. Then when she did, he sunk the vibe deep inside her and threw his head back as he came in the other woman's mouth.

Addison's body reacted. Her fingers swirled faster.

She turned.

"I need—"

Hunter shook his head. "Make yourself come. Now."

His demand sliced through her, and body followed the instruction. She arched into her own touch as she came on her fingers.

Then Hunter was on his knees in front of her, lapping at her, his strong hands holding her up as a second wave hit. His tongue slid in circles on her most sensitive spot and deep inside her, riding her orgasm further.

"You taste so damn sweet." He licked his lips as he continued to hold her up and stood. When he was towering over her again, he pulled her against him. "That was the most beautiful thing I've ever fucking seen."

She caught her breath and glanced around.

"I can't believe I did that."

"Felt good, didn't it?"

She nodded, and his lips claimed hers.

CHAPTER THIRTY-EIGHT

Hunter stood in the elevator, his cock stiff in his pants, and stared straight ahead.

Addison pressed into his side.

He could have fucked her at the club, but after what he'd witnessed, he wanted her at home, in his dungeon, so they were free to do whatever they wanted.

For as long as they wanted.

They stepped out into the entrance of his penthouse, and she turned to him.

"I know this isn't…"

"Don't. Just let us have this night," he said. "Without definition."

"Just one night." She nodded.

He wasn't sure, even now, he was able to let her go. After watching her pleasure herself in the viewing room, he'd just about come right there and then in his damn pants.

And he wouldn't have been sorry for it.

The fact he had an office with a change of clothes out back helped, but even if he hadn't, it wouldn't matter.

Addison was the sexiest woman he'd ever laid eyes on.

He pushed open the door to his dungeon, and she walked in. No questions. Just walked in and sat on the edge of the bed.

"Put this on." He handed her a black leather lingerie set that covered nothing, but would strap around her breasts, arms, and thighs. And had little hooks for some toys he was planning to use.

"It might not fit." She took it from him.

It would fit. He'd purchased it for her this week.

"Trust me." He winked, crouching down in front of her. "From this point onwards, you call me sir. You must obey my every word. I'm going to introduce you to things you have never experienced."

She swallowed, nodding.

"Do you want a safe word, or do you want to use no?"

"No is fine," she said softly.

"Good girl."

"Get changed and I want you to stand on that spot on the floor." He pointed to it as he stood.

"Then what?"

"The answer is, yes, sir." He took her chin. "We aren't playing now, Addison. From this point on, if you don't obey me, you will be punished."

Her mouth gaped open, then shut as she nodded. "Yes, sir."

It was the flush of panic and arousal on her face and chest that had him turning away before he fucked her right there and then.

He had promised her pleasure, and it was his job as Dom to deliver.

As she changed, he removed his clothes, placing them on the back of an armchair. When he glanced up, she was standing on the spot.

Hunter walked over to her and ran a finger down the front of her. "Turn around."

Big eyes held his for a moment, and then she did.

He reached around and placed a silk blindfold over her eyes, rejoicing as she drew in a breath.

"Drop to your knees."

Hunter walked to his cupboard and quietly began to remove a few toys, placing them on the bed.

While Addison waited.

Afterwards he stood watching her as he stroked his cock. Her rosy pink nipples were taut, and her breathing labored in anticipation.

What most people didn't understand about the Dom-sub relationship was the holistic nature of the play. It wasn't just about having dominance over another's body. There was another sex organ far greater.

The mind.

The anticipation and fear as a sub waited for instruction, to be touched, to not know what was next, was the greatest aphrodisiac on the planet.

She licked her lips.

Tonight he would find out if she was just a sub, or if she was also turned on by sado-masochism.

Pain.

It was the extreme side of his fetishes and the one most socially unacceptable to people like his brothers. As they'd admitted, they were dominant. Many men were. Many women enjoyed being dominated and challenging their Dom, eventually relinquishing control.

Receiving pain as a form of arousal was a whole other ball game.

He picked up the whip and slapped it in his hand.

She jumped.

"Hunter." She pleaded quietly.

He went to her and ran his hand over her hair. "You are doing well." Then he put the clamps they had used in the Hamptons on her nipples. "Remember these?"

She gasped and let out a little moan. "Yes."

"Sir."

"Yes, sir."

This time, he added a chain to each clamp and connected them to the hooks on her leather panties.

Crotchless panties.

"Oh, God." They naturally created a tug. The more she moved, the more they tugged. "Shit."

"That feels nice, doesn't it?" He ran his hand over her hair and then cupped her chin, lifting her face.

"Yes, sir."

Fire laced down his shaft as he ran his thumb over her lips. "On your hands and knees."

A moan escaped her lips as she bent over.

Slap.

The leather landed on her ass as she cried out.

Around and around her body he walked, whipping her ass between her legs, and then doing the same to her breasts.

"Hunter, please," she cried.

He grabbed a vibrator and slid it over her rear hole and down to her pussy, letting it tease.

Then stopped.

She was dripping.

Hunter slid a finger inside her pussy and Addison arched, pressing into him for more.

"Greedy girl." He pulled it out and licked her juices from his finger. "Nectar of the gods."

Lifting her to her knees, he let her get her bearings and then nudged his cock to her lips. Immediately she took him in her mouth, eagerly.

"Oh fuck, yes. Take me down your throat." He gripped the back of her head.

When he could think, he used the whip and slapped it against her ass.

Jesus.

She gagged around his cock, and it felt fucking awesome. Then she began to suck him hard, her hands gripping his hips.

He pulled out of her before he came, the sight of her mouth around him too damn incredible.

"Stop. Now pleasure your pussy while I watch," he ordered.

"Hunter, I need you inside me," she cried, but did as she was told.

Walking to the other side of the room, he sat down on the sofa, his legs wide as he watched her kneeling in the middle of the room with her fingers between her legs. The chains and leather worked to tug on her nipples.

He could do much worse.

He had cups that would pull her nipples so damn hard she would scream.

Would she want to scream?

"Remove your blindfold," he said.

Addison reached up and lifted it off, her eyes darting around the room until she found him. Need glistened from her face.

"Now come to me."

When she went to stand, he held out a hand, and she froze.

"Crawl."

"What?" she asked, her expression changing.

"I said crawl. On your hands and knees." Hunter stroked his cock.

Addison stayed where she was and stared at him. Her eyes dropped to his member, need fighting with the rejection of his demand.

Interesting.

Then she shook her head.

He arched a brow.

"Hunter please." She begged.

"Crawl."

She shook her head again.

"Then say no," he said. "Use your safe word or crawl on the floor and take my cock in your mouth."

Her eyes darted around the room, and landed on the swing hanging from the ceiling, the cross on the wall.

There was a reason he hadn't selected those tonight. This was a test. Hunter wanted to know her boundaries. He could have asked, but she wouldn't have known. This was the only way to know.

"All of this pleasure could be yours, but you need to crawl to me." He stood. "It is your choice, Addison."

A tear slid down her cheek and his heart nearly fucking broke.

Fuck.

He walked across the room and pulled her into his arms.

"I'm sorry." She spoke into his chest.

"Don't be. You did well. Really well," he said softly. "You are so fucking beautiful, Addy."

Hunter carried her into his bedroom and pulled her into his arms as they lay down.

"I need you," she said.

And he wasn't going to deny her, or him.

He lifted her leg over his and tugged her against him as his cock slid deep inside her.

"Harder," she pleaded, so he slammed into her with the next thrust. And the next. And the next.

Both of them needed this close, furious fucking.

As she tightened her pussy muscles around him, stroking his cock as he pounded into her, Hunter prayed this wasn't their last moment together.

He had been wrong.

He should have gone soft with her.

Instead, he'd terrified her.

Was that what he wanted? A reason to scare her off, or to find a reason to not want her? When he knew deep down he was falling for her?

I can't.

His cock swelled as she began to tremble in his arms, her fingers digging into his chest.

Hunter tugged her underneath him, and she wrapped her legs around his body. "God, you are gorgeous." He cried out as his mouth found hers and they kissed like it was their very last.

Reaching between them, he circled his fingers over her clit, and she exploded.

"Ohmygoddddd," Addison screamed and as he thrust harder, his own orgasm erupted, pouring from him and filling her.

As he collapsed, his head hitting the pillow beside her, Hunter didn't want to move. He feared she was going to leap up and run far from him.

But she didn't.

Slowly, their heartbeats calmed. He lifted her up and removed the clamps and slipped the leather and chains from her body.

Reaching for the tissues, he cleaned them both up as best he could for now and pulled her into his arms.

"Thank you." She wrapped an arm around his torso.

He closed his eyes, nearly purring at the feeling of her against him. Then he heard it.

"Hey," he said, lifting her chin. A tear dropped onto his chest. He sat up. "Talk to me. Did I hurt you?"

"No." She shook her head as his thumb ran over her cheek. "I'm sorry I couldn't do it."

"God, don't apologize, Addy. You discovered a boundary. That's a good thing. You are learning what you like and don't like."

But he knew what was bothering her. All subs felt like they disappointed their Dom when they found their limit. It was natural. Often times it meant there was an incompatibility but not always.

Hunter wasn't sure what it meant for him. But he knew, for Addy, it was a line in the sand she wouldn't go near again.

And that this was over.

"I'm not mad. Is that what you think?" he asked.

She sniffed and shook her head. "No. Perhaps disappointed."

Hunter drew in a breath, taking time to answer. Usually, yes, he would've been. For some reason, he had been okay with it.

While he was still working it out, he couldn't deny his reaction when he'd seen that damn tear of hers. He'd been across the room in seconds.

The dynamics ended without giving it another thought.

He cupped her chin. "Addy. I'm not mad. I'm not disappointed. I told you from the beginning you were allowed to say no at any point. And you did."

"Sure. But now it's over and... God, I don't know. I know you were never going to be the great love of my life—"

Ouch.

Why did those words bother him so much*?*

"But" she continued, "I... shit, I don't know what I'm trying to say."

"You think I don't want to fuck you again?" Hunter said as she lay her head back down on his chest and nodded.

The answer should be no.

But it wasn't.

"We said only one night." He pulled her closer.

"I know."

"So, if I asked you to stay the weekend, would you?"

Jesus, what was he doing?

"If I said I don't want to go back to that room, would you still want me here?" she asked, tipping her eyes to his.

"Yes." He said it way too fucking quickly.

They lay there for several moments, their eyes locked, until Addison finally nodded. "Yes."

Holy fuck, what were they doing?

Except, instead of panicking, he pulled her up his chest and softly kissed her mouth.

"I still own your body. I am a dominant man. That doesn't change," he said against her lips.

"Good."

The now familiar buzz of their bodies reared to life. "Go to sleep. You are going to need it."

He rolled her over and wrapped his arms around her, treading his leg between hers. Hunter felt her body relax and her breath soften as she began to slumber.

What had he agreed to?

More importantly, why?

The idea of driving her home tomorrow and not seeing her had created a tightness in his chest. Worse, when she'd said he wasn't the love of her life and he imagined some other man with their hands on her, he had shut those thoughts down fast.

"Addy."

"Yes."

"I don't want you seeing Trent." He knew he had no right. And yet he'd had to say it.

She nodded. "Okay."

And with those few words, they both stepped into a dangerous place he wasn't sure how to get them out of.

Because he could never let his brothers find out about his relationship with Addison, and he didn't want to let her go. He'd been worried about breaking her heart when it might be his that ended up being crushed.

CHAPTER THIRTY-NINE

Addison sat across the table from Hunter and watched him slice up his well-cooked poached eggs.

"I can't believe you don't like them runny."

"Ugh. Gross. You know what eggs actually are, don't you?" he replied.

She laughed. "Yes. And if you're that worried, why are you eating them?"

"Protein." He filled his mouth.

"There are plenty of other protein options."

"I like eggs. Just not runny ones. Now eat your, whatever that is, and then we can hit the road." He smirked at her.

She shook her head and dug into her kale and chicken salad. After a late and active night, they had slept in and then Hunter had taken her home to change and grab a bag.

Now, they were having a late lunch and heading to the Yankees versus Met game at the stadium. She wasn't a huge fan, but the buzz was addictive and Hunter had wanted to go. It had been years since she'd been to a game, so she was looking forward to it.

"You sure you want to get seats? We have a corporate box," Hunter asked, screwing his nose.

"You're lucky I'm not making you take the subway," she said. "I want to be in the action."

"I'd rather be by the bar." He leaned back in his seat and wiped his mouth on a napkin.

Addison tried not to react.

Hunter in casual clothes was a seriously sexy thing. Today he had a cap on backwards giving him that all-American boy vibe, and his chest looked even broader than usual in his navy Henley t-shirt. He didn't need to stand up for her to remember how great his ass looked in his well fitted, and likely stupidly expensive, jeans because she'd been staring at it all day.

And yeah, they were Prada, so stupid-expensive.

She lifted her coffee to her lips, and they simply stared at one another across the table. It was both comfortable and sent warm shivers through her body.

They had chosen a café a little way from Hunter's penthouse, so they weren't seen but she was still nervous. The media were always interested in the Dufort brothers, but even she agreed he didn't look like him once his sunglasses were over his eyes.

So here she was, spending the weekend with Hunter, and taking a risk at being found out. Addison couldn't explain why she was doing it, only that she hadn't wanted to be apart from him.

Which was concerning and something she'd have to think more about tomorrow.

Hunter had surprised her when he invited her to spend the weekend with him. She thought for sure after what had happened last night, he wouldn't want to sleep with her again. If anything, it seemed to have made them closer.

How, she couldn't say.

She knew he didn't think of himself as an intimate lover, but the way he'd held her and gazed at her when he'd entered her back in his bedroom had sent butterflies through her body.

It wasn't something she'd experienced before and while Hunter had introduced her to many things over the past few weeks, that had been the moment that stuck with her.

Her heart had... opened. And it shouldn't have.

This could only be temporary.

Hunter was out and proud about his sexual preferences—though not publicly—but Addison wasn't comfortable doing the same. Which meant a relationship, even if he wanted one, was not possible.

If Olivia or Harper found out, she would be so ashamed. Possibly lose them as friends.

She had been shamed by Rob during their marriage. Him telling her father had just been a cruel thing to do. He was lucky she'd mostly forgiven him.

The embarrassment she'd endured by learning some of their friends had been told had been painful.

Divorce was difficult when a couple had the same friends. Which they'd had, because they'd met when they were so young. Addison had reached out to one of her friends, Suzy, a month after she'd separated from Rob, hoping to keep the friendship.

Look, I'd love to see you, but Michael is homophobic. Wrongly, I agree. But he just wouldn't be comfortable, Suzy had said.

What are you talking about? I'm divorcing Rob, not gay. Not that there's anything wrong with it if I was.

Oh, I know. He explained to Michael about your... kink things.

He? What kink... what did Rob say?

Is it bondage stuff that you like? I really don't know much about it. Perhaps we just wait until Michael comes around.

Addison dropped her coffee down much too harshly and Hunter raised his brows.

"You okay?" She nodded. It still made her furious, even today, when she thought too much about it. "Just a flashback. I'm fine."

Whatever this was, she could never let her friends or Rob know she was sleeping with Hunter Dufort. She had lived through enough shame.

It wasn't worth the risk.

She cringed.

Wasn't he?

It was a moot point. Hunter had been clear there was nothing on the other side of this sexual experience together.

Wasn't that what she wanted, anyway?

Hunter stood, dropping some big notes on the table and took her hand. They walked out onto the sidewalk, and he told Trevor to meet them two blocks away.

"Yes, sir."

"Let's walk, and you can tell me what the dark shadow was that crossed your eyes."

"I'd rather not." She groaned.

Hunter took her hand and she tensed.

"Relax. Fletch and Dan don't hang out around here. Trust me." He laughed, then frowned when she plunged her hands into her jeans. "Addison, what is going on?"

She began walking, but he grabbed her arm.

"I just think it's better if we don't look all coupley. Anyone could spot us. You're Hunter Dufort. If someone took a photo then blasted it over social, the whole damn world would know about this."

He glared at her.

"No one is going to recognize me in this baseball cap. I'm not Ryan Reynolds."

True, but he was as hot. Not the point. Stay focused.

"What the fuck, Addison? I thought we were only hiding from my family?" Hunter said when her eyes averted.

"Yes, and… I can't be associated with your lifestyle." She grimaced as the words fell out of her mouth.

Hunter crossed his arms.

"*My* lifestyle? You mean the *lifestyle* where *you* had your fingers in your panties watching three people fuck each other last night?"

"Stop it." She spoke between gritted teeth, trying to tug him along the road.

"Or the *lifestyle* where your pussy was dripping while you were on your knees blindfolded being whipped? *That* lifestyle?"

"That's not me. It's not my life."

"Sorry gorgeous, but it *is* you," Hunter said, placing his hand on the small of her back and marching them to his car. "Get in."

When the door closed and they were moving, he stretched out one leg, looking powerful and masculine.

"Talk. Or I will take you home and this ends." He spoke firmly. Addison let out a long sigh and stared out the window.

"My ex, Rob, was very uncomfortable about the things *we* enjoy."

"You mentioned that. And can you stop talking like that? Call it what it is. Kink. Bondage. A Dom-sub relationship."

"Look, this is all new to me. I'm *not* like you," she said. "I've been shamed for having different sexual tastes. When I left Rob, he told my father and many of our friends."

She watched Hunter's jaw tense and those muscles flare either side. "What happened?"

"My father told me he was disgusted by me. I never knew exactly what Rob told him because we didn't talk after he confronted me about leaving my husband. Then a week later he was dead." A tear slid down her face. "In the months following I lost all my friends except Olivia."

"So she knows," Hunter said softly.

Addison shook her head. "No. She was the only one Rob didn't get to. And I threatened his damn life, so he never did. He lied and exaggerated everything because of his own ego."

"Because you left him."

"Yes." She nodded. "He made me see a shrink after telling me there was something wrong with me."

Hunter shook his head. "If he wasn't your daughter's father, I would drive there right now and pummel the guy."

Addison let a small smile hit her lips.

"Not everyone is that small-minded, Addy," Hunter said. "You need to be open about who you are. Forget about me or whatever this is between us. Don't you want to stop hiding? Or at least stop being ashamed?"

"I lost nearly everyone, Hunter. I can't live through that again. I love Liv and Harper," She cried. "I have no family except Sienna and my friends. Please understand."

HUNTER carefully watched Addison as she sat across from him fidgeting with the strap of her handbag.

What were they both doing together?

He didn't want a relationship, and even if he did, clearly, she was all wrong for him. Yet, she felt right in so many ways.

Not all, obviously.

Last night had achieved what he had wanted. Addison was a submissive, but that's where her kink ended. He was a dominant, who also enjoyed inflicting pain and humiliation. On those who also enjoyed it, to be clear, but the woman in front of him did not.

However, it had been an interesting learning for him as well. Usually something like that would have had his cock flatter than a pancake. Instead, it had triggered his protective tendencies, and he'd flown across that room in two point five seconds, pulling her into his arms.

And he'd still wanted to possess every inch of her body and being, but in a way he never had before.

Intimately.

Hunter had been thinking about it all morning. He cared for her; he had to stop pretending otherwise, but that didn't mean there was the potential for a relationship.

Yes, she was the first woman he'd really wanted to have in his life for more than pleasure. He loved her smile, her blushes, the little glances she thought he didn't notice. How she fidgeted and chatted away about things in her life, unwittingly giving away more about herself.

The fact remained he had needs they both knew she couldn't fulfill and ultimately that meant he would end up being disloyal.

Which Hunter could never do.

Not to Addison.

He knew if he let this continue, he'd fall in love with her.

He refused to go down the same path as his father and see her destroyed, like his mother. Addison deserved better than that. She'd already had one ex-husband who had disrespected her. He wouldn't add himself to the list.

Her or any woman.

Daniel and Fletcher were right. He was better off single and living the sex-club life.

Now she had shared her own concerns openly with him.

Hunter knew if she carried that much shame after losing people she loved, then being with him, even for sneaky weekends like this, was a huge risk.

Addison wanted to stay hidden, and he was the one man who could expose her. He couldn't risk that happening.

His jaw flexed.

They were playing with fire. After the game, he would take her home.

"I don't want you to lose them either, Addy." He reached for her and she climbed on the seat next to him. "Do you still want to go to the game?"

She nodded, and he leaned down to kiss her lips. "Good. Let's go have some fun."

She tucked under his arm and then a little voice said, "I'm sorry I couldn't be what you wanted."

His heart cracked.

Why did hearing those words from her lips suddenly seem so wrong? Hadn't he just thought the exact same thing?

It was him that was the problem. If he could control his urges… as he had last night. Then he would never let her go.

Fucking never.

Letting her think it was her fault was not okay.

Hunter turned and cupped her face. "That's not true. You are fucking perfect, Addison. If I could, I would never let you go."

And why did he have to go and say that?

Shit.

CHAPTER FORTY

"Here," Hunter said, tucking her under his arm as they pressed through the crowd after the game. The Yankees had won by three points, and he'd been obsessed with watching Addison's exhilaration during the game.

"My dad used to bring me here when I was a kid," she said. "I haven't been since he died."

Wow, now this perfect afternoon with her felt even more important. With two beers and two hotdogs under their belt, they had relaxed and enjoyed the game, sharing stories about being at the park.

As kids, he and his brothers had spent their lives traveling and learning the business or in the Hamptons, but his parents had taken them to the odd game. In the corporate box. Never down in the stands like this.

And he kind of loved it.

Fortunately, he hadn't been spotted by anyone while there, which he'd grown more and more concerned about after their discussion. Especially as they had done a little tongue dancing during the intermission.

The best part was watching her excitement about the game. All her stress had disappeared as she'd jumped up and down and yelled at the umpire, laughing with the people around them.

"I'm totally bringing Sienna to a game soon," she said as they climbed in the car. "It's just, you know, well you don't, but pricey and she's only six."

"I'll organize the box for you," Hunter said.

"Thanks, but I wasn't hinting at that. I want her to experience what we did today. Being in the stands with everyone. It's so fun."

Hunter laughed. "It's not action-less in the box."

Addison giggled. "I'm sure."

He pressed his lips together to stop from saying that *he* wanted to take them.

Hunter wanted to be the one to take Sienna and Addison, even though he'd never met the little girl before. But he had a sudden and overwhelming urge to organize it.

Then it just came out.

"Let's do it. I'll get us tickets for next weekend." He realized the mistake he'd made immediately. Addison's smile faded, and he turned away from her, looking out the window as they made their way through the traffic.

Pain sliced across his chest. Unexpectedly.

Fuck it.

"Ignore what I said." He spoke quietly. It could never happen. She didn't want him knowing her daughter or being in her life.

"Hunt."

"I said forget it."

Her hand landed on his leg, and he looked down, then up into her eyes.

"If we could, if it was possible, even though it's not, I want you to know I would love it."

He took her hand and nodded, then glanced away. It was time to stop pretending.

As they pulled up to his penthouse, Hunter pressed the intercom. "Trevor, give us ten minutes."

"Yes, sir."

He turned to Addison and saw those big cobalt eyes staring at him.

"You want me to leave?" she said softly.

"No," he said instead of sticking to his plan. "And that's a problem, Addy. I never seem to want you to leave. Last week, I thought about you constantly."

She swallowed. "Me too."

"Shit." He ran his hand through his hair.

"One more night." She placed her hand on his chest. He took it and squeezed.

"One more night. I'm going to pleasure you so damn good you will never forget me."

Her eyes filled with tears. "Hunter Dufort, you are unforgettable."

His mouth found hers and all the emotions between them exploded from his chest. This was going to be one hell of a night. He was going to give her all of him.

He opened the door, climbing out, then reached for her. As she took his hand and fell against his chest, their lips connecting for another kiss, they both froze when they heard the chillingly familiar voices.

"Hunter, there you are—oh, shit," Fletcher said.

"Addy?" Olivia called.

"Hunter?" Daniel said, Harper by his side, as all four of them stopped on the sidewalk.

Hunter stared down at Addison as his blood turned cold. Then she pulled out of his arms.

"Oh, God," she cried, burying her face in her hands.

CHAPTER FORTY-ONE

No, no, no.

How could this have happened?

Olivia followed her through Hunter's penthouse as she gathered up her things, her face bright red, her heart thumping.

"Just talk to me," Olivia said. "You told me you weren't seeing him."

She whirled as Harper stepped into the bedroom.

"I can't! I can't do this." She stuffed her—of course her damn red lacy lingerie—into her overnight bag.

"Is this just... are you sleeping together?" Harper asked.

Addison zipped up her bag.

"I. Can't. Talk. About. It," she said, barely able to look them in the eye.

"Why not?" Olivia asked. "I mean, it's a surprise, but... why didn't you tell us? Why lie to me?"

When her eyes lifted, she saw the questions on their faces. The judgment, though, they tried to hide it.

Tears began to fall.

"Oh, babe," Harper said, taking a step closer, but Addy held up her hand.

"Just... I have to get out of here. Please." She pushed through the door.

As she made her way into the living area, she found Hunter, Daniel and Fletcher standing together, arms crossed. Except Daniel, who had his on his hips.

"Addy, wait," Hunter said, coming over to her. Then he called out to someone over his shoulder. "Give us a fucking minute."

She ignored him and walked to the entrance, punching the elevator button. "I have to go."

"Addy, it's all out now. I want you to stay. Let's face them together," he said. "You don't need to be ashamed about this."

Stay?

Was he crazy?

"Oh my God, I told you what happened. I have to get out of here." Her heart thumped, panic setting in. "This is... please."

"I'm not letting you leave like this." He tried to pull her into his arms.

"I'll go with her," Olivia said, coming around the corner.

Her eyes flew wide.

"No. Stop. All of you. Just leave me alone," she yelled, and they all froze.

The door to the elevator opened, and she backed in like a crazy person. Her eyes found Hunter's, and she saw the hurt and anger on his face. Her chest pounded as it ached for what could have been.

But what they both knew never could be.

"I'm sorry," she whispered, and as the doors closed, she saw his barely perceptible nod.

CHAPTER FORTY-TWO

Hunter walked back into the living area, Olivia trailing him. He stared at his family.

"You were fucking her?" Fletcher growled.

"Don't say it like that," Olivia said, slapping his arm.

"How long has this been going on?" Daniel asked, his arms crossed now.

Jesus.

Did they think he was a child still?

"Why is she so upset?" Harper asked, confusion in her voice.

Hunter glared at Olivia with a raised brow. "Go on, ask your questions. Let's get them all out and then you can all fucking leave."

Fletcher took a step toward him, his brows dipped. "Don't speak to my fiancée like that."

Yet it was okay for them to storm into his home and get involved with his business.

"Okay, stop," Daniel said, stepping between them. Hunter had puffed his chest and was ready to punch either one of them. In fact, right now it was a choice between a face or a wall. He was so furious.

At Addison.

He was angry at her. She should have stayed.

But he knew why. He'd hoped she could face this now their secret was out, to see if there was a way they could make it work.

He didn't understand the shame and disgust written all over her face, as he'd faced who he was a long time ago. But it had told him everything.

She couldn't and may never be able to accept her sexual desires. And he didn't mean enough to her to push through her fears.

"I want to know why she wouldn't talk to me," Olivia said, emotion thick in her voice. "She's my best friend."

Damn. He felt that.

Addison had not just walked out on him. She had walked out on all of them, and they all cared for her.

"Oh, honey, I'm sure she was just surprised by us showing up," Harper said.

Fletcher glared at him. "Could you not have chosen someone else to fuck around with? Someone a little less close to home? She's Liv's goddamn friend."

Hunter's fury rose.

Daniel raised a brow.

"I wasn't playing with her." Okay, fine, he had been in the beginning but not now. "We are both consenting adults, for fuck's sake."

"He's right," Harper said, shrugging.

He glanced around the room. If he could give her one parting gift, it was to protect her. Something that was still sizzling within him.

She may not be his to keep, but she was his to protect.

"Look, you don't understand. Addy is not—" He began.

"Like you?" Olivia said, interrupting him, clearly now angry. "Of course she's not. Which is why you shouldn't have taken advantage of her."

Okay, ouch.

It was tempting to tell them how wrong they were, how absolutely gorgeous she was when tied up or blindfolded, being the sexual woman she was. But he would never do that to her. He would keep her secret and play the villain.

He let out a long breath.

"You're right," Hunter said. "I'm an asshole and should never have gone near her." He held both his brother's eyes as he said his next words. "Nothing happened."

They knew what he meant.

"So you didn't..." Fletcher glanced at Olivia. "Sleep with her?"

He nodded. "Yes, but not in the way you are all thinking."

"This is not okay to be talking about this," Harper said, planting her hands on her hips. "It's none of our business."

Daniel nodded. "She's right. It's not. But clearly Addison is upset for a reason. Why?"

Hunter shrugged. "She didn't want you to find out. It was meant to just be one night. I was taking her home when you arrived."

He'd never lied to his brothers before. Not like this. But to protect her, he would.

"We got drunk last night after bumping into each other downtown." He knew that sounded likely as she worked in the area. "Then we decided to go to a Yankee's game today when we woke. That was it. Addison knows what I'm into and was embarrassed you'd think she was, too. She's not."

Not a complete untruth.

"None of which you should have to explain," Harper said, and damn, he was grateful she was playing Switzerland right now.

Daniel narrowed his eyes.

"I am capable of having boring-ass sex, you know. Not that it was boring."

Shit, he was fucking this up.

"You know what, Harper is right. I don't have to explain this. Just don't judge Addison." He growled.

They all stood staring uncomfortably at each other as Fletcher ran a hand through his hair and let out a long sigh.

"I'm sorry. I just don't want anyone getting hurt," his brother said.

You mean except me?

If he hadn't been protecting her right now, he would have a whole lot more to say. That day would come. But not today. It was time his brothers learned some boundaries when it came to his personal life.

"What are you all doing here anyway?" he asked, suddenly wondering what they had been doing outside.

"We all went for dinner after Harper and I arrived back today. Your phone was off so clearly you didn't get the invite," Daniel said.

"Yeah, I had it off." He dug his phone out of his pocket and powered it up. He never turned it off, but he had wanted to give Addison his undivided attention.

"I'm just going to see if Addy left anything behind," Olivia said, pointing to his bedroom.

Hunter nodded as Harper followed her down the hall. He turned back to his brothers.

"You like her," Daniel said, studying him. "Addison."

Oh, no you don't.

He narrowed his eyes. There was no way he was sharing his feelings for her with them right now. Or ever. As soon as they left, he was calling Addison.

Right now, he was focused on getting them out of his house and finding out if she was okay.

"I'm not in the mood for the big brother act. Whatever it was, it's now over." He shook his head.

"Addison isn't the one for you, Hunt," he replied. "Find someone with the same tastes. She wants the ring and picket fence."

And you don't think I can give that to her?

Of course he couldn't. Not long term. It would never work. Least of all, because she couldn't face who she truly was. And there was the small detail of him needing more than she could give. Which meant he'd just hurt her down the road.

He walked across the room to full-length windows and stared out across the city. "You're right."

And they were.

He should never have touched Addison Hill.

CHAPTER FORTY-THREE

Addison swiped to reject the call.

She let out a sigh as she glanced out her office window. Hunter had tried to call her on Saturday night, but she'd let it go to voicemail. Then, when Monday morning rolled around, and when he hadn't reached out to her again, she'd burst into tears and taken a sick day after dropping Sienna at school.

She'd walked to the park and just sat there contemplating her entire life.

How could she have let it all get this far?

It felt like she was living a double life.

One where she had wild and delectable sex with Hunter Dufort, the other where she was a sensible mom and corporate woman hiding her true self. Not that one walked around with a t-shirt saying *I'm into kink, shake my hand*. It was more she was hiding from herself.

It had occurred to her, as she'd sat there for hours remembering the people in the club and how they were openly expressing who they were and being thoroughly fulfilled, that maybe—*just maybe*—she could be both.

She could be all that she was.

If she just gave herself permission and stopped looking for other people to accept her.

Addison could be a mom, a sexual woman with fetishes, and a businesswoman with friends who accepted her.

While she had enjoyed her experience at the sex club, she knew she didn't want to be a frequent member, but on occasion it might be fun. What she did need was a man who wanted more spice in their sex life than her ex-husband had.

But the humiliation play crossed the line. And she knew Hunter needed that.

She was grateful he had helped her discover what she did and didn't like while awakening the sexual goddess within that she had ignored for so long.

That she had been ashamed of.

Perhaps because of that, she felt a connection with him different from anyone else. The way he dominated her body and soul, and demanded she bare all of who she was to him.

It was intoxicating.

Over the past month or so she had seen him at Fletcher's side when Sammy went missing, Daniel and Harper's engagement party, when they'd gotten them out of jail, spent the week with him at the Hamptons and then most of last weekend at the club and ballgame.

Each time she had gotten to know him a little more.

Yes, he was dominant, but he was also loyal, caring, and protective.

And cheeky as hell.

Those faint dimples and golden eyes had her weak in the knees and practically willing to do anything for him. Even watching him eat eggs had been a stupidly happy moment.

Had she simply fallen for him without realizing?

Her heart physically ached as she recalled the way he'd looked at her through the elevator doors. The unsaid words loud and heavy.

And final.

So why did her body still crave his touch and need to hear his voice? To see his wonky smile, which promised complete pleasure.

The tears had fallen each morning and night when she had the privacy to grieve whatever she and Hunter had been in the face of his silence.

Then, last night, he had called.

Addison had stared at the phone until it had eventually gone to voicemail. She hadn't been ready to hear the words he would inevitably say.

Thanks for the wild ride and see you at the next Dufort event.

If she was even welcome after her shameful outburst. And probably by now, they knew who she was.

Sleeping with Hunter Dufort would do that.

There was no hiding it now.

Then she'd cleared the voice message. Hearing his voice had turned on the waterworks again, but his message had surprised her.

"*Addy, call me. I want to talk to you. Call me back. Oh, and you can stop worrying about what anyone thinks. I told them you weren't into anything kinky. That it had been a single night of boring-ass sex.*"

She'd let out a snotty laugh.

It was funny for a short moment until she connected the dots. He had lied for her.

Lied to his brothers.

God, what a mess.

He'd protected her by lying to the two people he was closest to. And she knew how close they were. Those three were impenetrable. Even Olivia and Harper agreed on that.

Yet what was she going to do? Text everyone and say, *sorry, Hunter lied. Surprise, I'm a kink girl.*

And really, was it any of their business?

More to the point, did it matter?

It was over.

Whatever they'd had, it was over.

Addison saved the document she was working on and opened her Instagram app. Hunter had posted a photo they'd taken at the game. It wasn't their faces. Just their knees and cups of beer.

Their private joke.

She kept going in and looking at it like a stalker.

Hundreds of people had commented on it because he had tens of thousands of followers. As billionaires did.

Gorgeous billionaires.

Single bachelor billionaires.

She chewed her lip as she flicked through his other photos. There were some great shots from the wedding. One of them was taken shortly after he'd made her come. His eyes sparkled with mischief, like he knew a secret no one else did.

And the truth was, he did.

One he was lying to his brothers about, despite the fact they had no right to ask about her sexual choices or their relationship.

Was it a relationship?

A sexual relationship.

Well, whatever it *had* been, Addison knew that Hunter would hate being dishonest to his family.

She didn't like she was the reason. These were her insecurities and yet again, he was protecting her. Despite walking away on Saturday.

She had to face them.

The damage had been done, and she had to apologize to Olivia and see if they could repair things. She was her best friend. They'd been through a lot together. Having babies, divorcing their husbands, Sammy's kidnapping. Liv's engagement to Fletch, and now she was pregnant.

She wanted to be in her friend's life. And Harper's.

It was time to accept who she was if she was to move forward in life.

Hopefully, Olivia wasn't as disgusted as the other friends she had lost. But she wouldn't know until she tried.

It was time to face the music.

Harper and Daniel were leaving for their honeymoon on Wednesday, so if she wanted to speak to them both in person, she only had tonight to do it.

A knock at her office door interrupted her thoughts. "Come in."

"Hey," Maggie, her PA said, walking in carrying what looked like the largest bouquet of orange roses she'd ever seen. "These came for you."

Holy heck.

She cleared a space on her deck.

"Thanks. Wow."

"Impressive. Who are they from?" Maggie asked.

Addison slipped the card out of the little envelope. "A secret admirer," she replied, holding back a teary smile as she read the note.

"Well, lucky girl," Maggie replied as she walked out.

Addy looked back at the note.

Do I need to come over there and smack that ass? Because I will. Call. Me. Back. Hunter x.

She flopped down in her seat and chewed her bottom lip. She didn't know what the flowers meant, but either way she couldn't hide from everyone forever.

First, she needed to speak to her best friend. She needed her support network if she was going to do the big goodbye with Hunter and break her own heart.

Because she was in love with him.

In love with Hunter Dufort.

CHAPTER FORTY-FOUR

Hunter stared at his phone and considered throwing it out the window. Not that the reinforced glass would allow him to do such a stupid thing from the seventy-second floor of the Dufort tower building.

Addison still hadn't returned his calls or messages. He had no idea how she was or what she was thinking.

He was worried about her.

And missed her.

Damn it, he wanted to hold her in his damn arms again and tell her it didn't matter what anyone thought. That she was exactly who she needed to be.

Except nothing he could say would heal her wounds. She needed to figure it out on her own.

Or never.

Some people never did.

But he had his own demons to slay.

On Sunday, his father had turned up, and he began to wonder if his place was turning into a damn hotel. Which was ironic, given they owned a bunch of them.

"Hey, you should have called," he said sleepily as he buzzed up his dad. In other words, *you shouldn't have come*.

When he stepped out of the elevator, Johnathan handed him a coffee. "Let's talk."

Hunter groaned. "Daniel called you."

"He texted me and it wasn't pleasant. Apparently, I'm to blame for the behavior of your nether regions."

"It's called a cock. And why is my cock your responsibility?"

He shook his head at even saying those words out loud.

Johnathan sat on one of the armchairs and lifted his ankle over his knee. "Two peas in a pod, or something like that," his father said. "What did you do? Did you cheat on that girl?"

The hell?

Hunter pulled his head back. "Addison? No. Is that what he said?"

His father shook his head.

"Calculated guess. So what did you do?"

Hunter had sat on the sofa and chugged back some coffee. "I slept with her."

"And?"

"Took her to the club," he confessed.

His father stared at him for a long moment. "Did she want to go?"

Did she? Had she wanted to go to the sex club, or had he coerced her into it?

"Look, you know I'm a dominant, right?" He felt really uncomfortable talking to his father about this.

"All three of you boys are if you uncomplicate it," Johnathan said, lifting a shoulder. "So what? Is there a point to that?"

Well, that was true. Daniel, more than any of them. Even perhaps his father.

"My point is the lines of authority in a Dom-sub relationship are different than in 'real life'. I don't know if Addison *wanted* to go, but she always had the option of saying no."

Johnathan narrowed his eyes. "So, what does this have to do with your brothers? Or me, for that matter."

Exactly.

But his father was here, so he may as well tell him everything. He'd caught him at a weak moment and the coffee hadn't yet kicked in.

"Fletcher and Daniel don't want me seeing her. Or anyone they know if I'm being honest. They're uncomfortable with my *lifestyle* as they refer to it."

Johnathan tapped his ankle and stared at him.

Blankly.

Yet he saw the judgment.

His father had taught them all how to manipulate and read people in the boardroom, and that translated just as much to everyday life.

"What? Do you agree?" Hunter asked angrily.

"No. You can do what you like with your cock. What I want to know is why you're letting your brothers tell you what to do."

He glared at his father.

"I'm not letting them do any such thing. Not only am I an active member of the club, I own fifty-nine percent of it," he snapped.

"So marry her."

He shook his head as if he hadn't heard him right. "I'm sorry, what?"

"Marry her."

"Okay, how did we go from taking her to a sex club to proposing?" Hunter laughed. "That's the absolute opposite of what I should do."

Johnathan stood. "No, Hunter. That's what your brothers have told you. They were both against the idea of marriage after what happened between your mother and me. You never had the same distaste of it as far as I recall."

Hunter pursed his lips.

"It's normal as the youngest to be led by your older siblings' beliefs. Just check in with yourself. What are you scared of?"

Christ, his father had turned into a shrink. But he was making sense.

"I don't want to hurt her. Like..." He didn't want to finish that sentence, so he let it hang.

"Like I did to your mom."

He nodded.

"I have my reasons for doing what I did, son. One day I may tell you, but that day is not today," Johnathan said. "I can tell you one thing I know for sure. All three of you are strong, loyal, and powerful men. I raised you to be like that.

"Look at how you stuck together and outed me from the board. I know it hurt you to do it, but your loyalty to each other and our employees drove you."

Hunter blinked.

All the feelings were rushing at him, his chest tightening.

Damn him.

"If you love her, or even think you love her, don't let her out of your sight. True love doesn't come around more than once or twice in a man's life," he said. "And when it does, if you're smart and commit to her for the rest of your life, you won't want anyone else."

Was that possible?

Even for him?

His father didn't understand. He was different. His needs, her desires. They weren't completely aligned.

"I need things she can't give me," he said, the words falling from his lips. Because who else was he going to talk to about this?

His father slid his hands into his pockets.

"Ask yourself if that's true. How important are those needs? More than a life with the woman you love? Or were they something that filled an empty space in you?"

Were they?

He didn't think it was that, but it was making him wonder how important *all* his fetishes were and if some were more entertainment than an actual need.

"Daniel is a smart and powerful man. He has strong beliefs. That's a challenge for a younger brother." His father added, "But he loves you. Make the decision for yourself, knowing both he and Fletcher will stand beside you no matter what you choose."

Hunter nodded.

Growing up with such a powerful father and two brothers probably had led him to having the desire for such control and dominance over another.

He'd never seen it like that.

It didn't make it wrong, but it made sense.

When he was with Addison, she felt like she was his. Not because he'd claimed her, although that too, but on some level they just fit.

He'd been honest when he said he hadn't been disappointed or less fulfilled by their time in his room together.

Hell, right now he wanted her in his arms and to be completely happy—no, fucking happy—to make slow sensual love to her if that's what she damn well wanted.

But he knew she liked his strength and control.

The more he thought about it, the more he could see what a long-term relationship and intimacy would look like. Hell, there was no way he'd be whipping or chaining her if she was pregnant or as they grew old together.

Not anyone else. It was Addison that he could see wearing his ring and taking his name.

"I love her."

"I know." His father smiled slowly. "I watched you with her last weekend."

"You could have told me." He felt like a little boy again.

Johnathan laughed and walked to him, slapping him on the shoulder and pulling him into a hug. "I can't wait for you to have kids. Letting them fall over and get back up is the hardest thing you will ever do. And it never ends, my boy."

When his father left, Hunter took the rest of the day to think about what they'd talked about. It was all very well deciding he loved Addison, but she had been clear about not wanting him in her life.

So, he had some work to do.

He needed to know how she felt and if she could open up to who she was and trust him.

This could be the hardest fight of his life.

Tonight, however, he had dinner with his family before Daniel and Harper headed off on their honeymoon in Hawaii.

Apparently, Jackson Wiles was still in NYC and Kristen had asked if he could be her date. Daniel was unimpressed, but Harper had said yes.

The background check on him had come back clean, so they'd decided to meet with other providers before making a decision.

These things took months, so there was no hurry.

And Kristen was returning to New Zealand in another two weeks, then he would be out of their lives.

Unless they decided to partner with him.

The guy probably just wanted their business. Dufort Hotels was a huge account for any supplier in the United States, not to mention a global reach like this app would have.

Ping.

A text arrived on his phone to say his flowers had been delivered.

His stomach tightened.

It was another step toward winning Addison's heart. The first had been speaking to his brothers on Monday when he'd arrived in the office.

"I don't know if she wants me, but Addison is mine," he'd told them. "Neither of you have the right to tell me what to do in my relationships *or* who those relationships are with. Including Addison. We're both adults and can make our own decisions. So I respectfully ask you both to back the fuck off and let me live my life."

Daniel had slowly raised his brows, while Fletcher had frowned. The staring had begun as he stood with his hands in his pant pockets not giving an inch.

"You're right," Daniel had finally said, causing Fletcher to glare at him instead.

"I'm not looking for your agreement, either. I'll let you both process it in your own time. But those are my rules."

"If you hurt her—" Fletcher had started to say, but Hunter had stopped him.

"I fucking love her, you idiot. If anyone hurts her, me included, I'll punch my own lights out," he'd growled.

"Good. Make sure I'm there to watch if you do," Fletcher said, but with a small smirk.

He'd rolled his eyes.

"About damn time you figured it out," Daniel said. "She's been making eyes at you for weeks."

"What?" Fletcher said, turning to him.

His father had been right. It was never their permission he'd needed. He was as guilty as Addison of caring what other people were thinking and saying.

Not the media. It was still not something he would publicize, but if it did leak, he would deal with it. For Addison, if she would have him, he would do everything in his power to ensure it didn't.

Now the rest was up to her.

Could she accept herself? And him?

Hunter would give her one more day to reply to him.

Then he was going to get her.

CHAPTER FORTY-FIVE

Addison walked into the café and spotted Olivia at a table near the back corner.

Tears prickled at her eyes.

As she got closer, she saw Olivia had also teared up. She stood and threw her arms around Addison, as they both said, *I missed you.*

Smiling and wiping tears, they sat down opposite each other, and Olivia pushed a coffee toward her.

"Almond milk mocaccino with a shot of vanilla," she said.

Addy's favorite.

"Thanks," she said, lifting it to her lips. "Liv, I'm sorry for lying."

"I'm sorry you didn't think you could tell me."

Oh.

She hadn't been expecting that. Although she should have because Olivia was a very thoughtful woman and they cared for each other a lot.

She had been a fool and didn't deserve the apology.

"Please, don't do that. I should have talked to you," Addison said, fidgeting with her mug.

"Well, I kept Fletcher a secret from everyone, including you, for a while. But I sense there is more to it and…"

Olivia drifted off, looking for the words, so Addison decided to help her.

"Because he's into kinky stuff and you're worried about me?" she asked.

Olivia nodded.

"He said it wasn't like that, but I just wanted to make sure... fuck, Addy. I don't even know what to ask or say. Hunter is a good person, but you both seem so different. Was it just one night?"

Addison let out a long sigh, drank another gulp of coffee, and looked her friend in the eye. This time, she was getting the truth.

"No."

She let that sink in.

"This is really hard for me to talk about." She tried to ignore Olivia's widening eyes. "When I divorced Rob, I lost a lot of friends. Not just because of the divorce, which is what I told you."

"Then why?"

Addison had to tell her story, tell the truth and trust that Olivia was a broad enough minded person, and their friendship was strong enough to withstand this. Because, despite her sexual desires being no one else's business, it was true she had kept a part of herself hidden.

Heck, it felt like she was coming out to people. When she really shouldn't have to.

"I left Rob because we weren't compatible sexually," she said and Olivia's mouth parted. "There was no passion and while I cared for him, I realized I wasn't *in* love with him or being satisfied. It got to the point where, when he touched me, I just cringed."

"Was he bad in bed?" Olivia asked, and Addison suppressed her smile.

Poorly.

"No. Well, yes. It was just boring. I have," she blushed, "I guess I have what people call kinks."

"I know what they are. I'm not completely naïve." Olivia laughed. "Is that what this is about?"

She nodded.

"You think I wouldn't understand?"

"I thought you would be disgusted." Emotion rose within her again.

"Oh, babe. I don't care what you do in the bedroom… or wherever you do it. Hell, Fletcher isn't exactly boring. That's no one's business but ours."

She nodded.

"So Rob flipped out and told everyone?" Olivia asked.

"And Dad. Remember when I told you we hadn't talked? That's why. He *was* revolted by whatever Rob told him. I don't know exactly, and I don't want to know."

"That asshole." She growled and Addison wanted to hug her friend. "I'm going to kill him."

She let out a little laugh.

"Okay, so I'm not disgusted. I still love you, and that's never going to stop. What I was concerned about was Hunter hurting your heart, not your… whatever. Your ass."

Addison let out an awkward snort.

The two of them looked at each other and laughed.

"Was Rob really that bad? I have to know."

"Liv, he didn't even want to try anal." She said it as if that was the most obvious explanation.

"Okay, well, I'm not into that either." Liv grimaced. "Hurts like a motherfucker. But yeah, I do it occasionally for Fletch."

Addison smirked. "Thanks."

"He would kill me for telling you that."

"I know."

They giggled some more.

"So, is it over with Hunter?" Olivia asked. "I get the impression his interests are extreme. But, before you answer that, I'm only asking because I care. You do whatever you want. I thought you wanted to get married again. Whereas Hunter has been open about not wanting that."

She nodded.

"Yeah, all of that is true. I did fall for him, but we're not compatible. And no, I'm definitely not explaining that," she said.

Hunter wasn't the falling in love type.

"If you hadn't busted us, I would have left on Sunday, and it would have been over."

Olivia was right. Hunter wouldn't want her. Not long term. She couldn't fulfill his needs and he would want more than she could give.

But hadn't Hunter said he thought she was perfect? That he felt something for her.

Had he meant it?

Addison turned around and found Harper standing in the doorway, looking sheepish. She called her over.

"I know we're not as close as you and Liv, but I was worried about you," Harper said, dropping her handbag and taking a seat. "Are you okay?"

So she shared her story again and Harper surprised her.

"Oh, you totally have to tell me what you've learned. I can use this for content in my romance novels."

With the ice broken, as only Harper could, Addison laughed and began to tell her about the club.

"Holy shit," Olivia said. "That's kinda hot."

"You have no idea," she drawled.

"Honestly, Daniel can be pretty aggressive sometimes. I personally love it," Harper said, leaning in conspiratorially. "I have my limits and he has his own boundaries, but we try different things. I highly doubt I'd get him to a sex club, but you have nothing to be ashamed about, in my opinion."

Addison began to relax as they all opened up a little more and, for the first time in her life, she felt accepted for who she was.

"Would either of you go to one?" she asked, curious.

Harper and Olivia shared a look, then they both shook their heads.

"I don't judge you at all. It's just not something I'd want to do," Olivia said.

"I'd go for research on a book, but not want to participate. And let's face it, Daniel would want to come with me, and he'd terrify everyone with his scowling."

They all giggled.

"Speaking of my gorgeous husband, tonight we are having dinner with everyone before we fly out to Hawaii tomorrow. Will you come?" Harper asked.

Addison chewed her lip.

"Can I answer that in about an hour?" she said. "I have one more person I need to apologize to."

It was clear who she meant.

"Addy, I know you said things weren't serious, but I got the impression that Hunter likes you a lot more than he's admitting," Harper said.

"I agree," Olivia said. "Despite what I said earlier. Look at us. We got Fletcher and Daniel to put a ring on it."

She smiled, knowing her friends were trying to help, but they didn't understand that they were sexually unmatched, so it was a moot point.

She said her goodbyes, then ran out and hailed a cab.

CHAPTER FORTY-SIX

Hunter stood by the elevator in his penthouse, waiting for the thing to open.

Addison was on her way up.

He couldn't believe she had just showed up.

The doors slid open, and his heart lurched at the sight of her. Her eyes were wide with nerves, but she was still gorgeous dressed in a pair of tight black pants, a fitted jacket and green cowlneck top. The sparkle of her gold necklace caught his eye.

"Hi," she smiled.

It had been three long days since he'd seen her, and he was done messing around. He took the few steps toward her and pulled her into his arms.

"Hi." He spoke into her hair. "Are you okay?"

"Yes," she said against his chest. "Thank you for the flowers. They're beautiful."

So are you.

"I'm sorry to show up like this," she said when he released her. "I thought we should talk. Clear the air."

Addison thought she was here to end things, but he had news for her. She was his. He just had to convince her.

He would be patient but firm, even if it took forever.

"Would you like a drink? Or something to eat? I am supposed to be going to the happy couple's dinner, but I can cancel," Hunter said.

She followed him into the kitchen.

"I've been invited. Don't cancel. But if things are awkward after I leave, I'll bow out. They are your family."

Hunter ignored that comment and grabbed a bottle of wine out of the fridge. He poured two glasses as she sat on one of the stools at the island in the middle of the room.

He slid the wine across the Italian marble counter.

"I'm sorry," she said.

"For?" he asked, lifting a brow. "Leaving or ignoring my calls?"

Addison took a large gulp of wine, and her eyes followed the glass, and she placed it back on the countertop.

"Both. All of it. This entire mess," she replied. "I needed time to think, and I suppose find the courage to own up to who I am."

Hunter hid his surprise.

"And have you?" He slid one hand into the pocket of his Tom Ford pants.

She nodded, taking another big sip.

She was nervous.

"Yes. I just told Harper and Olivia everything. Well, not in great detail, but they know enough."

"I see." He took a drink.

"I'm sorry you felt you had to lie to your brothers for me," she said. "Hopefully they'll understand why when the girls explain. Because let's face it, they will tell them."

Hunter snorted. "Pillow talk."

"Yes," she grinned shyly. "But I *am* sorry."

He dropped his glass, let out a sigh, and then made his way around to her.

"So you keep saying you're sorry, Addy." He stopped in front of her, leaning his hip against the counter. "But you could have texted or rung me to say all that. Why are you here?"

Her lips parted. "I—"

"Tell the truth." He tucked a hair behind her ear.

She swallowed. "I wanted to see you. To say goodbye. In person."

"A goodbye fuck? You want me to pleasure you one last time. The kind only I can give you?"

Desire pooled in her eyes.

"I thought so." He nodded, taking her chin in his fingers. "Go to my sex room, take off all your clothes, and spread yourself out for me."

"I thought we could—"

"Talk? No, you didn't. Go," he ordered. "If my mouth isn't on your pussy in three minutes, you need to leave."

That was the last thing he wanted, but she needed this. She had denied who she was and who they were for long enough. He wanted her to prove she had accepted it.

All the shadows disappeared, and she got off the stool and walked out of the room.

Good girl.

HUNTER waited three minutes, then walked into the room, unbuttoning his shirt, pulling it from his shoulders as he gazed upon the completely naked beauty stretched out on the firm bed.

"Did you touch yourself?" he asked, throwing his shirt on a chair.

"No."

"Why not?"

"You didn't give me permission," Addison replied as he smiled darkly and ran his finger lightly across her skin.

She shivered.

"Are you giving me control, Addy? Full control." He tugged on one of her nipples and then let it go.

She cried out. "Yes."

"Good, let's begin." Hunter reached above him to pull the sex swing over. "Up you get."

He helped Addison up into it, their eyes meeting each other's as he did the straps up on her wrists and calves.

"You can sit up or lie back." He ran his hands up the inside of her thigh. "Are you comfortable?"

"Yes."

"And you know you can say no at any point, and we stop."

She nodded, humming her agreement. "Please touch me, Hunter."

His cock jutted hard against his pants as he took in the wetness between her legs. Leaning forward, he gripped her thighs and blew.

"Fuck," she cried as he stepped away and unzipped his pants.

Addy arched, laying back in the swing, but when her head lifted, she glared at him. "Hunter, I need more. Please."

"I know what you need, baby." He kicked his pants off and gripped his cock. "Lay back."

"God, please."

He walked to the counter and grabbed two nipple clips, then placed them on her, gripping her hair in his hands as he licked her lips.

"Are you mine, Addison?"

"Yes."

Hmm, no, she wasn't yet, but she would be.

He stood back between her legs and gripped her thighs.

"Look at you glisten for me." His fingers brushed around her pussy, but he didn't give her the satisfaction he knew she craved. She moaned and arched eagerly, wanting more.

Then he slapped her over the clit.

"Ohfuckkkk."

He did it again.

And again.

Her cries filled the room.

He slowly leaned forward and as he spread her cheeks, his tongue found that sensitive space between her holes and licked along her flesh until he found the sensitive bud with his mouth.

And sucked.

"Hunter, God, oh my God."

Slipping his fingers inside her, he worked her until her body began to tremble.

She was putty in his hands, her body singing to the song he was strumming, and yet Hunter felt a disconnect. He wanted more from this woman and while he had no idea what would happen after this, they had this moment.

He needed the connection they'd had the other night. He wanted a closer intimacy that he'd only felt with her before.

As she was about to come, he withdrew. His mouth, his fingers, everything.

"When you come, it will be around my cock." He unstrapped her and pulled her into his arms.

"I need you." She wrapped her arms and legs around him.

"You have me," he said, sitting on the bed and lifting her body as he gripped his cock. "Kneel over me and align your pussy."

Addison did as he ordered as he took her hips, guiding her. With his cock still in his hands, he swirled the head through her moisture.

"Now, Addy." He tugged her face to his and claimed her mouth. She slid down his cock, and they both groaned against each other's lips.

"Fuck," he cried as she began to ride him. "More. Deeper. I need more of you."

Addison ground into him, her breasts bouncing, her head thrown back. When his thumb pressed against her clit, she screamed her orgasm.

Hunter wasn't done.

He was going to claim this woman.

Flipping her onto her back, he lay over her, tugging her legs around him and plowed into her again.

"Say you are mine."

"I am!" she cried, fingers digging into his shoulders.

"Don't you fucking leave again." His hands were under her hips, slamming them together as if his life depended on it. "You are mine."

Fire sliced through his spine, his cock swelling as his body prepared to fill her. Hunter lifted and arched, his hips pounding as she clenched him, milking him dry.

Her hands were tight around his arms when he collapsed, laying a forearm beside her head, panting as he gazed down into eyes full of confusion and emotion.

They should have talked first.

But he'd had to show her how he felt. Had to prove to her that she needed him.

And that leaving wasn't an option.

Not for either of them.

HUNTER carried her into the shower and let her legs drop down to the floor.

"Can you stand?"

"Yes. I think." She let out a little laugh.

As the water sprayed over them, he grabbed the sponge and began to wash her.

Caring for her.

Slowly and gently.

"It's never going to be enough for you," she said, when he had finished washing her back. "I can't ask that of you."

"You haven't."

When she nodded, he turned the water off, and they stepped out of the shower. He wrapped her in a huge white towel, put one around his waist, and led her to his bed.

Now they would talk.

He sat her on the bed and crouched in front of her.

"I didn't think men like me could have relationships." He shared his inner thoughts. "The idea of one woman who I'd ultimately be disloyal to was distasteful and unappealing."

She chewed her lip, nodding.

"I knew you were different the night we were on the beach in the Hamptons," he said. "Do you remember?"

Addison grinned. "Yes, Hunter, I remember. You tortured me."

He smirked. "You loved it."

"Yes."

"It terrified me," he admitted. "When I pleasure women, there is a sense of satisfaction. I don't always need to be pleasured in return, so it's not necessarily sexual. That's been confusing to me. Occasionally, a woman is more pleasurable than another and I sleep with them a second time. Rarely."

"Why are you telling me this?"

Hunter shifted his weight to his other leg. "Every single moment with you, I have been in denial. I held you that night on the grass in my arms, but against my heart. I freaked out after we fucked that first day because I knew I didn't want to let you go. I wanted to rip Trent's fucking head off for just talking to you. But I never thought I could be worthy of you."

"I understand. This isn't—"

"No, Addy. You don't." He needed her to understand everything. "My father cheated on my mother and destroyed her. I promised myself I would never do that to a woman. God, the thought of hurting you. Betraying you, Addy. I'd never let myself do that to you."

She nodded, her eyes meeting his.

"I know you wouldn't." She reached out and placed her hand on his heart. "You are a good man, Hunter Dufort. I know that."

He gripped her hand.

"Not that good, sweetheart. Because I can't let you go. I am in love with you, Addison Hall. And you are mine."

Her little gasp made him smile. "You love me?"

"With my entire black heart."

"I thought… you love me?" she repeated. "I…" She fell into his arms. "I am *so* in love with you, Hunter."

She was?

His heart swelled and as he dragged her against him, and their mouths were about to meet, she pulled back.

"What about the other night? I can't do those things. And you need them."

He shook his head.

"Sweetheart, I need you. You are enough. *More* than enough." He sat back on his ankles. "I'm still working it out, but I don't believe the sado-masochism is a need as much as a fantasy. And that isn't something I'm willing to hold on to and lose you over."

She looked unconvinced.

"Life won't be boring with me, Addy. Sexually, I will always be the dominant one. There is more than enough for us to play with that will satisfy me," he said. "Like any area of relationship, there is compromise and it's not like you are a vanilla lover."

Addison blushed as a little grin hit her lips. "Well, no."

"Nothing matters except having you in my life. I've said it one hundred times. You are mine."

"I am yours." She nodded.

"So, that means letting me into your life. With Sienna. And that fucking asshole of an ex-husband."

Addison shook her head. "He was just hurt. His pride wounded. He's a good father."

He let out a grunt.

"And the answer is yes. I want you to meet Sienna. I want this. With you," she said, tears brimming.

Thank fucking God.

Now he needed to start from scratch and woo this perfect woman. He wanted her to know she was special and meant the world to him. He wanted to know everything about her, build a relationship with her daughter, and create a new world together.

"I'm going to make you so damn happy, baby," Hunter said, cupping her face. "But first things first."

Her brows lifted.

"Will you go on a date with me?"

Addison let out a laugh. "Yes, Hunter, I will go on a date with you."

"Good, because I have tickets to the game this weekend and I'm hoping you and Sienna would go with me."

Addison smiled, those tears spilling over. "I truly do love you, Hunter Dufort."

"Ditto, gorgeous." He stood and pulled her into his arms, claiming all that was now his.

EPILOGUE

Hunter held the door open for Addison as they stepped into the restaurant. They made their way through to the private dining room and found they were the last to arrive.

He guided Addison to her seat.

"Can I please have everyone's attention?" Hunter said, and the table quietened. "This is Addison. My girlfriend. End of story. Great, okay, so what else is happening?"

"Girlfriend?" she asked, staring up at him with mischief in her eyes. "I agreed to one date."

He ignored the giggles around him and sat down, draping his arm over the back of her chair. Then winked at her.

"Oh, they are adorable together," Harper said, clasping her hands.

Daniel rolled his eyes.

"Wow, what did I miss?" Kristen said. "How did I miss this?"

"Nice to meet you, *Hunter's girlfriend*. We met at the bar that night," Jackson said to Addison. "I'm Jackson Wiles."

"Oh yes, hi Jackson. You saved Harper's ring," Addison said, then laughed. "And got us arrested."

"Totally worth it," Harper said,

"Ah, no. Next time, let the guy take the damn thing.," Daniel said. "Actually, there is no next time."

Harper raised a brow at him. "Oh, there will be more girls' nights."

"Not like that one. Not while this thing is growing inside me," Olivia said, pointing at her stomach.

Hunter glanced down at Addison and wondered if she wanted more babies. The thought of her carrying his child was terrifying and wonderful.

She turned to him, and a small, knowing smile hit her lips. He lowered his mouth to hers, and the silence as they kissed made him grin so much he had to release her.

"They *are* cute together. Ah, young love," Kristen said, and he watched Jackson glance away.

So the guy was just fucking her.

Which left only one reason he'd be here tonight. He wanted inside the Dufort family.

Hunter glanced around the table and caught Daniel's eye. They shared a knowing glance. They would be careful what they said tonight, and it would all be focused on the happy couple. No business, which sometimes slipped in.

Hunter lifted his glass. "So, happy honeymoon or whatever we are here for."

"Let's wait for Dad," Daniel said.

"Your father is coming?" Jackson asked, stiffening.

And paling.

Interesting.

Very fucking interesting.

"Yes." Daniel narrowed his eyes. "Why?"

Fletcher caught his eye. Finally, it was if the penny had dropped.

"Ah—" Jackson began, and his chair shifted.

"Sorry I'm late," Johnathan Dufort said as he walked up behind them. "I got..."

Hunter watched his father take in all the members of their dinner party and land on Jackson. He felt like he was in a movie as the room blurred and went deathly silent.

Daniel's face turned dark red as his eyes slid from his father to Jackson. Then back to his father. He cast one look at him and back to Fletcher.

How had they not fucking seen this?

"Who are you?" Daniel demanded, his voice a low and dangerous growl.

Jackson stood, his chair noisily grazing the wooden floor.

"What's going on?" Kristen asked, looking back and forth between everyone.

The poor girl.

She had been used.

If Addison hadn't been in his life, he may have paid more attention. But now the pieces of the puzzle were coming together. When he looked at the guy, it was so fucking obvious.

Johnathan continued to stare at him.

"Are you going to tell them who I am? I know you know," Jackson said, with a small shake of his head.

"You know?" Johnathan asked.

"Jesus," Fletcher cursed, shaking his head. "I can't fucking believe this."

Kristen stood. "What's going on? Who are you?"

"Shit," Johnathan said, running a hand through his salt and pepper hair.

"Fuck me," Hunter said, doing the same with his own dark hair.

Jackson turned to Fletcher, then to him, and lastly looked at Daniel. A token glance down at Kristen.

"I'm your brother. Half-brother. Johnathan Dufort is my father."

AS the gasps let out across the table and the shock settled in, Kristen jumped to her feet. "You bastard. You used me to get to them. How dare you?"

She slapped him.

Hunter flinched.

Then she threw her napkin on the table and bolted from the restaurant. Harper, Olivia, and Addison stood in tandem and went after her.

Jackson's palm went to his face. "I deserved that."

"Yeah, you did, asshole. Now sit down and talk," Daniel said, then glanced at his father. "And you aren't going anywhere. Sit down."

As his father circled the table and found a seat, he waved down the waiter for a whiskey.

"Bring the bottle," Daniel said.

Hunter caught his father's eyes and, for the first time in his adult life, realized that he wasn't anything like this man. He had a lot of secrets, and his words to him the other day were starting to unravel.

Jackson Wiles might be their half-brother, but now the question was, what did he want?

Because when you were a billionaire, someone always wanted something. Especially if they were claiming to be a blood relative.

Hunter got comfortable. This was going to be a long night.

Damn it.

He'd had other plans. Much more enjoyable ones. But there would be tomorrow, and the day after that. He planned to put a big sparkling ring on Addison's finger.

She would be a Dufort one day very soon.

Addison Dufort, the woman he had chosen and would pleasure for the rest of his life.

Get Jackson and Kristen's steamy billionaire romance, Desire Unbound **by going to this link:**

books2read.com/desireunbound

Or turn the page to read the first steamy chapter of their story.

LOVE STEAMY ROMANCES?

Start my paranormal romance series **FREE** with The Vampire Prince. With over **1100 ratings on Amazon**, The Vampire Prince is the first in this long ongoing series much loved by fans.

Order your eBook or Paperback at this link:

https://books2read.com/thevampireprince

ALSO BY JULIETTE N. BANKS

The Dufort Dynasty
Steamy billionaire romance
Sinful Duty **(FREE)**
Forbidden Touch
Total Possession
Desire Unbound

The Moretti Blood Brothers
Steamy paranormal romance
The Vampire Prince **(FREE)**
The Vampire Protector
The Vampire Spy
The Vampire's Christmas
The Vampire Assassin
The Vampire Awoken
The Vampire Lover
The Vampire Wolf
The Vampire Warrior

The Moretti Blood Wolves
Steamy paranormal shifter romance
The Alpha Wolf
The Unbound Wolf

The Protective Wolf

Realm of the Immortals
Steamy paranormal fantasy romance
The Archangel's Heart
The Archangel's Star

DESIRE
UNBOUND

CHAPTER ONE

Yesterday

Never in a million years did Jackson Wiles think he would be sitting at a table full of billionaires. A table full of Dufort's. Six months ago that felt like the furthest thing likely to happen to him.

Not that he wasn't an extremely rich man himself. He was.

Now.

His hand lay casually along on the back of Kristen's chair, and he was mindlessly drawing little circles on her shoulder while everyone at the dinner table chatted easily.

Huh, he laughed inwardly. There was nothing mindless about it. He was highly aware of Kristen's sexy body. Every damn inch of it.

If only he'd seen more of it.

One kiss.

That's all they'd had, and she didn't even fucking remember it. It had been the best goddamn kiss of his life. His entire body had burst into flames.

It was lucky he was a gentleman, or he would've been tempted to take full advantage of her drunk state.

Since then she'd played this coy game with him. If she was American or lived in Los Angeles where he did, Jackson might have had more time for it. But they didn't. In a week she was returning to the other side of the world. New Zealand.

Could you live further away, you sexy thing?

He would also be leaving New York City and heading home.

So they had days, not weeks. And not a lifetime.

Being a red-blooded male, he had made it clear what he wanted and, after that kiss, he knew she did too.

Yet, she had returned from Southampton with her best friend Harper, who had just married Daniel Dufort, and rejected all his requests for a date.

Finally, after his tenth message, because he hadn't become a successful businessman by taking no for an answer, she'd given in and invited him to the group dinner he was currently sitting at.

Talk about luck.

Jackson might want to fuck Kristen into next Sunday, but it was her connection with the Dufort's that had seen him pursue her.

Not those emerald green eyes that took his breath away. Not the soft curve of her hips that he liked under his touch. Or the long blonde hair she constantly flipped over her shoulder. Or the way she looked at him with hunger in her eyes, then blinked as those lashes lowered in submission and looked away.

Before he left Manhattan, he was sinking inside this woman and holding those eyes in a locked gaze while she screamed.

He was determined to unearth her inner tiger.

It was there; he knew it.

She turned to him as if surprised to feel his touch and he gave her a small smile.

"You shouldn't do that." She leaned in. "This isn't a date."

"So you keep saying." He also leaned in, as if they were in a conspiracy.

"Keep those dimples to yourself, mister. This is just dinner."

His smirk grew wider as he sat up, distracted by the new arrival.

"Oh, my goodness," Kristen whispered as Hunter Dufort arrived with a woman he recognized.

Jackson raised a brow.

"Can I please have everyone's attention?" Hunter said, as the woman sat at the chair he'd pulled out. The table quietened. "This is Addison. My girlfriend. End of story. Great, okay, so what else is happening?"

"Girlfriend?" Addison asked, staring up at him with mischief in her eyes. "I agreed to one date."

Well at least she was admitting it was a date. He glanced down at Kristen who poked her tongue out at him.

Do that again sweetheart, and I will bite.

Hunter sat and laid his hand on the back of Addison's chair, mirroring Jackson's pose. Unsurprising given they were brothers.

And that was why he was here.

A few months ago he had discovered Johnathan Dufort was his father. He'd never known who his father was before then. His mother had always said she didn't know.

Jackson was still processing the information but one thing he'd known for sure. He had to meet the family. Having a tech company who created apps for hotels, and many other industries, was a huge coincidence but one he had capitalized on immediately.

He'd secured a meeting with Fletcher Dufort, the middle brother, and met Hunter while he'd been there.

Then days later another coincidence occurred when he'd been having a drink in a bar planning his next steps when Harper, Kristen, Olivia—Fletcher's fiancée—and Addison had stumbled in drunk during Harper's bachelorette party.

And that was how he met Kristen.

He'd recognized Olivia immediately as she'd been in the meeting, and Harper from media photos. But it had been those green eyes of Kristen's which had captured him and given him reason to cross the room.

Yes, he'd felt like life was handing him opportunities to meet his blood relatives. Yet, this sexy blonde was like a cherry on the top. The weeks following he'd taken her out a few times, but when she left for the Hamptons, she'd indicated she wouldn't see him again.

Yeah, so that wasn't happening. Kristen had been a huge gift. It had allowed him to spend time with the Dufort brothers, Daniel, Fletcher and Hunter, without having to tell them who he was or be some creepy sales guy pushing his app.

It was the perfect situation.

And he might get laid if he could find out what was stopping Kristen from just having a good time. They clearly had chemistry.

"Oh, they are adorable together," Harper said, clasping her hands at Hunter and Addison.

"Wow," Kristen said. "How did I miss this?"

"Nice to meet you, *Hunter's girlfriend*. We met at the bar that night," Jackson said to Addison, referring to the bachelorette evening. "I'm Jackson Wiles."

"Oh yes, hi Jackson. You saved Harper's ring," Addison said, then laughed. "And got us arrested."

"Totally worth it," Harper said.

As the conversation continued around them, Kristen smiled up at him.

"You did save it."

He winked at her.

Instinct had just kicked in that night when they heard Harper scream that some guy had pulled her kabillion-carat diamond engagement ring off her hand and run for the door. He'd leaped and caught the guy's foot, and they'd both crashed to the floor.

Harper had ripped her ring out of his hand and moments later the cops had arrived. When the guy claimed he'd been assaulted all of them had stood silent, while Jackson had pulled Kristen aside.

He could see exactly what was going to happen. As a tourist in the city, being arrested could have resulted in her being sent back to New Zealand before seeing her best friend get married.

Why he cared, he didn't know.

"So, happy honeymoon or whatever we are here for," Hunter said, lifting his glass.

Jackson began to lift his when Daniel held up his hand.

"Let's wait for Dad."

He froze.

Oh my fucking God.

Johnathan Dufort was joining them? His fucking father?

"Your father is coming?" Jackson asked, feeling the blood rush from his face.

"Yes." Daniel narrowed his eyes. "Why?"

"Ah—" Jackson began, and his chair shifted.

"Sorry I'm late," Johnathan Dufort said as he walked up behind them. "I got…"

Jackson turned and stared at the salt and pepper haired man who was built just like his sons. Broad, tall, and strong. Power and confidence rolled off him.

He was dressed in black designer pants, a black shirt and a button-down cardigan which was done up.

Johnathan had a light dusting of facial hair and a thick head of hair. He was only fifty-five, so it wasn't like he was ancient, but clearly, he was in great condition.

But that wasn't what froze him in his tracks.

The senior Dufort knew who he was. Jackson wasn't sure *how* much he knew, but he was aware of Jackson's existence. After all, he'd paid for Brown University. So he recently found out.

But his father didn't know everything.

He didn't know Jackson was a twin.

He wasn't going to find out either. Jackson had protected Jessica all his life and he wasn't going to stop now.

To keep reading Jackson and Kristen's steamy romance in Desire Unbound go to
www.juliettebanks.com

Or

books2read.com/desireunbound

ALSO BY JULIETTE N. BANKS

The Dufort Dynasty
Steamy billionaire romance
Sinful Duty (**FREE**)
Forbidden Touch
Total Possession
Desire Unbound

The Moretti Blood Brothers
Steamy paranormal romance
The Vampire Prince (**FREE**)
The Vampire Protector
The Vampire Spy
The Vampire's Christmas
The Vampire Assassin
The Vampire Awoken
The Vampire Lover
The Vampire Wolf
The Vampire Warrior

The Moretti Blood Wolves
Steamy paranormal shifter romance
The Alpha Wolf
The Unbound Wolf
The Protective Wolf

Realm of the Immortals
Steamy paranormal fantasy romance
The Archangel's Heart
The Archangel's Star

LOVE STEAMY ROMANCES?

Start my paranormal romance series **FREE** with The Vampire Prince. With over **1100 ratings on Amazon**, The Vampire Prince is the first in this long ongoing series much loved by fans.

Order your eBook or Paperback at this link:
books2read.com/thevampireprince

MORETTI
BLOOD BROTHERS
Bestselling paranormal romance series

Juliette N Banks

www.juliettebanks.com

LET'S STAY IN TOUCH

Join my **VIP BOOKCLUB.** Go to
www.juliettebanks.com and sign up there.

AND

Join my private Facebook Group:

facebook.com/groups/authorjuliettebanksreaders

Follow me on Instagram:

Juliettebanksauthor